OMEGA FOUND

EVELYN FLOOD

First published by Evelyn Flood in 2022

ISBN 9798416728014
Copyright © 2022 by Evelyn Flood

Cover and formatting by Diana TC, TriumphBookCovers.com

A word to my loving family

Dear family,
Thank you for the support. I love you.
Now turn around, and walk away from this book.*
Do it now. I mean it.
Sunday lunch will never be the same again.
And no, none of you are in it.
*This also applies to my very supportive boss. Soz for being so
extra x

TRIGGER WARNING

This book contains themes and scenes of sexual and physical assault, torture and suicide which may be distressing.

(Family, if you're still here, consider this your final warning.)

All abuse takes place outside of the harem.

If this means you're not comfortable reading Omega Found, please don't risk it. Nothing is more important than your health.

If this is okay with you, then please keep reading!

Evelyn x

ABOUT THIS BOOK

This book is an **omegaverse**. That means that the characters have some of the characteristics often seen in wolves, but they **do not shift.**

PROLOGUE
THE OMEGA CREED

1. All omegas become the property of the Omega Compound upon awakening
2. Omegas must obey alpha commands at all times
3. Omegas are not permitted to own or use soft furnishings or participate in any activity that may be considered 'nesting'
4. Omegas are not permitted the use of a bed
5. Omegas are not permitted to initiate bitemarks or participate in heats outside of those permitted by the Omega Compound
6. Omegas must kneel in the presence of alphas unless permission is granted to rise
7. Omegas are not permitted to make eye contact with alphas
8. Omegas must consume food or drink from the approved list compiled by the Omega Compound
9. Omegas are not permitted to own property or drive
10. Omegas must wear the allocated collar when outside of the Omega Compound

Exceptions to the creed may be made under agreed circumstances, such as mating, with the permission of the guardian alpha.

Any Omega found to be in breach of the Omega Creed must be returned to the Omega Compound for correction.

CHAPTER ONE
HARPER

My knees are fucking *burning*.

Wincing, I try to shift my position before our instructor makes it down the line. The pain catches in my throat and a groan slips out before I can stop it.

Hale swivels on her heel, stalking back down towards me. I see the black boots heading closer in the corner of my eye, but I keep my head down. If I move any more, I'll be punished.

Again.

I keep my eyes fixed firmly to the floor as Hale comes to a stop before me, her boots shining in the harsh light from the strip of naked bulbs above us. I breathe in and out lightly. Silent and still – just how a good omega should be. I hope that it's enough, that Instructor Hale will just move on.

But today isn't my lucky day.

The swish of the cane whistles just before it slams down on my thigh. It's a test I'm unprepared for. My cry comes out as a high-pitched wheeze, thin lines of scarlet blood already welling up on my bare skin.

The other omegas don't make a sound, keeping their heads down. They're glad it's me again. I always take the attention away from them. It doesn't help that the rice I've been kneeling on for the last two hours is digging in like tiny sharp razors burrowing under my skin.

I don't move an inch, so at least they can't punish me for that. As a final warning, Hale places her boot on top of the marks she's just made with her cane and presses down, pushing my leg deeper into the rice. The pain is indescribable, and my vision flashes white as I fight not to pass out.

Breathing slowly through my mouth, I track Hale's movements as she moves her boot across, holding it over my other leg in a silent warning. I brace myself for another push, but Hale seems satisfied, moving further down the line to inspect her other charges. The *good* omegas. I'm the only one here being punished today, the only omega with bloody knees from tiny pieces of white rice.

The bell will ring soon though, and I can go and get something to eat. My stomach grumbles noisily at the thought, and I fight back an instinctive cringe. Hale won't punish me for it. They like to hear that we're hungry. As if on cue, the clanging of the dinner bell echoes through the room, and our group waits to be dismissed. If anyone moves before Hale confirms we can go, we'll wish for more time on our knees.

She keeps us waiting for another minute or two before we're finally free to leave. I ease back on my ankles slowly as I wait for the blonde girl next to me to move, getting ready for a painful crawl across the compound grounds to the dining hall. We're not permitted to walk when there are alphas in the vicinity unless we have permission.

We never have permission.

And since all of our instructors are alphas, we're basically not allowed to walk at all, apart from our exercise sessions and when we're locked up in our tiny cells at the end of each day. It's four steps to get from one side to the other.

I hiss quietly as I start to move, slowly following the line as we crawl out under the watchful eye of the beta guards. My thigh burns, pain shooting down the strips Hale has left on my skin. A few grains of rice stick to my knees, making it even worse. I try to roll my knees on the ground against the gravel to work them out, but I haven't managed it by the time we reach the dining hall.

"Up."

The order is given briskly, instant obedience our only option. Our response isn't quite as swift as the instructors would like, I'm sure. After several hours in the same position, it takes us all a few precious seconds to stagger to our feet. One girl trips as the cramp in her legs proves too much and the guards are quick to pull her away. Her bare feet scrabble for purchase against the rough ground as she wails. We all keep our eyes averted. I learned a long time ago not to get involved.

Thankfully, the alphas don't attend the dining hall. It's hard for us to collect our food and take it to our table if we're not able to stand up.

Joining the queue of omegas, I stand quietly in line, twisting my torso from side to side to work out the kinks in my back. I'm starving, but my expectations are low. The slop they serve is never enough to feel full. Enough to keep us alive, maybe. Thriving and healthy? No. Thin and weak is how they prefer to keep us.

I grimace, wrinkling my nose as a plate is dropped in front of me by an expressionless beta. A small helping of plain rice and a banana. I wonder if Hale knew this was on the menu today. It wouldn't surprise me. I debate leaving the rice, my stomach twisting at the thought after this morning's punishment, but my hunger wins out.

Scanning the room and finding a table, I settle down, making sure my back is to the wall. I shovel the food down my throat, ignoring any sort of manners. There are no alphas here and the omegas are too focused on our meager meal to pay attention to me. *Red velvet cake*, I tell myself, closing my eyes and choking down the dry food, chasing it with my water. *Red velvet cake and pepperoni pizza.* God, I miss pizza.

Pushing the empty plate away, I casually scan the room with quick glances from under my lashes, searching for a familiar head of curly caramel hair. Ava has been in the interrogation unit today. That's our name for the psychiatry team at the compound.

Every month, we're forced into mandatory psych sessions. They don't want to hear the truth, though. Instead, it's an opportunity for the compound to poke and prod at us, looking for weaknesses.

We sit there quietly as they talk at us about our 'dangerous omega behaviors', testing how close we are to potential breakdown. Even better if they can get us to admit to anything, like nesting instincts.

Beta doctors sit there in white coats as you perch on an uncomfortable seat in a freezing sterile room, nodding with false sympathy if you tell them anything. Of course, their notes are handed straight to the instructors, who'll spend the next month 'training' any non-compliant thoughts out of us.

A good omega is a silent omega.

A good omega does as she's told.

A good omega follows the omega creed.

I've been living at the Omega Compound since I was fourteen. I perfumed early, a strong cinnamon scent bursting from my skin one summer morning as I had breakfast with my mom and dad. My *beta* mom and dad.

They had me packed up and dumped at the compound doors before I even knew what was happening. They wouldn't talk to me on the drive over, my mom pale-faced, my dad ignoring my frantic questions with grim determination, his only words telling me to get out when we pulled up.

I'd screamed and begged them to stop as they drove off,

desperately throwing myself after their car as the guards pulled me through the gates. My parents didn't look back. They didn't even wait for me to get my bag out. I was dragged into the Omega Compound with nothing but the clothes on my back.

I wish I'd known then what I know now. I would have thrown myself from the moving car before the OC ever had a chance to get their hands on me.

The Omega Compound is the Government's way of keeping control over the omega population. It hasn't always been this way, though.

Around twenty-five years ago, the Omega War decimated omega numbers, taking us from uncommon to rare.

First, the beta birth population rates started dropping. Slowly, then faster. Betas used to be able to bear children, but nobody could work out what the problem was. Every year for four years, it became lower, and fewer babies were born.

Eventually, omegas were the only race that could carry a child. A beta hasn't given birth for more than twenty years, and most children born now are beta. Alpha births are unusual, but an omega awakening is as rare as finding a diamond on the street.

Only an alpha-omega pairing can produce an omega child, and it's not guaranteed by any means. Even then, omega genes are impossible to detect until an omega awakens, normally between the ages of seventeen and twenty-one. Lucky me, awakening at fourteen.

There used to be more omegas than there are now. But the declining birth rates caused a war, with alphas and betas fighting over the limited numbers of omegas.

When public conversation turned to government control over omegas to stop the unrest, only the alphas stood up for us.

I read once that it's not power that corrupts. It's fear. History tells our story differently. But then, history is always written by the winners.

The winners say that omegas are dangerous. We controlled the alpha population, using them as shields to avoid our duty to society and forcing them to turn on the betas. We used our scents, our pheromones, to remove their free will and control them completely, turning them into mindless violent beasts.

Then the Government came up with a solution. Bag and tag the omegas and keep us in controlled environments away from alphas where we wouldn't be a threat. Lock us away and make us provide children until a cure could be found for the beta birth issues.

The beta population overwhelmingly voted for the move, and the Government was quick to disband any alpha packs that wouldn't comply. By lethal force, if needed.

It only took another few years for the last of the free omegas to be hunted down and the system to slide neatly into place. Sometimes I wonder if there are any omegas still out there, living under the radar. *Free.*

I hope so. I wish I was one of them.

It's also our fault that betas can't have children, of course. How, I don't know. But that's what society thinks. We're not to be trusted. Our only use is to pop babies out as quickly as possible until our bodies give in. It's our punishment for taking the option away from everyone else.

Now, all omegas belong to the Omega Compound, and the Omega Creed sets out the rules that we all must follow.

We're not permitted to do anything that might *influence* an alpha – not even looking them in the eye or standing at the same level as them. Certain foods and materials can trigger our scent markers, so we eat from a prescribed list of food and only drink water along with taking daily scent-blockers. And you can forget any kind of omega rights, like driving, holding down a job, or living alone – all omegas must be given over to the compound as soon as we start to perfume for our training to begin.

I've been in training for seven years. I'm still not the perfect omega they want me to be.

If they ever decide that I meet their impossible standards, there are two options. The compound could sign me over to an alpha pack, where I'll be bitten in and bred in the hope of bearing omega children, at the mercy of whoever owns me. Only packs who demonstrate complete obedience to the government are eligible for bitemarks, and if they're anything like my instructors suggest, I'll be better off dead.

I've never wanted a bitemark or a pack. I'll never condemn a future child of mine to this life. But if I'm not matched with a pack, then I'll be sent to the heat nests, where I'll be drugged and available for hire by anyone who can afford it. Any children I bear will be placed into a government surrogacy program for betas.

Either way, I'm fucked.

My mind has wandered as I wait for Ava, and I finally spot her caramel curls as she moves into the room, a dejected slump to her shoulders. I can see from one glance that she's upset, since she's normally a bouncing ball of sunshine – which is unusual in our life, to say the least.

Catching her eye, I quietly motion for her to come and sit with me. Worry forms a pit in my stomach as I wonder what the doctors have said to her. Ava's turning twenty-one soon and has always been impeccably behaved, so she'll probably be given to an alpha pack. She puts on a brave face, but I've heard her crying at night in the cell across from me. She's absolutely petrified.

Ava's tray lands on the table with a slight crash, making the omegas around us jump and look over with frowns. It's drawn the guard's attention too, and I curse internally as Jason makes his way over to us.

Jason is a *creep*. I mean, all the guards here are awful. Seriously, I've never seen one even crack a smile. But Jason is particularly deviant. Nothing makes him happier than doling out a punishment.

And if I'm involved? Even better.

Ava bites her lip, her hazel eyes filling with guilt as she sinks down into her seat next to me.

"I'm so sorry," she whispers to me, panic in her voice.

I don't get the chance to respond before Jason kicks my stool out from underneath me. My elbow makes a loud crack as it hits the ground, and I swallow back a whimper. No way will I give this asshole the satisfaction of hearing my pain. He's had more than enough of it in the past.

I glance over at the other two guards on duty, but they have their gazes fixed firmly on the opposite wall. No help will come from them. They won't risk their jobs for Jason. His father is on the board of governors for the OC, and it pretty much gives him a free pass to do whatever the hell he wants.

Normally, I let him get on with it. The quicker he gets his kicks, the quicker I can get away from him and lick my wounds.

But then Ava reaches down, grabbing my hand and trying to pull me up. Jason is faster than me. Before I can do anything, he cracks the back of his hand across her face. Ava crashes back off her stool with a cry of pain as Jason pulls back his leg to kick her in the ribs.

That's it.

I'm so done. Me? I can cope with anything this asshole throws at me.

But I won't let him turn that on Ava.

I've never understood the meaning of the words 'seeing red', but I get it now. There's a real red mist descending over my eyes. I've hit my limit.

I'm going to give this fucker absolute hell.

With a snarl of rage, I throw myself at Jason's leg and knock him off balance. We hit the floor in a tangle of limbs. I'm *growling*, ripping at his hair and scratching his face with my short nails. I know it's futile – the guy is a strong beta and I'm a weak-ass omega.

There's no way I'm going to win this fight, but I'll leave my mark on him if it's the last thing I do. Years of pain and frustration explode from my skin, years of living my life as a fucking omega in this world.

Ava gasps my name as she crawls towards me with her hand outstretched, to try and stop me or help me, I'm not sure which. The guards are paying attention now, racing forward from the walls to try and pull me off. Jason stops them with a growl. An *alpha* growl.

I freeze, the tone of his voice making me shrink back. What the actual fuck?

Jason is an *alpha*. Not a beta after all. My head spins at the realization. Everyone knows that alphas aren't allowed to be guards and near the omegas on a regular basis. Even our alpha instructors are on rotation to stop them from getting too close.

Shock holds me for a split second – and a second is all Jason needs to grab my hair and pull me down. His hands tangle in my waist-length hair, holding on at the roots as he drags me underneath him, pinning me to the floor with his bulk. Tears of pure frustration roll down my cheeks as I hiss at him. Incoherent anger flows out of my mouth as I curse him and every single damn speck of this compound.

His knee comes up to force my legs apart and he barks a single command.

"Yield!"

My useless omega body has never frustrated me as much as it does right this second. My legs fall apart of their own volition, opening to him as a commanding alpha. My head turns so that my throat is bared in submission, and I catch a quick glimpse of Ava's tear-filled eyes before Jason's hand grips my neck. My whole body relaxes, submitting to the alpha on top of me, even as fury fills me from my head to my toes.

Fucking omega instincts.

Jason's rancid breath ghosts over my face as he twists my neck to face him. I expect an explosion, a slap. I'm completely taken aback when he *laughs in my face.*

Bright red blood is smeared across his cheek from the scratches I laid on him, but he looks absolutely thrilled. His laughter booms across the completely silent dining hall as he throws his head back in a deranged cackle.

"What the fuck is so funny?" I manage to rasp through his fingers on my throat, my eyes blurring.

His laughter finally comes to an end. Leaning down, he holds my throat open for him as he runs his nose down it, breathing in the scent of my skin. The scent blockers stop my perfume from being too obvious, something I'm suddenly grateful for.

My stomach twists in revulsion.

He raises his mouth to my ear and licks it. My body shudders, biology betraying me. In my head, I don't want anything to fucking do with Jason, but all my body feels is an alpha and it's sure as hell not listening to me. Hot breath invades my ear as he takes his time before he whispers.

"Thank you, omega."

I have no idea what he means, but the joy in his voice sends nausea up my throat until I think I'm going to heave.

Whatever happens now… it's not going to be good for me.

CHAPTER TWO
HARPER

M y feet scrabble on the black and white linoleum as Jason drags me out.

The other guards stand around, uncertainty on their faces, and even the omegas are all out of their seats watching. Normally, that would be definite grounds for punishment, but clearly, I'm the star of this show. It's not every day that an omega goes batshit crazy and attacks a guard, after all.

Jason doesn't spare them a glance as he yanks me through the doors of the dining hall, fingers gripping my arm in a way that I just know will leave pleasant little crescent moon shapes embedded into my skin. I catch a final glimpse of Ava's pale face, her eyes wide with fear, before the door slams shut with an air of finality.

Jason doesn't push me down on my knees to crawl, even though we're passing instructors who call out to him, confusion on their faces. He ignores them completely as he strides across the compound grounds confidently.

I'm too busy trying to get my feet under me to look at where we're going. Jason loses patience and drags me upright. I jerk against his grip, and he snaps a growl at me that makes me stand up straight and follow.

Dread slithers down my spine as I work out where we're going. I try desperately not to panic as Jason tows me towards a grey brick building, pulling me up the stone steps and through the huge wooden doors.

The Directors' office.

The Director of the OC is responsible for keeping the system running smoothly and upholding the rules of the creed within the boundaries of the compound walls.

He's a phantom. None of us ever get to see the Director, but we hear plenty from the instructors and guards. They like to threaten and intimidate us with a visit to the Directors' office. There's a rumor among the omegas that once we go in, we don't come out.

My feet still follow Jason like an obedient little toy, and I try to pull away from him as he drags me down a dimly lit corridor.

The carpet is red, the walls stone. There are actual candlelit sconces lining the walls. I try not to snort in derision even though my stomach is churning. I mean, seriously, they could make it look a little less Transylvania. I wonder hysterically if the Director is actually a vampire and that's why we never see him.

Jason's not letting up, almost jogging in his haste. He finally stops in front of a large walnut door with an antique brass door knocker. Glancing at me, his thin lips twist up into a malicious smirk as his meaty fists lift the knocker. One, two, three times.

We wait for a minute, Jason vibrating with impatient energy. My eyes flicker up and down the corridor, searching for any potential hiding or escape spots, even as Jason's arm grips me tightly. If there's an opportunity, I'm taking it.

Finally, a low voice calls out for us to enter. Jason sweeps into the ornate office, yanking me with him so hard that I trip and land on my abused knees. I stumble to my feet hastily.

Looking up, I finally lay my eyes on the Director for the first time in my seven-year stint at the compound.

He's not as forbidding as I thought he would be. His dark hair is slightly messy, sticking up at the back. He's older, but still clearly fit. His shirt bunches where his muscles strain against the fabric. It's when he raises his eyes to me that I flinch back.

There's nothing there. His pale green gaze is completely empty, almost as if he doesn't see me at all. My heart kicks uncomfortably in my chest. Belatedly, I drop my gaze to the floor, realizing that not only am I standing in the presence of two alphas, but I also just made eye contact with the most senior alpha at the compound.

Fuck my actual life. I'm definitely gonna get a beating for this. Jason kicks the back of my leg and I collapse back down to the floor with a pained grunt. Hardly the picture of a graceful omega.

The Director says nothing, tapping his fingers on the desk as he waits for Jason to explain why we're here.

"Sir," Jason rushes out. "There's been an incident in the dining hall. I was forced to discipline 792 for displaying negative behaviors and she *physically attacked* me."

He points dramatically to his cheek, smears of blood turning to rusty brown around the scratches I made. I clench my fists, wishing I'd made better use of the opportunity and kicked him in the nuts. The world would be much better off without any future tyrannical little Jason brats running around.

The Director catches my movement, flicking his pale gaze down to my side. I force myself to relax.

"I had to use the alpha bark to subdue her, Sir."

The Director shifts in his seat, and Jason falls quiet.

I fight not to roll my eyes at the use of my designation.

792. Here, omegas are just a number. I mean, God forbid they think of us as *people*.

After a moment, the Director sits back in his seat, clasping the tips of his fingers together.

"What do you want, Harding?" His voice is harsh, impatient, but he speaks quietly. "Clearly there's something, or you wouldn't be here bothering me."

Jason hesitates before speaking this time. I suck in a breath, holding it in anticipation.

What's it going to be? Isolation? Reduced food rations? A whipping?

Been there, got the fucking t-shirt.

"Sir, we have previously discussed 792 acting as the first trial subject for the Phoenix project. I believe that her behavior today has demonstrated once again that she is the perfect candidate, and I propose that we move ahead with the trial."

My forehead crumples with confusion. *What in the ever-flying fuck is this?* I've never heard anything about a trial. A trial for what?

Glancing up from beneath my lashes, I see the Director lean forward as he considers Jason's words. I find myself praying that he says no.

Anything that gets Jason this excited will not turn out well for me.

Finally, he speaks. "The Phoenix project is still in development, Harding. We're not at the stage where it's been categorically confirmed that the project is even viable."

Jason puffs up his chest, his words dripping with self-importance.

"The board is very keen to progress with the pilot, Sir. My father has spoken of it to me on several occasions. I'm sure he'll be delighted that we have identified such a *suitable* candidate."

There's an inherent threat in his words. This isn't good. My stomach starts churning, and I watch the Director's response closely.

The man in front of me sighs. For a second, he looks tired. It's just a flash, though, before his face settles back into expressionless lines.

Reaching down, he pulls a manilla folder from a drawer in his desk, flipping through it. The folder has my number on it, and he pauses on some of the pages, his eyes scanning the contents.

"I can see why 792 has been identified." His gaze suddenly moves to my face, and I drop my eyes again, caught out for a second time. Stupid fucking rules.

"You can look up, 792." The quiet offer shocks me for a moment, but I'm not about to lose the opportunity. My head shoots up and I look straight into the Director's green eyes.

"Do you know anything about the Phoenix project, Harper?" The use of my name makes me jolt. I don't think I've ever heard an alpha use it before. He speaks slowly, deliberately.

He motions at me to speak when I remain silent. "No, Sir. But it doesn't sound good."

Immediately, I want to shrivel up as he raises a brow at me. He didn't ask for my opinion. Why do I always let my mouth run away with me?

The Director's lips twitch upwards at the corners with the hint of a smile. It drops away quickly though, as he looks down again at the folder. It seems like he's reluctant to move ahead with whatever-the-hell this is all about, but my hopes are dashed when he speaks again, his voice flat.

"I'll agree to a short trial period, Jason. Two weeks, and I want to see your progress before making a decision on whether to move forward."

Fuck.

The Director beckons me to stand up, and I curse my knees as it takes me a moment to catch my balance. I see the Director staring at them before he moves his eyes back to my face. God knows what they look like.

"The Phoenix project is a new initiative developed by the psychiatry facility at the compound." I snap to and pay close attention, shocked that he's even taking the time to explain this to me. The mention of the interrogation unit makes my stomach clench as I remember Ava's pale face. Is she involved with this? God, I hope not.

"The aim of the project is to fully enable omegas to fulfil your core responsibilities to society in a more… effective, way. As things currently stand, you have an amount of autonomy over your life here-"

He falls silent as my snort of derision rings through the room. Mortified, I shift my feet from side to side. "Sorry."

The Director clears his throat, ignoring me.

"As I was saying. The Phoenix project works on the basis that even this *small* amount of autonomy is not a suitable fit for omega biology, and in fact, can be more damaging for omegas in the long run. By introducing a more rigid structure and enhanced training, omegas can live a peaceful and fulfilling existence."

I'm starting to freak out. This sounds… *horrific.* My breathing speeds up. The government wants even more control over omegas. Over me. I look across at Jason and the leer on his face draws a whine from my throat. The OC already controls every single aspect of my existence. What more can they possibly take from me?

"You will be the first test subject in the Phoenix project, 792. You'll be allocated a single trainer, who will have sole responsibility for your activities and wellbeing. You will also be placed into a rigorous, one-on-one training program. The pilot will test if this approach may be a viable option in the future to expand to all omegas."

The words are delivered flatly, almost as if the Director is bored. Then he drops the worst part.

"At the end of your training, should it progress satisfactorily, you will receive a bitemark from your trainer, and you will be allocated paired lodgings outside of the compound. You will be required to breed within twelve months. Any children produced will be placed into the surrogacy program, pending confirmation of their omega status in the future."

I don't feel my bruised knees hit the rug. I don't feel much of anything, except white-hot terror splintering up my insides, threatening to twist me inside out. This is everything I've feared from the day I got here. Every beating, bruise, limited meal is *nothing* in comparison to what Jason will do to me.

I fix my gaze down at the floor and plead for my life.

"Please," I beg, a whine slipping through. "I know I haven't done as well as I could, but I'll do better. Just please don't make me do this."

The Director stares at me impassively.

"My hands are tied. You will be the first test subject, 792. I suggest you think carefully about your behavior from now on. You will not be afforded the same leniency again."

Fuck him and his damn *leniency*. I'm sobbing now, incoherent sounds squabbling to make their way out of my throat. They can't do this to me.

"I'm a person too," I try one more time, broken pleading noises spilling from my lips. "We're people, same as you. Please don't make me do this. I don't consent. *I do not consent!*"

My last words come out as a scream as Jason grabs hold of my arm and I pull away. The Director shakes his head at me and looks back down at his paperwork.

I crumple down into the thick red carpet, my legs collapsing underneath me as sobs rack my body. Jason moves closer, his slimy touch roaming over me as he pulls me into his arms and turns for the door. I try frantically to pull away from him. This can't be happening. It doesn't feel real. He barks and my traitorous fucking body just gives in, relaxing even as the tears blur my vision.

I hate him. I hate Jason, the Director, this compound, this fucking life I've had the bad luck to be allocated. Most of all, I despise my own fucking body. The way any alpha can make my body crave him no matter my feelings. I'm a hostage to my own instincts.

"Jason."

The Director stops us as we leave. My breath hitches with sobs as Jason turns, affording me a final glimpse of the man that's condemned me to a monster.

"Two weeks," the Director confirms, although it feels like a warning. Jason tenses beneath me. "And no bitemark before then."

The implications of this hit me all at once. No bitemark... but everything else is on the table. Jason can do whatever he wants to me, as long as his teeth don't end up in my neck.

Jason pulls me closer, cradling me in a gesture that might be considered protective from anyone else. He whispers gleefully in my ear, hot breath dampening my hair.

"We're going to have so much fun together, 792."

CHAPTER THREE
ROGUE

My team is a bunch of immature assholes. Absolute assholes.

It's like herding fucking cats.

"Ace," I snap into my comms speaker. "Quit messing around and do what you're actually paid to do."

A snort is my only reply. A shadow flits across the dirty window lined up through my scope, completely ignoring my order to stay put.

Our team has been assigned to extract a pallet of illegal tranquilizer guns from a group of omega traffickers and get the two omegas they currently have in captivity safely to the Omega Compound.

We've been staking out this warehouse for two days, and tonight we're moving in. It was all going well up until my team decided to completely ignore my orders.

Ace shimmies his body like a cat as he climbs up the drain-pipe, his combat boots finding a hold in the wall as he hauls himself silently through an open window and into the warehouse.

I curse as Devlin hisses into my ear. "Rogue—"

Of course it's a goddamned trap. I've been distracted by my team dynamics, and gunfire erupts from inside. Swearing, I push myself into a flat run, shooting at the door of the warehouse and slamming myself against it to burst it open. We've given away every advantage that we might have had, but I'm not leaving Ace in there to defend himself alone. *Asshole.*

I burst through the door, attempting to dodge the gunfire as Devlin crashes through behind me with a whoop. He lives for these moments – where everything goes to shit, and you have no choice but to fly by the seat of your pants. Me, I'm more of a planner than a pantser.

We take cover behind a pallet – hopefully, full of the guns we're looking for – and Devlin covers me as I reload. He returns fire against the cocksuckers shooting at us as I hiss through the comms for an update.

It takes a moment, but Ace's cackle comes through loud and clear. A lump of relief fills my throat before I force it back down. No time for sentiments in this shitstorm. After, maybe. Once I've battered them for being assholes.

"I'm clear, Rogue. Up on the beams – I'll take them out, you get the girls and the guns."

Apparently, Ace is now leading this fucking mission.

I wait to hear the gunfire switch to another direction before scanning the surrounding area. The light dips in and out as a few bare lightbulbs swing, highlighting the damp floor and a couple of rickety chairs.

The flickering light briefly illuminates two girls huddled in a cage in the corner. They're young, too, and my stomach turns at what they might have been subjected to since they were taken two weeks ago. I turn to Devlin beside me, knowing better than to send him over there.

"I'll get the guns," he mutters before I even have a chance to get the words out, slinking out and keeping his gun up and ready.

For the love of fuck.

"Am I actually in charge of this fucking mission or what?" I snarl, before stomping over towards the cage. I can't hear any more gunfire so I'm assuming that the traffickers are dead. Ace is an actual shadow in the field. No bullets ever seem to even get close. By this point though, I'm grumpy enough to tie him to a tree and use him for damn target practice.

The girls are silently gripping each other tightly for support and warmth. Motioning with my hand, I tell them to move to the back of the cage, before shooting the lock and pulling the door open. The oldest girl protectively covers the younger, keeping her eyes on me and refusing to move.

"It's okay," I tell her. I'm not the softest, but I try to keep my voice low and soothing. "We're getting you out of here."

She considers my words for a moment, glancing down at the shaking omega in her arms. I like the way she doesn't immediately jump, even though I'm an alpha.

"What will happen to us now?" the older omega asks warily. I notice that her gaze keeps shifting to the gun in my hand, and I slowly reach to the floor and place it down, holding my hands up to reinforce that I mean them no harm.

"We'll take you to a safe place. The Omega Compound."

Her eyes widen at my words, and she frantically shakes her head from side to side. Far from the reassurance I thought it would be, the girl clutches the younger omega tighter and pushes herself even closer to the bars of the cage.

"No," she states, her voice shaking. "Not there. We won't go there."

Her voice holds the barest trace of an omega whine, and I wince as Devlin comes up behind me, huffing in frustration at my slowness. I throw out a hand in warning to stop him from moving closer to the frightened girls. Dev isn't a big fan of omegas, and I don't want to scare them any further.

His gaze sweeps over them, lingering on the smaller girl.

She's even younger than I thought, barely a teen if that. Incredibly young to have awakened, probably why she was taken.

Nausea threatens at what would have happened to them in the hands of omega traffickers. Dev takes a step back, his hard eyes softening slightly at the two shaking females. It's hard not to want to do as they ask. But then that's the issue with omegas, isn't it? They're supposed to be master manipulators, using their hormones to influence others to their will.

And alphas don't?

I push away the uncomfortable thought.

"They don't want to go to the OC," I mutter to Dev.

I don't really get it. The Omega Compound is *safe*. It's a haven for unmated omegas. They're offered training and support to adjust to their omega traits, and then they're either matched with suitable packs or single alphas when they come of age, or they enter a strictly regimented surrogacy breeding program.

It sounds brutal, but with omegas the only race who can bear children, there has to be a structured way for that to happen. Even then, adopting a child is a one-in-a-million chance. There just aren't enough omegas.

Sure, I've heard it's strict. There's the Omega Creed and its archaic rules. But the reality is that our world isn't kind to omegas. It may have been years since the omega war, but people – especially betas – haven't forgotten. And they certainly haven't forgiven. It's better for the omegas that they stay under the care of the compound.

It's hard to reconcile the images in my mind to the two girls before me. I've never really interacted with omegas much. Truthfully, I've never really wanted to. Everyone knows that they're a risk to alphas.

These girls don't seem like that, though. Devlin's brow furrows, and he turns his back on the cage.

"I'll get Ace," he says, shouldering past me. It's a good shout. Ace is much better with females than either of us.

We wait for a moment in uneasy silence, the older omega not taking her eyes off me. The little one peers out from under her arm, curiosity in her face as she stares. Her eyes slip to Ace, widening as he slips past me. Dev mutters that he'll get the van ready and retreats hastily.

Ace takes a step towards the cage door, kneeling down.

"Hey," he murmurs softly to the girls. "I know this is scary, but we really do want to help you. The Omega Compound isn't something to be afraid of. They can help you learn more about being an omega and how to control it, and you can't stay here."

He lowers his voice, saying something I don't catch. The older omega stares hard at Ace as he holds out a hand, and he shifts back slightly to give her some more space. Her shoulders slumping, she looks down once more at the young girl held tightly in her arms. Murmuring soothing words, she gets the younger omega up and they hesitantly move towards the cage door.

Ace and I step back to give them space, and they emerge slowly, limbs shaking. They've been in the cage for at least a few days, and I can see that it's taking effort to keep their legs from folding.

"Here, lean on me," I offer, reaching out a hand slowly.

It takes them a moment, but the younger girl reaches out for me, small hands curling around my arm before grasping on tightly. I hear Ace behind me offering the same, and we slowly move out towards the vehicle. Dev is there, leaning against the door with his arms folded. His eyes flicker across the two omegas and tighten before he swings around to the driver's seat.

We get the girls situated comfortably and Ace pulls out a blanket from the box we brought in case it was needed. It's a breach of the creed, but they'll freeze without it. Handing it to the cold omegas, I watch them for a second as they huddle in the corner together. Something stirs uneasily in my gut at the idea of handing them over to the OC, but I dismiss it and move away towards the front of the van. It's not my place to get involved with omega politics. Ace throws himself in next to me, avoiding my gaze. He knows he's in for trouble after the stunts he's pulled today.

Dev is already on the phone to call in a clean-up crew and secure the warehouse. Our part of the mission is over – or it will be, once we deliver the omegas to their new home.

It's not a long trip, and we're soon pulling through the gates of the OC, moving through the three security checkpoints they have in place to prevent unauthorized access. I twist in my seat to check on the omegas. The small one is dozing. The older girl is staring out of the window at the electric wires and guards with guns strapped to their hips. There's a look of defeat on her face.

Pulling into the courtyard, I get out and head to open the door for them, Dev exiting the driver's seat. Before they can step out, I step closer and murmur to the older omega. "What's your name?"

Her blue eyes pierce mine for a moment before she begrudgingly responds.

"Gabrielle. This is Molly".

Gabrielle steps out carefully, and Molly blinks sleepy eyes as she looks around whilst Ace helps her gently down. He heads to the boot to unload the pallets we collected from the warehouse, waving a guard over to help. Two of the matrons are already coming down the steps to the main building, ready to collect their new charges.

"This is Molly and Gabrielle," I say, wanting to give them a good introduction before we have to move on. "They'll need some warmer clothes, a medical check-up, and time to settle—"

"Yes, thank you." The matron cuts me off abruptly. "We're aware of what an omega needs. We'll take it from here."

She grabs Gabrielle by the arm and pulls her away from us as my brows raise. Catching her wary eyes as she turns, I try to offer a smile of reassurance. It feels a little flat though.

I'm not sure why I feel so uncomfortable. There's a similar look on Dev's face as he reluctantly returns the small wave Molly sends him, before his features retreat to his usual 'don't fuck with me scary-killer face' (Gabe's words, not mine).

Hoisting myself back into the truck, I wait for Ace to return from offloading the pallets, checking my phone, and returning Gabe's message. Devlin hesitates before pulling out, and I resist the urge to look back.

"What now, boss?" Ace pokes me in the side, and I growl at him, pushing the omegas from my mind.

"Home. We've got a debrief and you have some explaining to do."

Both of my pack members groan in unison.

CHAPTER FOUR
GABE

I flit around the kitchen, putting the finishing touches to a lasagna. My phone beeps and I back up, carefully balancing the ceramic dish in my hand as I check the screen. The pack are on their way back, a typically brisk message from Rogue giving me a 15-minute ETA.

I slide the meal into the oven, emitting a soft growl of satisfaction as I close the oven door.

I'm not really your typical alpha. Sure, I've got the build. I'm nudging six foot and even though I'm slighter than the rest of my pack, I still work out and have the muscles to show for it. But I've never been a typically *dominant* alpha. Rogan, Devlin, and Ace pulled me into their pack in school almost by accident. They thought they were defending a beta. They soon realized I was alpha, though, when I knocked out the beta who tried to jump Ace when he wasn't looking. I might not be the first to throw a punch, but I'll happily finish the fight.

Humming quietly, I whip up a salad and throw some chopped potato into the frier. Ace will give me the puppy eyes if there's no fries. My stomach flips at the thought. Pushing away any thoughts of Ace's eyes, I finish up laying the table and head up for a quick shower before the pack gets home.

Home. It's a funny word. It means something a little bit different to everyone. It does to my pack. My throat closes at the thought of another awkward meal as I lean up against the wall of the shower, taking a moment to let the hot water batter my tired bones. Raising a hand, I trace the scar running from under my hairline down my left cheek. It goes straight through my eye.

Our pack is falling apart at the edges. We all know it.

Don't get me wrong. We'd give our lives for each other in an instant. I'd do anything for my brothers, and I know they'd do the same for me. I've never doubted it, even during our time with Elinor, and what happened afterwards.

But lately, our pack has become…cold.

We used to spend so much time together, all of us in this beautiful farmhouse we picked out. Our touch is all over this place. Rogue's books take up space in every corner, Devlin's art is hanging in the hallway. There are polaroid prints of us in our younger days dotted across the kitchen fridge. It should be perfect.

But the atmosphere is missing. Every day, it feels like we're going through the motions whilst we wait for something to happen. For *someone* to happen.

Our pack is missing a female. Alpha packs need a relationship in the pack bond to stay sane. We rely on it, can even go feral if we go too long without one. Our pack has buried itself in work and home to try and push off the feeling but it's starting to colour every interaction we have. We're all on edge, quick to anger and harsh words.

All of us have been reluctant to go near the OC, even with Rogue's connections. Devlin turns pale at just the thought of bitemarking an omega. And Ace… Ace is complicated. My heart jumps into my throat.

What happened with Elinor tarnished our relationship. She took what we had and twisted it, broke it into pieces. Now, we're so far apart I can't see us ever finding our way back to each other.

Maybe it's for the best. Focus on finding a female, and we can fix the main issue with the pack. Ace and I will sort ourselves out eventually.

We don't have to bring in an omega though. They're rare as fuck, for one. Devlin's aversion is another good reason to avoid the OC. We could always try and bring in another beta female.

My head pounds at the thought, and I close my eyes tightly. I need to get a handle on this. Between me and Devlin, there won't be any type of suitable female to bring in. Alpha females don't settle with male alpha packs, only betas.

My fingers follow the familiar path down the side of my face, tracing the memento Elinor left me with.

I switch off the shower and my attention is caught by the glare of lights sweeping across the window. Quickly dressing, I head downstairs to check on the food.

The silence as the kitchen door swings open speaks volumes.

Blowing out a breath, my gaze sweeps between them.

Rogue's face is a picture of frustration, his dark hair flopping into his eyes as he impatiently sweeps it off his face. Devlin's face is thunder whilst Ace is pure lightning, his eyes flicking around the kitchen as he takes in the nicely laid table, the candle, the basket of salad and our 'good' place settings. A little twist tugs in my stomach as his eyes meet mine, his gaze moving to my scar. I turn to fuss with the food, breaking eye contact.

"Let me guess," I drawl. "Ace went off like the lone ranger and Dev decided to just do his own thing?"

Rogue bristles, swinging around to point a finger at them

both, swinging between them like he's not sure who to ream out first.

"This is the last time," he snaps, his frustration scenting the air sharply. "Do you hear me? We are a *fucking team.* If you don't start to act like it, you'll be fucking benched, and I'll recruit new blood in."

Ignoring them both as they start to protest, he flops down at the table with a groan. I pass him a beer and he taps my wrist in quiet thanks, throwing a wink my way when the guys aren't looking. I shake my head at him. Rogue would never go on a mission without Ace and Dev. Even when they've gone maverick, they're still twice as effective as any other team.

I point at the two empty chairs until Dev and Ace sit their asses down, still grumbling at Rogue as he pointedly ignores them. Grabbing the lasagna from the side, I set it down in the middle with a flourish and Ace whistles in appreciation.

"Damn, Gabe, that looks good."

There's a flip of pleasure in my stomach at his words. I just nod, pushing away the guilt as his face falls.

It's all quiet for a few minutes as we focus on our food. Dev groans, leaning back in his chair and giving me a thumbs up.

I wasn't going to say anything tonight. But the tension seems to have settled into a tentative truce, so I'm seizing my chance.

Clearing my throat, I catch Rogue's attention.

"What's up?" he asks, settling his green eyes on me. I brace myself, shifting uncomfortably.

"I've been thinking..." I say hesitantly.

"Dangerous," quips Ace. He grins at me tentatively when Dev elbows him in the side. I ignore him and focus on Rogan and Devlin. I know Ace will support me. My heart twinges at the thought.

Rogue raises an eyebrow. "Go on," he encourages, motioning with his hand for me to get on with it.

Blowing out a breath, I go for it.

"I think we need to look at bringing in another female."

The table goes silent. Ace turns to look at me with wide eyes, and Devlin and Rogue still in their seats.

"I know things... didn't end well with Elinor." I stare down at my plate, clenching my fists and resisting the urge to touch my face. "But I can feel the tension in the pack bond. I don't want to hold us back anymore."

The pack immediately let out sounds of protest, and I wave them off.

"You've been holding back because of me, and I'm *ready*. I'm not saying I want to jump immediately into a bitemark—" Dev growls at the thought, "—but I want to at least start looking into betas again."

Ace sits forward, a serious expression on his face.

"I agree with Gabe."

Sagging in relief, I smile at him, an edge of sadness in my face. Maybe we'll actually get somewhere productive tonight.

"But I don't think a beta is a good idea." Ace's words are careful and pointed, and he holds my gaze. I suck in a breath as a stab of pain lances through me. I might have started it, but he's taking this conversation into unchartered territory.

"You can't be serious." Devlin's face twists in horror at Ace's words.

We all ignore him for the moment. He was always going to react badly at even the suggestion of an omega. I glance at Rogue to gauge his response. He looks deep in thought, his brow furrowed.

"We met two omegas today," he starts, but Dev interrupts him.

"Are you fucking serious? They were children!"

Rogue is on Devlin in an instant as he snarls, dominance leaking into his voice.

"Will you let me finish? I'm not suggesting *them*, you

goddamn idiot. I mean that we should look again at the OC. Those girls today didn't come across as controlling or manipulative, and they weren't even trained. I think it's worth at least looking into."

Dev rubs his throat angrily as Rogue releases him.

"I don't want an omega here," he snaps. The scent of anger and frustration cuts through the air like a knife, making the hair on the back of my neck rise.

Frustrated, I lean over to catch his eye. Dev has some deep issues around omegas from his childhood. I don't want to make him do anything he doesn't want to do, but the pack is at risk. We need to think of the bigger picture here. Part of me is relieved we're talking about an omega rather than a beta though. I shoot Ace a side-glance and see him watching me, a furrow between his eyes.

"Can't we just look into it?" I plead. "Maybe it won't come to anything. They might not have anyone suitable, and it might not work. We might not even be in the running for an omega. But if we don't try, then we'll never know. You *know* that we need someone, Dev. If not the OC, then who? Ace is right. If I'm completely honest, I don't want to try another beta. I know that makes me a hypocrite, but that's where I'm at. I will though, if you're absolutely set against an omega."

He looks away at my words, jaw ticking. I quickly finish before he can interrupt. "If we don't all agree, then they don't stay. That goes without saying."

Devlin nods his head slowly in reluctant agreement, rubbing a hand over his face. Ace whoops, an excited grin on his face. My stomach flips with excitement at the possibility. An *omega*. Not a beta. Relief forms a lump in my throat.

Rogue looks between us as he pushes his chair back and stands, pulling his phone from his pocket. "I'll call Dad now and see what we need to do to get in."

As he heads towards his office, I'm cautiously hopeful that

this might work. I can't believe it. Maybe we'll get somewhere this time.

Either that, or it'll tear the pack apart for good.

CHAPTER FIVE
ROGUE

Pouring myself a large measure of scotch, I sink down into the welcoming leather of my office chair and run a hand down my face.

An *omega*.

Even Devlin has agreed to give this a go. It's a sign of how bad things have become in the pack that he'd ever agree to something like this. And Gabe had to raise it. Some pack leader I am.

Pushing the negative thoughts away, I take a long swig of my drink for courage and dial my father's number.

I don't have a bad relationship with my dad. He's just distant. When I was a kid, he was the best father anyone could ask for. His booming voice used to echo through the house as he searched for me during our hide and seek games, exaggeratedly ignoring my toes poking out from underneath the curtain. He'd make a point of sitting in his office chair, tapping his feet in patterns whilst I giggled from underneath his desk. He'd dance with my mother around the kitchen, singing in his deep baritone while she laughed and made pancakes every Saturday morning, piling my plate high.

Life was good. But then my mother left.

One day when I was seven, she didn't pick me up from school. I sat on the steps, waiting, far past the time when everyone else had been collected. It was dark by the time my father arrived, his face pale and stricken. He'd scooped me up and hugged me tight, and in the car, he'd explained that my mother had to go away for a while, and hopefully, she would be back soon. But a week stretched into months, and then years. After a while, I stopped asking my father when she'd be back.

I knew she wasn't coming back.

Dad turned into a ghost overnight. He went through the motions, and I was always fed and clothed and had everything I needed. But he drifted through the house like a wraith, until one day he told me he had a new job. That was the day I saw the spirit back in his eyes. He seemed more like himself, throwing himself into his work at the Omega Compound. I bounced around from nanny to nanny, seeing him less and less as he progressed through the ranks until he became the Director.

"Rogue?" He picks up the phone quicker than I expected, his voice concerned. Has it been that long since I called him?

"Dad. Have you got a minute?"

"Sure, hang on." I hear him mumbling apologies as he moves away from whatever he's doing. "There we go."

"Sorry, I didn't mean to disturb you."

"Don't be. It was a boring meeting anyway. Are you alright?"

"Yeah, everything… everything's fine." There's silence on the line from my dad. No matter how long since we've spoken, he can always tell when I'm hiding something. "I wanted to speak to you about the OC."

"Oh?" There's a hint of surprise in his voice. I've always shied away from anything to do with the compound. When I was younger, I thought they'd stolen my dad from me, and over recent years it's had more to do with Devlin's history. On the rare occasions we have to go there, like today, it's in and out as soon as possible.

"Yeah," I clear my throat. "We've been talking about bringing in a new female to the pack, and I was wondering if you'd be able to help through the compound."

Dad goes quiet for a moment. "And Devlin is alright with this?" His dislike of omegas isn't exactly a state secret.

"He's agreed to try, trial period only for the time being."

Dad hesitates, seconds stretching out as he considers my words.

"Well, that's great news," he says finally.

"I think we'll be able to help, and it'll be good for the pack to have that stability. Can you come in tomorrow?"

After agreeing to meet him at the OC in the morning, I hang up and consider what this might mean for us.

Having a female in the house will be a big change. Having an *omega* here will be challenging. Our previous efforts nearly ripped us apart, and Gabe... we nearly lost him.

I wonder if an omega will work better. Heading back into the kitchen, I let the team know and Gabe smiles brightly, nervousness and a hint of excitement I haven't seen since the incident creasing his cheeks. Ace offers to come to the OC with me, but before I can agree, Dev cuts in abruptly.

"Can I come?"

We all stare at him in shock. Ace recovers first. "That's fine. I'm trusting you both to pick someone pretty, though. A redhead would be a bonus."

"Being female is a bonus at this point," Gabe mutters in exasperation. Ace flinches at his words, and I frown, staring between them for a moment. They pointedly look away from me with matching expressions of false nonchalance. I thought things between them might have been getting better.

Making a note to pull them both aside and find out what's

going on, I head back to the solitude of my office. I work late into the night, reading the same lines repeatedly as my thoughts drift to tomorrow.

I pull up information on the Omega Creed on my laptop and flick through it. My back straightens, unease and distaste trickling into me with every word. It's a lot stricter than I realised. I mean, they're not even allowed a *bed*. What's the point of that?

Molly's face fills my mind, Gabrielle begging us to take them somewhere else. My hand clenches, the plastic protesting with a large crack. I shove away my broken mouse and lean back with a sigh.

I'm not responsible for them, I tell myself. *This is the law.*

But something isn't sitting right with me.

CHAPTER SIX
HARPER

I don't feel like me anymore.

The water is freezing, but I stopped feeling it a while back. I just feel numb. My body is completely submerged, and the shaking has stopped. I don't think that's good, but I can't bring myself to care.

Maybe this is it. Maybe I'll just drift away.

I'm so tired. I think I'm ready.

My thoughts wander, taking me away from the feeling of ice sloshing against my skin. For the first time in years, I let myself think of my mom and dad. We were happy, once. Childhood memories of family gatherings and the sweet scent of baked goods wash over me, and I surround myself with better times, picking through memories like pages from a book until my mind grows fuzzy as my face slips below the surface.

Let this be it, I think. There's a haziness to my thoughts.

Let me be free.

A hand grasps my hair and yanks me out of the water. My legs can't hold me up and I cry out as my full weight dangles. Jason rips me from the comforting numbness, dragging me across the floor towards a second tub. My legs scrape over the rough concrete, new bruises springing up amongst the field of purple and green. My body shakes violently, teeth chattering with the aftereffects of the ice bath.

He forces my legs into the warm water and agony sears up my limbs as steam rises. I scream, my legs feeling like they're on fire.

It lasts for a handful of seconds at most, but tears are falling when Jason pulls me out again. I land heavily on the floor and don't move, my legs twitching as the pins and needles hit them.

Jason leans over me, stroking my hair back from my face. I flinch before I can control it, and his hand whips out, slapping me across the face. A stab of pain flares as my lip splits again, blood trickling down my chin.

"Kneel." It's a growl, not a bark, but I still comply.

Every inch of me hurts, but I drag myself onto my knees, keening in pain at the pins and needles and burning in my legs. I'm not quick enough for Jason and a bamboo cane slaps the bottom of my feet, making me cry out.

"I'm sorry, Sir!"

He only hits me twice, so maybe I wasn't so slow this time. My feet sting with the feeling of the thin cuts.

Kneeling obediently with my legs pressed together, I face the floor. I stare forwards, my gaze unfocused as I rest my palms on my thighs.

I don't know how long I've been in this room. It feels like months. And every waking moment has been filled with *him*.

Even my sleep doesn't bring peace. When I'm allowed to sleep at all, Jason is either next to me, his hands roaming my body, or I'm in the cage, shivering on the plastic matting. There's no sheet. Nowhere to hide in this room.

I think I've only slept a handful of times since I've been here. My reality is hazy around the edges, exhaustion pulling at me.

In the back of my mind, I know that it can't have been longer than two weeks. The Director said that he'd want to see Jason's progress, and I haven't seen anyone apart from him since I've been here. Jason is my whole life now, and he's loving every second of it.

My stomach gurgles, crying out for food. I'd take a meal of plain rice in the dining hall with a smile and grateful thanks at this point, rather than Jason putting his fingers in my mouth and feeding me his leftovers.

Maybe they've forgotten about me. Maybe this is it.

Cold hands caress my messy hair, and I close my eyes for a second, hating myself for leaning into it.

This is what they want me to do. They want me to rely entirely on him, to be a good omega, a good pet. To follow the three stages of omega submission – kneel, spread, present. To set me up for breeding.

I think they're going to get what they want. I've tried so fucking hard, but there's no fight left in me.

"Spread."

This time, he uses his bark. I'm quicker now. I don't even feel nauseous at the thought anymore. If I please Jason, then he might give me something to drink. My throat is bone dry and if I cough, I'll be back in the ice bath.

My knees spread apart, hands obediently resting on my thighs in the correct position as I rest back on my heels. My chest is pushed out, displaying my body for him, the thin underwear doing nothing to hide me.

Jason's alpha bark rings through me and I feel a gush of wetness between my legs as my body responds. Two weeks ago, I would have panicked. Now, I feel nothing.

Reaching down, he strokes his fingers against me almost gently. My body tenses up even as my hips shift, my body seeking more as a low whine comes out of my throat.

He hasn't mated me yet. He wants me to beg him for it. It's

the one line that I haven't crossed, and Jason's doing everything he can to drag me across it.

I won't present for him. Presenting is the ultimate omega submission. Elbows down, ass up. It's permission for an alpha to *take*.

This is the only thing I have left, and I won't give it. So, the punishments continue.

But I'm so tired. I'm so close to giving in.

I keep my eyes focused on the floor as his finger strokes back and forth over my thin underwear, his pungent lemon scent burning my nose like bleach.

His eyes never leave my face. Inside, I'm screaming. I'm fighting a battle with my own body. The screaming is so loud I'm surprised Jason can't hear it.

Nobody is listening.

Nobody is coming to save me.

My instincts are crying out for me to obey, raking claws down my insides. To do exactly as he tells me, to be a good omega, to have privileges and be warm and make my alpha happy.

But I've already given up so much. My full submission is the only thing I have left, and even if Jason takes it from me, I won't give it up willingly. I don't know how much longer I can keep this up, though.

Jason's scent sharpens as his anger spikes. Withdrawing his hand from between my thighs, he shoves his meaty fingers into my mouth as far as he can. I taste myself on his fingers as I choke, falling backward onto the floor.

He follows me, bringing his weight down and shoving himself between my thighs. I try to push him away, but my efforts are pathetic.

Weak.

"Beg," he demands, but he stops short of using his alpha bark. I shake my head frantically and a moan slips out as he grinds himself into me. I can feel his knot swelling up. As he stares into my face, greasy and lank blonde hair hanging down, realization fills me.

He's not going to take my silence as an answer anymore. He's just going to *take*.

He reaches down to unbuckle his trousers, pulling his leather belt through the loops. Stretching up, he easily catches my flailing hands and ties them above my head. I cry out thinly, but there's no strength left in my body or my voice. I keep trying to shout, heedless of the silence telling me that no one will hear me.

Shifting down, Jason brings his face between my legs. I moan in horror as he places his nose against my dampness and inhales deeply. Traces of my own perfume start to appear. The scent blockers are wearing off, since Jason hasn't given me any since I've been here. *Cinnamon and oranges.*

It's been years since my scent appeared at all.

This is happening. This is really happening. In my panic, I remember the Directors words. "You can't bite me," I rasp. Not responding to my words, he pulls my head to the side and drags his tongue up my throat.

He's going to do it. The Director might be angry, but he won't break a bitemarked pair. And my consent doesn't mean a damn thing. Alphas don't need an omega's permission, only the OC's.

My only hope is that he hasn't injected me with the hormones to trigger a heat, so I won't get pregnant. Not this time, anyway. My lungs close at the thought and I gasp for breath, my legs flailing as Jason holds me down.

Then I hear a bang. One, then another. My gaze flickers desperately to the closed door as Jason growls, baring his teeth at the interruption. He pulls away from me and stands, doing up his trousers. Sobbing, I drag myself away from him, folding into a corner and looping my tied hands over my knees to hug them tightly. It's a reprieve at best.

Staring around, I look desperately for something I can use as a weapon, but Jason is careful not to leave anything within reach. I'm not even allowed to use cutlery because he feeds me by hand.

It takes a minute for Jason to work through the four locks he's installed on the door, but eventually he rips it open, and I catch pieces of the conversation.

"*Director… progress…omega…,*"

The relief that fills me is staggering. They didn't forget about me.

This is it. I'm going to get out of this room. This may be my only chance to escape, and I need to be ready.

CHAPTER SEVEN
DEVLIN

I grit my teeth as I follow Rogue and Christian down the hall. Christian is talking animatedly, but his tone seems… off.

Maybe it's me. Nausea swirls in my stomach. This is such a bad fucking idea.

I *hate* omegas. Anything to do with them. Omegas are the reason I don't have a family anymore. The only thing stopping me from pulling Rogue to one side and demanding we leave is the look on Gabe's face when he asked about a female last night.

I know he's right.

The pack is falling apart. Ace's mood swings are affecting us all, and I can barely get a sentence out without snapping at someone. Rogue is more centered, but as pack leader, he's still picking up on our emotions through the bond and it's affecting his ability to think rationally. If we don't sort ourselves out, things will get worse and one of us will end up in a frenzy. A rabid, snapping, snarling beast.

We tried a beta before because of me. Guilt stabs me at the thought. Elinor caused so much damage that we nearly split up in the aftermath. Gabe still isn't himself, pushing back his own instincts and tearing Ace apart in the process.

I owe it to them to try. I owe it to all of us.

Christian ushers us into his office. It's plush, thick red carpet holding a large walnut desk. Books surround us on every side, and a copy of the Omega Creed hangs on the wall. I push away the twinge of discomfort I get when I look at it. It's in place for good fucking reason.

Christian and Rogue are talking quietly, Rogue settling into one of the fancy chairs in front of Christian's desk. We don't see Christian often. His role demands a lot of his time, so it's good to see them together.

Christian looks up and waves me over.

"How are you, Devlin?" I don't know why, but the question makes me uncomfortable. Christian's gaze is a few shades paler than Rogue's, but he has the same piercing stare. If I didn't know him, I'd call him a cold motherfucker.

Shrugging, I play off the awkwardness.

"You know, usual shit. Hands full with this lot."

"Not too full for an omega though?"

I jolt, betraying my discomfort with this whole idea. I'll see it through for my team though. I have no doubt that any omega we choose will soon show her true colors – and I'll be showing her the door as I kick her out. It's a short-term solution, but maybe we'll find a beta Gabe can work with in the meantime.

Christian hums and leans back, shifting his gaze between us.

"I do have an omega that I would like you to meet."

Rogue shifts forward, his interest clear. "What's she like?"

A grimace flits across Christian's face before he schools his expression, and I wonder why he looks so uncomfortable.

"She's… unusual. Been with us for seven years, and she's currently participating in the pilot of a new project. I've actually asked for her trainer to bring her in and give us a demonstration of their work so far."

My neck prickles, and Rogue's brow furrows. "What kind of pilot are we talking about?"

Christian clears his throat. "As you know, the OC trains awakened omegas to manage their instincts before matching them with appropriate alpha groups."

We nod. The general work of the OC is common knowledge.

"In recent years, the board has been clear that they don't believe our work goes far enough. Rumors surrounding the omega war and some unfortunate incidents mean that public sympathy is growing for omegas. There are discussions in play over whether the work of the OC is still needed. It also takes up significant government funds, and we're being pushed to look for more cost-effective alternatives that result in more children being born."

Anger swirls through me at the thought of releasing omegas into the general public, free to wreak havoc and work their influence, controlling alphas until they become mindless rutting beasts. "That's bullshit."

"Do you think so?" Christian raises his brows at me, but he doesn't look surprised. "Well, you might be a fan of the new scheme then."

He doesn't look like much of a fan himself, and Rogue pulls him up on it. "So, what's the deal with this new project? The OC already owns all omegas. Surely there's not much else that can be done?"

"There's always more that can be done." Christian's voice is dark as he gets up, facing away from us and staring out of the window.

Curious, I step up alongside him, taking in the guards lining the fence, guns at their hips. Seems a bit overkill, but who knows what they have to put up with. The space directly under his office looks to be some sort of exercise area, and there's a handful of omegas there stretching.

My lip curls automatically, and I head back to my seat, not wanting to see any more.

"The Phoenix Project aims to remove all autonomy from omegas. By binding them to a single alpha trainer who will have full control over every aspect of their lives, they will undergo a significantly intensified training program from what we currently offer, including behavioral and emotional aspects. At the end of this training period, they will be bitemarked and enter the surrogacy breeding program alongside their individual alpha on a permanent basis. It's more focused, will cost less and has a higher chance of successful breeding than the current arrangements."

My stomach clenches. Glancing at Rogue, I see a similar expression on his face. "Alpha, as in singular? No more packs?"

Christian nods, the expression on his face betraying his distaste. "Exactly. Omegas will no longer be matched with a pack if the project proves successful. The government has always been aware of the influence of alpha packs, especially given the issues we had during and after the omega war. They wish to dissolve that influence and think that this may offer a joint opportunity – true control of the omega population and limiting the capability of the alphas."

Just the thought of being separated from my pack makes my teeth clench. "It'll never happen," I scoff.

"Not immediately, perhaps. But over time, who knows?" Christian challenges. "Once, we would never have thought omegas would be where they are now, but things change. Not always for the better." He mutters the last part under his breath.

Rogue turns to me. Before he can speak, a knock sounds at the door.

"That will be Jason and 792," Christian looks concerned. "I

wanted to explain more before you met her, but we're out of time. Just keep an open mind – and whatever you do, *stay calm*. Your reactions are likely to be reported back to the board."

What the fuck? Firstly, omegas have names, so why are they referring to this girl by a number? Secondly, what exactly are we going to see that will make us react badly?

Rogue and I share a quick glance and his concern is clear.

What the hell have we gotten into here?

CHAPTER EIGHT
ROGUE

Something's not right. I've never interacted with my
father at work, but the way he's behaving is strange. My
neck prickles at his final words. They sound like a
warning.

Devlin's unease pulses through the pack bond. I reach out a
hand, squeezing his shoulder. His tension is clear, and I'm
starting to second-guess this whole arrangement. It's too late to
leave without meeting the omega now, though, as my father
calls out for her to enter.

The door swings open to reveal a stocky man in a grey
guard's uniform. His dirty blond hair is sticking up and his
sweaty brow furrows over beady muddy brown eyes. Distaste
fills me.

He's clearly an alpha. His scent leaks into the room, and I bite
back a snarl at the acidic citrus tang. This guy's giving me the
creeps. A side glance at Devlin shows me that he feels the same way.

My eyes sweep around, looking for the omega, but a sound
from Devlin draws my attention back to him. His face has
paled, brows dipped in trepidation as he stares down at the

floor. A pulse of anger echoes through the pack bond. I follow his gaze, and that's when I see her.

Stunned shock fills me, quickly followed by absolute fury.

The girl at his side shuffles forward on her knees, keeping close to him. It takes me a second to see the collar around her neck, linking to a chain-link leash wrapped around the guard's pudgy fingers, and I can't stop a growl emerging. The *fuck* is this?

The girl's eyes sweep up to me at the sound. We lock gazes for a second. Her eyes shimmer the purest shade of gold, like sunlight through a glass of whiskey before she quickly drops them down to the floor again. The agony in them almost brings me to my knees.

Devlin has turned to stone next to me. I don't think he's even breathing. Whatever his thoughts on omegas, neither of us expected this. My thoughts fill with Gabrielle and little Molly, waving as she trustingly walked into this place because we told them – *promised* them - they would be safe.

I think I might be sick on the floor of my father's office.

Silence fills the office for a moment until this asshole decides to open his mouth, smirking jauntily at my dad like he's presenting a prize. His eyes pinch at the corners as he moves closer, and the smirk drops off slightly.

I watch him carefully, noting the way he winds the leash in around his fist, forcing the girl closer to him. He's possessive of her.

"Well, sir, I think you'll be pleased with my results," he simpers.

His weaselly voice goes through me. He gives the leash a shake, and the omega's neck pulls sharply upwards. It must hurt, but she doesn't react, staring straight ahead.

Devlin hasn't moved, his eyes focussed on the broken girl in front of us.

My father clears his throat again, and I whip my gaze over to him. He meets my eyes steadily, with no hint of distress.

I wonder what happened to the man I used to hero-worship.

"Thank you for bringing 792 in for a viewing, Jason. As you can see, we have two alphas with us today, who would also like to witness the progress you've made. If progress is sufficient, we may look to match 792 with a pack because of your efforts."

I can't even be angry at him for throwing us under the bus. One look at the bruised omega in front of me and I want her out of here, safe at home where Gabe can fuss, and we can work this out as a group. Even if she's not for us, I'm not leaving her here with this toad of a man. I move closer to Dev, brushing his arm with my own. He tears his attention away just enough to give me a brief nod before it returns to her. We're on the same page, his dislike of omegas pushed aside for the moment.

The guard – Jason - obviously isn't happy with my dad's words. He starts to splutter, his fingers holding so tightly to the leash that they're white at the knuckles.

"But, Sir – we've made so much progress, it would be an awful shame to see that go to waste. I think I've proved that the Phoenix project has real potential, and my father won't be happy if we abandon at this stage,"

I tune his whining drivel out. Clearly, my father is pushing us towards this girl. Whatever his reasoning, I'm not going to argue with him about it. I let him handle the dickhead whose face is turning redder and redder.

Scanning my eyes over the omega, I force myself to detach from the emotion hitting me like a battering ram and clinically assess her in her measly clothing. It's cold out today and she's wearing hardly anything, a filthy underwear set with a camisole that looks like it might have been white at one stage. It's ripped in parts and she's dangerously close to exposing herself, but she stays perfectly still while Jason rants above her.

There are bruises littering her creamy skin, shades of purple and green made over several days. One particularly nasty purple bruise looks like a large boot, and there are smudges of dark finger marks dusted over her chin and neck area.

Her wrists aren't cuffed, but the marks covering them tell their own story. She's been restrained recently for a substantial period. I can't see her legs properly from this angle, but her feet are bare. Her tangled, damp hair is a beautiful shade of copper and swings down either side of her face, hanging off the floor by a few inches.

She's breathing quickly, her ribs clearly visible as they move in and out. I can *feel* how petrified she is. The scent permeates the room, making me shift restlessly, but she's trying to hide it. She keeps perfectly still, trying to avoid attention even though every alpha in the room is focused on her.

I swallow back the urge in my chest to go to her, to rip her away from the guard. Is this what they mean when they talk about omega control? It feels like there's a rope in my chest that's tugging me to move straight for her.

I need to get her out of here.

My father is trying to get my attention, so I turn to him reluctantly.

"Let's sit down, shall we? Jason, please demonstrate your progress with 792 as requested and we can discuss from there."

Every mention of this girl by number makes my hackles rise. Dev sits reluctantly in his chair but leans forward, laser-focussed on the omega in front of us. I follow his lead and take a seat, hating the feel of soft leather when the girl in front of me is on the floor.

The Director gives Jason a nod, and he snaps his fingers.

"Kneel."

The omega moves quickly, her hair catching the light like

liquid fire as she pulls herself into a kneeling position. Knees pressed together, she sits back on her heels, placing her hands on her thighs. The whole time, her gaze remains downwards.

Jason waits a moment, and my father jumps in. "How has she behaved over the course of the pilot?"

His face twists unpleasantly. I can see him battling with the urge to boast and wanting to keep her here, with him.

"Improving, Sir," he says reluctantly, "but she needs more work. It took a while, but by using the continuous training techniques identified in the earlier stages of the project, she now responds well to most commands."

He strokes a hand over her hair gently as he speaks, and revulsion fills me as she leans into it. What kind of conditioning have they given her?

Dev clears his throat next to me. "Tell us more about this *continuous training.*"

If Jason hears the dangerous threat in his voice, he doesn't react to it. His chest inflates with pride as he launches into an explanation.

"It's a series of techniques originally developed during the omega war. By subjecting the omega to these on an ongoing basis in a restricted environment, it was discovered that complete obedience can be achieved much more quickly than by the years of training the current programme offers."

"What techniques have you used?" I ask. I've studied some of this previously, but surely, he can't mean—

"She responds especially well to sensory deprivation, along with temperature control. Iced baths work well as a quick method, and we also trialled the Chinese water method. We haven't had a huge amount of time to see that one through, but it had promising results during the three hours we tested it. Bamboo canes have also been successful, although more for punishment than conditioning."

The fuck. I bite back a snarl.

Chinese water torture. It's a miracle she's even functioning. Prolonged water torture can cause a psychotic break in a matter of hours. I swallow down the sick feeling in my gut and wave a hand at him to continue. Catching Dev's eye, I shake my head slightly to stop the protest I can see forming on the tip of his tongue, remembering my father's warning.

Do not react.

If we want to get her out of here, we need to be as nonchalant as they are.

Jason waits for my father's nod before continuing to the second step. I recognise the commands now from my reading last night. The three stages of omega submission. I find myself holding my breath, dread pooling at the base of my spine at what's coming next. Devlin's hand is clenched so tightly on the end of the chair I swear I hear it creaking in protest.

This time, he uses his alpha bark. *"Spread!"*

Our omega immediately spreads her legs, revealing the tiny scrap of lace between her thighs. Her hands press against the inside of her thighs as though she's holding herself open for inspection, and she thrusts her chest out invitingly. Even battered and bruised, she's absolutely mesmerizing.

Devlin swears under his breath, and I shift in my chair, my slacks suddenly feeling tighter than they did a second ago. I wrestle the feeling down, hating myself for reacting to this horrific situation. This is an absolute violation in every way.

Then a low, pained whine fills the room. Dev and I immediately jump to our feet, taking a step towards her as the omega's scent surrounds us. Cinnamon and oranges rise up in the air, drawing our alpha pheromones to the surface.

Ours. Protect.

The urges hit me like a freight train, and aggression taints the air as Jason blocks our view, a low growl rumbling from his chest.

"Enough!" My father's bark holds enough dominance to make each of us take a step away.

He barrels between me and Dev and grabs Jason by the throat. His weaselly face purples, and he tries to back up, but my dad grips him tightly.

"Have you bitten her?" he demands.

Dread fills me as Jason chokes in response, his eyes rolling back in his head as he shakes it from side to side. If he's given her a bitemark then we won't be able to separate them without causing her pain, possibly death. Bitemarks link omegas to the alphas they're allocated, an extra layer of control.

I drop my gaze to the omega. She hasn't moved, although her scent is much stronger now. Glancing down quickly, I rip my eyes away. There's a damp patch spreading across her underwear as her body responds to the hormones in the air. Her shoulders are shaking and there are tears rolling down her face, cheeks flushed red with humiliation.

I desperately want to drop to my knees and comfort her, give her something to cover herself with. My hands fall to the end of my shirt to tug it off before I remember Dad's warning. My hands clench against the white material.

Is this really the infamous omega control they talk about? Because I'm not seeing any manipulation here. Just a petrified, abused girl at the mercy of an unforgiving regime.

I turn away from her in case my urge to go for Jason's throat overwhelms me and drag Devlin back to his chair by his arm, shaking it until he looks at me. *Hold it together, and maybe we can all walk away from this.* I push reassurance down the bond and he grimaces, nodding slightly. I can see his clenched fists shaking. The last thing we need is for Devlin to lose it.

Dad throws Jason away from him and he hits the floor. Colour rises on his face as he pulls himself up, and he makes a move towards the omega before my dad speaks, his words cutting and dripping with ice.

"I've seen enough. I find myself… unhappy with your progress."

Jason immediately starts to protest, and Dad slams his hand down on the desk. Jason shuts his mouth with a snap.

"You may leave. I'll be in touch."

The girl lets out a single, broken sob as Jason reaches for her leash. My heart just about tears from my chest and I take a step forward, but my father gets between them, his hand on Jason's chest.

"Your services on the Phoenix project are no longer needed. Return to your post."

Jason splutters in shock. "But – but my father—"

"*I* am in charge at this compound, and I'm ordering you to return to your post immediately. You can expect a performance review in the next 24 hours where we'll be discussing your future employment. I'll also be speaking to your father about this, believe me. The pilot was not an open invitation for sexual abuse. *Get out of my sight.*"

Jason stays where he is for a moment, his beady eyes focused firmly on the omega. For a moment, I think it's going to come down to a fight. The idea excites me. Part of me hopes he stays put. This dickhead needs a taste of his own medicine.

Devlin cracks his knuckles threateningly and the sound makes Jason's head turn to us, scowling. Alpha or not, we're two highly dominant males. We'd break this little rat in a second and he knows it. Swallowing, he backs away and spins to storm out of the room without another word, slamming the door shut behind him.

CHAPTER NINE
HARPER

The door bangs shut, but I stay where I am. I don't trust that this isn't another trick in Jason's endless toolbox. Heat creeps up my neck, embarrassment at being exposed like this in front of these men lighting my cheeks on fire. I bite down a whimper.

The silence in the room stretches, and my breathing slows. I can feel the gaze of the two new alphas on me. Rather than making my skin crawl, I feel warm. Their scents are comforting rather than jarring, like Jason's acidic tang. Something is pushing me to look up, to move closer, but I snap it back.

Breathing deeply, I make the most of it while I wait for orders. I expect that someone will be in shortly and they'll hand me over to another trainer. I pray that whoever it is, they're better than who I've spent the last fortnight with.

I shudder and another growl creeps through the room. I really want to look up and get a better look. I saw one of the alphas briefly when I first came in, but I didn't have a chance to see him properly. His eyes were beautiful though. A deep, emerald green framed with long, light lashes.

Footsteps thud into the carpet, and I tense as the Director

comes to a stop in front of me. His hand curls around my chin and it's unexpectedly gentle as he nudges me to look up.

"It's alright, Harper, you're free to look around. Just relax for a moment," he says quietly. Looking up at him, I'm surprised to see sadness on his face. His eyes look haunted now, rather than empty.

Letting go of my face, he turns to the alphas.

The green-eyed alpha watches the Director with a frown, his face holding a familiarity I recognize as I glance between him and the older man. I think they're related. Similar noses, similar bone structure in their faces.

The rest of him is as attractive as his eyes. A black curl falls lazily across his eye, and he pushes it away from his face impatiently. My eyes trace his hawkish nose and mouth. It tilts up at the corners, as though he's used to laughing.

The second alpha clears his throat and I whip my gaze to him. Russet brown hair, short at the sides but longer on top. It's his eyes that grab my attention though. So dark they're almost black, he watches me with an intensity that I'm not sure is a good thing. His face is expressionless, arms crossed. He looks like he'd rather be anywhere else than here.

Just to make this awkward situation even better, my core clenches, another wave of cinnamon perfume rising up in the air. I can't stop it, and I push my legs together tightly. The two alphas inhale deeply, nostrils flaring as my cheeks flush in mortification. I could blame it on the scent blockers wearing off, but there's something about these two that makes me want to roll over and freaking *beg* for their knot.

I've *never* been attracted to an alpha before. I could definitely make an exception for these two, though. Flicking my gaze between them, I nickname them *Green* and *Brown*. Not the most imaginative names, but they'll do.

The dark-eyed alpha, Brown, shifts. Breathing deeply, he holds my eyes for a moment more before turning to the discussion happening between father and son. A whine reverberates in my throat when he looks away, but I manage to reign it in. My omega instincts are all over the place. I don't want to make things any worse than they already are.

A wave of dizziness hits me hard, and my eyes start to flutter. I dig my nails into my hands, willing myself to stay conscious. The last two weeks are finally starting to catch up to me, the aches and pains in every inch of my body making me want to curl up in a ball and push the world away.

I've been surviving on pure adrenaline. With Jason nowhere to be seen, I feel safe for the first time in days.

I'm not sure what makes me think that when I'm going to be handed to someone similar, but I have a feeling it's the alphas. I force my eyes open wide as scents fill the room, a smoky leather aroma entwined with the fresh scent of cut grass swirling in a heavenly mix that makes my mouth water.

Just for a moment, I wish things were different. I wish I could stay with them.

I've stupidly ignored the discussion and when they turn to me expectantly, all I can do is blankly stare at them and hope not to pass out. Wouldn't that just be the cherry on top of a shit sundae?

Brown steps forward. "She's going to pass out."

"'M not," I mutter. My voice sounds slurred. I hear a curse as I slump to the side, and suddenly I'm engulfed in warmth, scented leather surrounding me. Letting out a small moan, I can't help but bury into it, rubbing my nose into a soft shirt as my eyes drift shut.

CHAPTER TEN
DEVLIN

Fuck.

The omega – no, *Harper*, nuzzles into my chest again, and something tugs at my chest. My scent rises up in waves, leather and woodsmoke filling the room. I can't help but respond to her. She feels ice cold to the touch, and I pull her a little more tightly against me as I run my hand up and down her arm. Turning, I face Rogue and Christian. They both look a little shellshocked at how quickly I caught her.

I haven't taken my eyes off her since she crawled through the door, and I know a stress reaction when I see one. She's light as a feather, the edges of her ribs protruding underneath my fingers. She needs food, warmth. My instincts start to take over and I growl at Rogue when he reaches out to take her from me, a deep warning sound echoing through the office and making his eyes fly wide in shock. He raises his hands in surrender but growls back at me, and my head drops slightly in a show of submission. I don't let go of her though. I'm not sure I can.

Christian moves forward and I back away. Sighing, he steps

further away from me and points to the two-seater against the wall.

"Put her down there," he murmurs. "She needs to rest, and we need to discuss what happens now."

I move over to the leather seat but rather than placing her down, I turn and sink into the cushions, keeping hold of her and raising my brow in silent challenge. Christian huffs at me but leaves it there, settling back into his chair as Rogue takes a seat beside me.

Rogue doesn't waste any time in getting to the point.

"You owe us an explanation," he challenges. He keeps his voice low as he flicks a glance at the sleeping girl in my arms.

Wincing, Christian looks penitent. "I apologize. I wanted to discuss this with you before he brought Harper in."

"You're *torturing* them." Christian flinches at my blunt accusation, but he doesn't deny it. Blowing out a breath, he squares himself and meets my eye. "Yes."

Growls echo as Rogue and I both respond to his words.

"Why?" Rogue barks, and Christian curls his lip at the inherent demand. Normally, an alpha using a bark on another alpha outside of the pack leader relationship causes issues, but as Rogue's father, Christian manages to resist snarling back.

"I want to explain now, but I can't." He cuts our protests off, holding up his hand.

"You deserve answers, but we don't have time. I'm sure that Jason is already contacting his father and Harper needs to be away from here before there can be any further developments."

The thought of that idiot getting his hands on the omega again makes my hands clench around her instinctively, and she lets out a plaintive mewl of protest in her sleep. Stilling, we all look down, and I loosen my hands, flexing my fingers against the bruising on her soft skin. Rogue reaches out and strokes some hair away from her face, watching me carefully. The pack bond recognizes that he's not a threat to her now things have settled down, though, and I nod.

"Fine." Rogue says the word through gritted teeth, but Christian obviously isn't going to give us anything else right now. "But you *will* explain."

Christian nods, relieved. "Our priority now is to get you both out of here with Harper. Unfortunately, there are normally a number of steps involved in an alpha-omega pairing. I can bypass some, but others will be noticed if we skip them. You'll need to attend the pairing induction, at least."

Pressing a button, he barks into a receiver. "Induction needed in room four. Send a matron over. I also need Hunt here in the next five minutes, have him wait outside my office."

A tinny voice confirms, and he sits back in his chair. For the first time, I realise how much he's aged since I last saw him. His salt and pepper hair is more salt than pepper now, and lines mark his face that weren't there a few months ago.

"Something's going on here," I watch his face twitch and know it's true. "Something you can't talk about." Christian jerks his head in agreement, but we're interrupted by a knock on the door.

"That'll be Hunt," he says, standing. "Leave Harper here. I won't let her out of my sight," he promises, clearly scenting the aggression from both of us at the idea leaving her in this room unprotected.

Too much, too soon.

I need to clear my head of her fucking scent. Cinnamon and oranges twist around me like a drug. My head spins and I force myself to stand and settle Harper back on the seat. She curls into the warmth I've left behind, shivering slightly as we step away. I flex my fingers, fighting the urge to go back to her. Determinedly, I push myself towards the door, every step a battle not to turn back.

"I'll make the arrangements whilst you're gone and you can

head off as soon as you're finished with the induction and paperwork," Christian motions for us to head out.

With one last look at the flame-haired girl that's flipped my world upside down in the space of an hour, I follow Rogue out.

We silently follow the guard down the corridor to an unmarked door, where he shows us into a bland room filled with chairs, a large projector screen aimed against the wall. When the door closes behind him, I round on my alpha, nostrils flaring.

"What," I hiss, careful to keep my voice down, "the *fucking hell* was that?"

Rogue looks strained, running a hand through his hair. "I honestly don't know. I had no idea that the compound ran like this. My dad…" shaking his head, he tails off. My heart tugs at the look of betrayal on his face. What's Christian playing at?

Moving away from Rogue, I start to pace up and down the space between a row of chairs.

"There's clearly something up. He wanted you in here today and he wanted you to see… her." My voice stutters over the words.

792. *Harper.*

I might hate omegas, but I'm not sure I can hate this one. She's clearly been through hell, and although the voice at the back of my head is shouting that this could be manipulation, I'm sure enough of my own instincts to realize when someone's been a victim of severe abuse.

"What about those girls we brought here?" I growl at Rogue. "What's happened to them? They're barely adults." Just thinking of what we might have handed them over to draws a red haze over my eyes. If anyone's touched them, I'll rip them apart.

"I'll find out," Rogue promises. He grabs my shoulder, pulling me into an embrace. I need the touch from my pack. I can feel myself spiraling. This is so much more than I expected. A visit, maybe having to meet an omega or two. Not this.

We pull apart as a light knock on the door announces the return of the guard, this time with one of the matrons responsible for looking after the omegas. Some fucking care provider.

My lip curls as she enters the room, and the beta woman recoils slightly. Avoiding my gaze, she nods at Rogue and edges around me, walking to the front. As we take a seat, she launches into a spiel about omega matches.

"As alphas, you have a societal responsibility to fully control your omega by means of the Omega Creed," she begins with a slight lisp, hands clasped behind her back as she drones on.

"Omegas are a unique and rare opportunity. Handled carefully, they can be a valuable addition to any alpha pack. Particularly as they also provide the possibility of children."

A sudden image of Harper, cheeks bright with a rosy hue and belly rounded with pregnancy comes into my head, making a prickle slide down my spine. Swallowing uncomfortably, I push the image away and try to concentrate in case the beta says anything useful.

"However, if handled badly," the beta continues in a grave tone, "then the consequences can be severe."

She clicks a button on a remote in her hand and images flash up on the screen behind her. Omegas with sunken eyes staring emptily at the camera. Alpha packs fighting, violence on the streets. Images from the omega war. The montage ends with a close-up of an alpha's face twisted in an unnatural snarl, and I flinch.

I breathe in and out, slowly, fighting the will to just get up and leave. Rogue's hand lands on my knee, stopping it from jiggling up and down in nerves.

"The Omega Creed was carefully developed over a number of years, designed to offer true protection for omegas whilst accounting for their unavoidable behaviors. They are, after all, the key to our future." The beta grimaces as she says the words, and I wonder what her personal feelings are.

"It's absolutely critical that you, as responsible alphas, follow the rules set out in their entirety in order to make sure your omega remains healthy and obedient."

I roll my eyes slightly and glance at Rogue. He's paying full attention, brow furrowed slightly in concentration. I half expect him to whip out a notepad and dutifully write all this shite down.

The beta jabbers at us for a good thirty minutes, talking through diet, exercise, appropriate activities, and a particular warning about restricting access to soft furnishings. Apparently, omegas will turn into some sort of rabid beast if we give them a blanket. My mind starts to wander back to the omega we left in Christian's office until her words draw my full attention.

"Now, heats. When in an uncontrolled state, omegas will go into heat approximately four times per year. These can last a number of days and are notorious for bringing alphas under full control of omegas through *sexual means*." Her voice drops slightly on the last phrase, a hint of scandal lacing her prim tone.

"Sometimes, smaller heat spikes can also occur in the build-up to a natural heat. The hormones emitted by omegas during a natural heat can induce a trance state in alphas, like being drugged. Alphas are drawn to obey every whim of the omega. These periods are highly dangerous, and uncontrolled heats are not permitted under any circumstances. Following the rules of the creed will prevent a natural heat from occurring."

I feel a sliver of relief at the thought.

"However, heats are the only period in which omegas become fertile. Therefore, the Omega Compound has developed a secure way to safely replicate a natural heat environment without the impact on alphas."

The beta talks through the artificial heat process. It involves injecting the omega with heat hormones and keeping them sedated for a 48-hour period while the alphas… use them. My stomach knots when I imagine an unconscious Harper in that position, and I swallow hard to get rid of the sick feeling. Rogue looks green at the thought too. I didn't know much about the artificial heat process, but if there's one thing I'm sure of, it's that I don't want anything to do with it.

The beta must catch our expressions because she stops and flaps her hands. "Oh, not to worry! I understand that despite the restraints, many omegas find it a wonderful and fulfilling experience."

We both stare at her.

"Well, moving on." Glancing down, she shuffles some papers.

"You will be provided with a starter pack for your omega. This includes appropriate compound-approved bedding and sleeping arrangements, a short-term supply of nutrients and some changes of clothing. Where additional equipment is required, this can be collected from the omega store. An artificial heat pack is also included, although this should not be used until the match has completed the trial period and been signed off by the Director. Additional equipment to support the heat process will be delivered to you in around two weeks' time."

It's like we're collecting a dog.

"The omega will be supplied on a trial period at first. Should your pack provide the appropriate level of care and command, the Omega Compound will authorize a full handover after appropriate checks have been made. Please note that although bitemarks are not permitted until handover, we do encourage alphas to make use of the trial period through general mating activity. It's important that omegas are able to please the pack they are being placed with."

God, please get me out of here.

Thankfully, the beta seems to be winding down. She hands

Rogue a thick booklet and package and disappears, leaving us both to stew over what we've just heard.

"I'm really not sure about this," mutters Rogue. "But we can't leave her here."

As much as I want to pretend this whole day didn't happen, I can't disagree with him. Sighing, I push myself up. "I know. So, let's get her and get out of here."

"How do you think Gabe and Ace will feel? Should we call them?"

Snorting, I shake my head. "Let them find out when we get home. They're the reason we're in this mess. Besides, I want to see Gabe's face when we rock up with an actual omega."

Rogue lets out a gruff bark of amusement.

CHAPTER ELEVEN
HARPER

The scent wakes me first. It's mouthwatering. Woodsmoke and leather, warm and comforting. It wraps around me like a blanket.

Whose scent *is* that?

I blink my eyes open and take in my surroundings. Holy shit. I jack-knife into a sitting position and yelp as the Director looks up from his desk. Panicking, I throw myself off the sofa. My limbs aren't working properly, though, and I stagger a few steps before my legs collapse altogether and I end up in an ungainly heap on the Director's carpet.

Oh gods. I'm so fucking dead.

I can't hear anything over my panic, and I flinch back with a whine when firm hands grab hold of my arm. The Director hauls me upright, his grip strong but not bruising as he lifts me easily and braces me until I'm able to stand alone. He meets my eyes steadily, no hint of his feelings creeping through. Ice cold.

"My apologies, Harper," he says politely. "I didn't mean to scare you."

"I…" I'm floundering. I mean, what do I say? What am I supposed to be doing? I should be kneeling, but he's just pulled me up. Confused, I settle for dropping my head and tilting it slightly to the side to show off my throat.

"I'm sorry, alpha," I whisper. I'm not entirely sure what I'm apologizing for, but it seems like a safe bet.

The Director sighs and touches my arm again. I stiffen as he guides me to a chair in the corner of the room and pushes my shoulder gently in a silent demand for me to take a seat.

Handing me a glass of water, he perches at the end of the desk and stares at me while I try not to chug the whole amount in one. I can't remember the last time I had a drink. My mouth feels like I've been chewing on chalk.

I'm too scared to say anything else, so I sit there in silence, staring at the carpet. The Director sighs.

"I know this won't make any sense to you now," he starts. His voice sounds slightly warmer, and I straighten slightly, cocking my head so he knows I'm listening.

"But I hope that in time I'll be able to explain everything. For now, I have pulled you from the Phoenix project. I apologize for the experience you had."

If I was standing, I'm pretty sure I would have collapsed with the rush of relief that comes over me. There's a hint of shock there too. Why is the Director apologizing to me? I mean, he fucking should apologize, but still.

I chance a glance up, and he reads the expression on my face.

"You can speak," he offers. I lick my lips.

"I...," my voice is rusty, my lip splitting slightly. "I can go back to my room?"

I need to see Ava. She must be worried sick. I doubt anyone told her anything, so as far as she knows, I just disappeared from the compound after the fight in the food hall with Jason. I hope she's alright.

The Director taps a finger on the desk. "Ah, no. You won't be going back to your room."

My whole body locks up in sheer terror as my perfume explodes out of me, metallic and sharp with anxiety. The Director inhales sharply and coughs.

"Good god," he chokes out. "Your scent."

I ignore his words and stare at him intently, waiting for more information.

"Yes, so," he moves abruptly away from me, distancing himself from the spice rolling from my skin in waves, and opens a window, staying close to the fresh air.

"Jason will not give up on the project so easily, I'm afraid. Nor will other members of the board. Therefore, I think it would be safest if you were placed with a pack as quickly as possible."

I just stare at him blankly. A pack?

Heats, my mind whispers. *Children.*

That's a firm 'fuck no' from me.

I shake my head determinedly, throwing any sort of obedience to the creed out of the window. "I'd prefer to go back to my room."

"I'm sorry, but that's not possible," the Director says. I'd almost say he sounds genuinely apologetic. "Your room has been reallocated, and your things are here." He opens a cupboard and pulls out a small bag. Gingerly, he reaches out and hands it to me, careful not to make contact. Pulling the zipper down, I see my hairbrush and toothbrush inside.

Yep. That's everything.

I gape at him. "This was stored in your cupboard?"

He raises an eyebrow at my incredulity. "Yes. The two alphas you met earlier are my son and a member of his pack. I'm placing you with them, at least on a temporary basis, to prevent the board interfering and you being returned to Jason's care."

I scrunch the thin blue material of the scruffy bag in my

hands. This seems like an awful lot of trouble to take for an omega.

"Why?" I ask quietly. I hold his eyes for as long as possible until a small ripple of dominance forces mine back down.

"A question for another time, I'm afraid." He says the words just as softly.

Sounds come from behind the wooden door, and I press myself back into the chair as the two alphas barrel in.

Their eyes widen as they get a full hit of my scent like a bat to the face. Gazes swing to the empty seat where I woke up, and then back to the Director.

"Where is she?" Green demands. His voice is rich, a slight lilt to his words.

I'm motionless in the corner. A trace of their scent reaches me; a mixture of freshly cut spring grass, woodsmoke, leather. So, it was them. An appreciative murmur slips out of me, and I clamp my lips shut in mortification.

Down, girl.

The two alphas swing their impressive glares to me at the noise and falter. We stare at each other for a moment. They're huge, both packed with muscle. Each must be over six feet easily, and I probably won't even reach their shoulders. But I don't feel intimidated by them.

Definitely feeling a little something, though.

Maybe it's because I've never spent time around alphas outside of the trainers, but I feel drawn to these two. Brown clenches his fist slightly, and I bite back a moan at the way his muscles shift. What is *wrong* with me?

The Director interjects, breaking up the awkward silence. "Harper's scent blockers have been removed, so you may notice her scent fluctuating over the next few weeks. It will settle."

They both take a deep breath, inhaling deeply as if they're tasting the air. I swallow, hard, and press my legs together. Oh god.

"I've explained the situation," the Director moves on smoothly as if the three of us aren't frozen in some awkward instinctual sniffing ritual. "Once the paperwork has been signed, you're free to leave." He crosses to the door, opens it, and retrieves something from the person on the other side.

Leave. Leave the omega compound. *Freedom.* My mouth dries up at the thought. I haven't seen the outside world for more than seven years.

My jubilant thoughts soon come crashing down to earth, and I force myself to be realistic. I'm just swapping one prison for another. And even if the guards are seven million times better looking than Jason, with cheekbones that could cut glass and scents that make me want to *lick* - they'll still own me.

I watch from my corner as the alphas crowd around the desk, studying the paperwork closely and clearly trying to avoid looking at me. They murmur questions to each other, and I wonder what the contract says. I don't need to see it. Or sign it. Because if the Omega Compound wants to sell me at auction, hang me from the wall by my ankles or bury me in a shallow grave, that's their right.

Finally, they turn to me. Green gives me an awkward half-smile that doesn't reach his eyes. Brown doesn't even look my way, arms crossed and mouth flat in a way that tells me he's not particularly happy with this arrangement. *Join the fucking club, buddy.*

Then again, I suppose there's no easy way of saying, "Oh, hi. We're going to be your new owners."

The door knocks again, and a beta matron enters. She shoots me a scandalised look when she sees my ass firmly planted in a chair, but I turn away. I'm leaving anyway, and nobody told me to get back on my knees.

The Director clears his throat. "It's time to go. Harper, if you would?"

He motions to the door delicately. Right. Back down I go.

I push myself away from the comfort of the warm leather and drop down to the floor. There's a soft growl, but nobody speaks. We all shuffle in a weird line out of the office and back down the hallway, the three alphas a few steps ahead of me. It's slow going, and they keep pausing for me to catch up. I can't go any faster though. My knees are screaming, and I bite back tears as pain shoots through my legs. It was only a couple of hours ago that Jason was swapping me between ice baths, and my body is seriously feeling the last two weeks.

I hesitate at the doorway, the gravel of the courtyard and the distance to the van in front of us feeling like a 10-mile trek through a pit of venomous snakes. My lip wobbles, and I suck it into my mouth. I won't show them how much it hurts.

A pair of black boots appear in front of me, perfectly shined.

"May I?" a low voice offers.

I glance up quickly, surprised at the offer. Green's arms are held out, and I cast one last look at the yard before nodding quickly. I don't think I'll make it otherwise.

He sweeps me up, strong arms drawing me into his chest as he turns and strides for the vehicle. The director and Brown are standing next to the open door. Brown looks furious, speaking in low tones to the expressionless director. He breaks off as we reach them and throws his arms up, disappearing around the side. A door slams.

Green growls in disapproval, and I stiffen in his arms. He doesn't even look down, just rocks me gently from side to side. His grass scent gently nudges me, reminding me of summertime and lazy afternoons reading books in our garden. The soothing motion makes my bones soften and I list against him. God. These alphas are like my very own kryptonite. I wonder how many others are in their pack. If they all smell as good as these two, I might actually be tempted to roll over and play 'hide the knot'.

Looking towards the open door, I realize what the issue is. The cage sits neatly in the back of the van. The metal door is open, the scent of the hard plastic mat making my nose wrinkle. Green takes a step away from it and the Director leans in, putting a hand on his arm and speaking quietly.

"There are eyes on us," he mutters. "Just do it."

Green drops his gaze to mine, and it almost looks like an apology in his emerald depths as he gently places me down on my feet. When I wobble, he grabs my elbow, the steadying warmth sending a pulse through me.

"Thank you," I whisper quietly, and he grunts.

Green and the Director wait patiently as I climb awkwardly into the cage, shuffling backward on my ass and pulling my knees up until I can wrap my hands around them. The cold bars press into my back through my camisole, making me shiver.

Green scans my face with one last searching glance as he shuts the door, and then there's silence. I can't see the front from where I'm sitting, but the soft sound of breathing tells me I'm alone with Brown. His breath hitches and I wonder if he's going to speak. Before I can find out though, the other door slams, and we're pulling out.

I crane my neck to try and see through the tinted glass, barely able to believe I'm leaving the compound walls after all this time. A pang of sorrow hits me as I think of Ava. I might not ever see her again.

On the bright side, every turn of the wheels is taking me further away from Jason. Just the thought of him makes me tense. Something tells me that when I finally have a chance to breathe properly, to have a moment to myself…

That's the moment I might break.

CHAPTER TWELVE
ACE

G abe and I are watching a film in awkward silence from opposite ends of the snug when the SUV lights flash into the room. Sharing a brief look, we both spring up and race into the kitchen. They've been gone for hours, and I've been sitting here wishing that I could have gone with them. The silence has been deafening. Three would've been overkill though, and I didn't want to push it when Dev asked.

Gabe is practically shaking. He forgets himself in his excitement as he leans up next to me to look out of the window, the pack contact relaxing my tense muscles. He stiffens when he realizes how close we are. I wait for him to step away, bracing myself for rejection, but he surprises me and stays where he is. He cranes his neck, but it's too dark to see anything useful.

"Relax," I laugh, carefully nudging him. "It's not like they're going to rock up with a girl. There's probably weeks of paperwork to get through."

He deflates slightly but doesn't stop straining for a look. "I know, but I want to know how it went. What if they met some of them?"

"I doubt Dev would've been up for that. Guess we'll find out, though."

Gabe made the right choice bringing our pack dynamics up last night. The last few weeks, we've all been on edge, me especially. I'm starting to make rash decisions and it came out in the mission, which was unacceptable. Rogue was right to pull us over the coals. I'd never forgive myself if one of my pack were hurt because of me.

I'm excited too, but there's also a dull ball of pain sitting in my stomach that I'm trying my best to push down so it doesn't flicker up the pack bond and tell everyone exactly what I'm feeling. Pack bonds can be really fucking inconvenient.

Our pack is close. Closer than many families. With omegas thin on the ground and it being hard to find a beta that will accept a pack, it's common to have at least one inter-pack relationship between alphas. A strong alpha relationship helps to center the group - especially with so few omegas out there.

Gabe and I used to be that for our pack. We used to joke that we were the glue holding the pack together.

But then he got hurt. And our bond *snapped*. It's a miracle that the pack has lasted this long without tearing each other apart. And I can't stop feeling like I'm the reason our pack is so destabilized.

Casual sex doesn't help, not that I've had any in months. It doesn't have any impact on our pack bonds. There have to be feelings involved.

I glance down at Gabe's disheveled blonde hair, wondering how he'd react if I pulled him closer. If I pinned him up against the counter and ran my nose up his neck, breathing in the scent of fresh bread, comfort, and *home*. I stir uncomfortably, swallowing hard and willing my scent to stay down. This is the closest I've been able to get to him for months. I don't want to scare him off.

What happened with Elinor hurt him deeply, and he has

the scars to show for it. Mentally and physically. I don't give a flying fuck what scars he has, but I don't think he's ever truly believed me. I'll never push him, but I miss him. I miss *us*.

This new omega? She might help Gabe come to terms with what happened, might help him settle. And maybe he'll want to be with me again.

On the other hand, she might rip us apart forever.

I take a chance and lightly wrap my arm around him, holding my breath. Gabe tenses slightly, but he doesn't pull away and his scent deepens. Breathing in deeply, I let myself have a little hope. *Please,* I pray silently. *Please be good for us. I don't want to lose him.*

The car door bangs and Gabe hisses with excitement. He darts back from the window, and I ignore the pang as he tears himself away from me. He leans casually against the wooden counter, crossing and uncrossing his arms. Chuffing in amusement, I pull up a seat at the table. "At least put some coffee on, Captain Obvious."

Gabe rolls his eyes at me but turns to get the cups out.

Rogue comes in first, his strained face telling me that their time at the compound might not have been the easiest. Dev is close behind him, brow furrowed as he mutters something fervently that I don't catch. Gabe is too wound up to notice.

"You're back! How did it go?"

I see the look they share and my suspicion jumps. Gabe seems to twig at the same time, slowing his exuberant bouncing and glancing between them.

"Sit down, Gabe," Rogue suggests. He grabs Gabe by the shoulders and manoeuvres him into a chair. Rogue and Devlin both stay standing.

"Okay, now I'm worried," Gabe laughs, a hint of nervousness in his tone. "What's the matter? Was it not good? Can we not get one?"

Devlin opens his mouth and closes it again. He looks to Rogue for help. What's with the weird expressions and secrecy?

"You didn't kidnap someone, did you?" I'm joking, but they don't respond.

"Holy shit. Did you actually kidnap someone?" I start to calculate possible exit routes in my head in case we end up surrounded by police.

Rogue shakes his head abruptly.

"No, nothing like that. But… we did bring someone home with us."

There's a stunned silence in the kitchen, Gabe and I taking in the news. Gabe is first to recover and flies out of his seat eagerly with a whoop as elation trickles through me.

"Fuck yes!" he crows. "You should have messaged – we haven't got a room set up; I haven't put anything together for dinner because I was too excited- where is she? Is she driving – oh no, I forgot. Why did you leave her in the car? Is she nervous?"

His excitement sinks like a stone in the quiet, the grave expression on Rogue and Dev's faces telling me that not everything is as it seems here.

Shooting out my hand, I grab Gabe by the wrist as he darts past me towards the fridge. "Sit down," I urge him gently. "There's something going on."

Gabe looks around at the solemn faces and his excitement ebbs away, belated realization setting in. "Oh."

CHAPTER THIRTEEN
HARPER

oft fur brushes against my cheek. Nuzzling into it, I relax into the softness and stretch out my legs. They hit something hard. Realization jolts into me, making me sit up sharply and bang my head on the metal bars with a yelp.

The two alphas, the Director, Jason... I sink my face into my hands as emotion overwhelms me. He didn't bitemark me. I got away. I'm not bonded to him. I'm safe.

Pull yourself together, Harper. You have no idea what you're heading into.

This situation might be much, much worse. Although thinking back to the Director's office, I didn't get a bad vibe from either of these alphas. Drawing in a deep breath, I realize their scents are all around me. Brown's smoky leather scent fills my nose like smooth whiskey, Green's freshly cut grass dancing around the edges.

It's mixed with a hint of something fresh. Almost like the coast. *Sea salt and driftwood*, my mind supplies. And is that... my mouth waters at the faint scent of fresh bread. It reminds me of the baking my mother used to do so well, laughingly pretending to smack my father and me with a spoon when we'd try to sneak cookies off the tray as they were cooling.

Maybe they cook. Not that it really matters. I won't be allowed to have any anyway.

Curling my fingers around the wire bars of my cage, I press my face to the cool metal and look around. I'm still in the back of the truck but it's dark, and I can just make out lights through the window. Maybe we've stopped at a gas station? There's a chill in the air, and I pull the blanket around me, frowning as I run the material through my fingers. I can't remember them giving me a blanket. It's definitely not from the OC. The matrons would lose their shit. We must have stopped at some point, and they put it over me. A little flurry of warmth fills me at the thought, and I turn my head to inhale their scents again. These are so much nicer than Jason's harsh lemon.

The sound of footsteps crunching on gravel breaks the silence, and I instinctively huddle into the corner of my cage like a scared animal.

I remind myself to behave. I don't want to be sent back to the OC. They might decide to put me back in the Phoenix project, and with a failed match behind me, I won't get another shot. It'll be straight back to Jason, and I won't make it out a second time. This is my one and only chance.

Forcing myself forward, I push the blanket away and assume the kneeling permission, awkwardly twisting my limbs to fit within the confines of the cage. I force my head down, although I'm desperate to look around at my new surroundings. The beep of the car signals the alpha's approach, and the door opening sends a wave of frigid air flowing over me. I shiver, wishing I'd kept the blanket around me.

The footsteps pause for a second, and a throat clears.

"You can… you can look up."

It takes me a second, but I sweep a quick glance from

beneath my lashes. It's Green. His form is shadowed, the lights from the house behind him obscuring his features, but he sounds subdued. Confusion draws my eyebrows down for a second. He doesn't sound that excited to have an omega here. Not that I think I'm some fantastic prize or anything, but it doesn't gel with what I've been taught over the last five years. I thought there'd at least be a touch of crowing. Having an omega is supposed to be a pretty big social jump.

A noise sounds from behind him, and he shifts over, allowing me to see another two figures heading towards us. Trepidation tightens my throat and I shift back slightly, a slight whine slipping out of me. The figures both stop abruptly and Green shoots a look over his shoulder.

"Guys, back off a minute. Let's get her inside first. She'll freeze out here." I'm shivering, the cold air pushing into the open doorway. I'm pretty sure I might poke him in the eye with a nipple if they don't let me inside soon.

The footsteps retreat and Green reaches for me with his arms outstretched. I shrink back, looking from his hands to his face uncertainly. What does he want me to do?

"You can't walk," he says gently. His voice is warm and raspy. "You haven't got any shoes on. Let me carry you again."

Oh. My mind goes back to him carrying me to the truck. That he's asked again rather than just grabbing me, even now we're in his territory and he can behave however he wants, is another point in his favor. At my slight nod, he gingerly steps forward. Sweeping an arm behind my back, I'm in his arms before I can do more than blink. He smells divine, and I fight the urge to bury my nose in his jacket. I do breathe in deeply though to inhale his grassy scent. It's soothing, my body relaxing as he turns for the doorway.

The scents are even stronger here, mingling with each other in a way that screams familiarity. There must be four in this pack, and the freshly-baked bread I picked up in the car is front and center. All four call to me in a way I didn't expect, and my perfume rises up in an unexpected cloud. Deep, spiced cinnamon with a hint of orange works its way into the air. Shit. My scent blockers have well and truly worn off.

Green sucks in a breath, and a rumbling sound flutters against my side. My core clenches at the sound of his purr and I slam my eyes shut, gritting my teeth and tensing against him as I battle to stop the rush of heat between my legs.

"Whoa," a deep voice chokes out, and I feel the stares of the other alphas on my face. Their scents combined with the purring from Green is too much, and I whine softly. Curses echo around the room from four different voices.

Abruptly, I'm dropped into a chair, and my eyes fly open at the loss of Green's warmth. He backs away from me, moving around to keep a table between us. His nostrils are flaring, and his purr turns into a deep, hoarse growl as he fights to get his instincts under control.

"Holy shit," one of the men whispers, and I get the first proper look at my new pack.

Two men are staring at me, one with a shit-eating grin on his face and the other with a hopeful small smile. They're both incredibly good-looking, and I can feel my body responding. *Why, hello there.* My scent is practically screaming an invitation at them.

The grinning alpha is tall, well over six feet, heavily muscled with lightly tanned olive skin and deep blue eyes that twinkle in amusement as he meets my eyes. I'm not sure if he's laughing at me. It doesn't feel like it though. More like we're sharing our own private joke. I hesitantly twist my lips into a small smile, and his grin broadens, eyes crinkling in delight. The shape of my lips feels unnatural. I wonder how long it's been since I truly smiled. A long time. Even longer since I've laughed.

The second alpha bounces lightly on his feet. He's not

much smaller than his friend, but just as easy on the eyes. My eyes jump to the jagged line running down his face. It's vicious, as though he's been slashed with a knife. The pinkish line runs from under his rumpled ash blonde hair and down across his left eye, which is a cloudy brown. It looks… not new, but recent. Maybe a few months. I have enough scars to know.

He catches my look and flinches, taking a step back. I immediately drop my head, staring down at my hands and clasping them in front of me as I wonder how he lost his sight. A wave of sympathy clenches in my stomach. They seem… nice, this pack, and a cautious optimism fills me. Maybe things won't be so bad here after all. It can't be worse than the compound. I shudder at the thought and a low growl of distress comes from the blonde alpha. Looking up, the tall one is frowning, his lips pulled into a thin line. The blonde alpha turns away from me and I realise that he probably mistook my shudder for disgust.

Wetting my lips, I consider staying quiet, but I don't want him to think I'm judging him.

"I'm sorry," I whisper in apology. "That wasn't…I didn't…"

My words flounder as I search for the words to explain. "I was thinking about something else."

The blonde stares at me, the rich brown of his remaining functional eye holding my gaze steadily. His face softens, and he nods at me, accepting my weak apology.

"Don't worry about it," he says kindly. "Everyone stares at first."

I swallow, offering him another small smile. The other alpha moves away, breaking the moment with a clap of his hands.

"Well, this is awkward, so let's move on," he quips. "Have these two bothered to introduce themselves at all, or have they just steamrolled everything?"

My smile grows slightly, but my gaze sweeps the room. I'm

looking for Brown, the woodsmoke and leather alpha who held me tightly in the Director's office. I find him leaning against a wall in the corner, arms crossed. Moody and mysterious seems to be his MO.

He looks like he'd rather be anywhere else than here, and a small swell of disappointment fills my stomach at the look on his face. His lip is curled in derision as he runs his eyes over me. I want to shrink away, but sit up straight and meet his angry eyes head-on, satisfied when they widen in surprise for a moment. If he thinks I'm gonna be cowed by a look, then he needs to take a closer look at the compound's extra-curricular activities.

They haven't made me kneel or drop my eyes yet, so I'm seizing the opportunity while I have it. I move my gaze past Mr. Grumpy, taking in the farmhouse-style kitchen. Exposed beams run along the cream ceiling above us, the dark wood matching the table we're all sitting around. Lighter wooden counters line the sage green walls, a large refrigerator humming in the background with a separate door next to it. I'm guessing it might be a cellar.

A strand of wistfulness winds through me. It's cosy, warm, and comforting. I *love* this kitchen.

The blonde alpha clears his throat, drawing my attention back as he motions to himself.

"Hi," he says, a small grin on his face. "So, I'm Gabe. That's Ace," he throws a thumb at the taller alpha, "and then we have Devlin, and Rogue, who's our pack leader. Well, his name is Rogan, but we call him Rogue. We're the Winter pack." A light blush stains his cheeks as he explains.

Rogue. That's the green-eyed alpha, and Devlin is my cold-faced dark-eyed savior.

There's a silence, and I realize they're waiting for me to respond. "And you are…" Ace prompts.

"792."

The two new alphas jerk at my quiet answer and Ace's brows fly up into his hairline. Frowning, Gabe looks to Rogue and Devlin before settling on me, confusion on his face.

"You don't have a name?"

Rogue has been silently watching us, and he sighs before answering Gabe. "I said it was complicated. Turns out the compound doesn't use names for their omegas."

Gabe's mouth twists, a look of disgust creeping over him.

"That's fucking barbaric. You need a name. I'm not calling you 792!" Ace shakes his head next to him, clearly in agreement. His eyes sweep down to the collar around my neck and his lips thin in clear disapproval.

I stay silent and glance at Rogue. I don't want to tell them and then be punished for it. Devlin cuts in before he can speak.

"Harper," he barks. "Her *name* is Harper." Although he still looks angry, he shrugs when everyone glances at him in confusion. "Christian said it. And I'm not using a number either. Even dogs have names."

I'm not sure if the barb is intentional but it hits me all the same, and I flinch at the reminder that my omega status essentially makes me no better than their pet.

I drop my eyes to stare at my hands. The room is quiet until the chair next to me edges out with a screech. I hold my breath before the scent of baked goods invades my nose. Gabe. That's definitely Gabe. Staring at my lap, his hand carefully moves over until it's over my hand, and he gently clasps it for a second.

"Harper is a nice name. It suits you," he whispers. I don't know what comes over me. It would get me punished at the OC, but... I'm not at the compound now. I turn my hand, wanting to feel his palm against mine. I can't remember the last time I truly felt a normal human touch.

Gabe sucks in a breath at the contact but curls his fingers gently over mine. The contact settles me, something inside calming at the feel of his warmth. A low thrum of approval sounds in Gabe's chest, and I flush lightly.

The moment is broken as Ace interrupts.

"So, what now, Rogue?"

We all look over to the pack leader. He shrugs, looking slightly uncertain.

"I guess we get her stuff in from the car. There's a manual you'll both have to read, and we'll need to talk over how this will work."

Looking at me, he adds, "It's been a long day. Harper, maybe you'd like to rest for a while?"

The last thing I want to do is go back inside my cage. But I need to show that I can be obedient. Nice or not, they'll still follow the law and I'll be sent back if I don't at least follow the basics of the omega creed.

Omegas must follow alpha commands at all times, I remind myself, and nod at Rogue.

Gabe pulls back and jumps out of his chair.

"C'mon, I'll show you to your room. It's only the guest room. We didn't know that you'd be here today, or I would have sorted it out – but it's quiet and cosy."

Interrupting him, Devlin says to Rogue, "What about the cage?"

Ace whips his head between the two, as Gabe stops to stare at Dev in confusion. "What cage?"

Rogue waves him off, saying "We'll sort that later when we get everything out of the car. It won't hurt for a couple of hours. Take her up, Gabe."

Devlin presses his lips together but doesn't argue. I panic as Gabe grabs my hand to pull me up. Do I need to kneel? I should kneel. I move off the chair and drop down to my knees, wincing slightly at the discomfort. Was it only this morning that I was kneeling on rice? And now here I am, away from the compound… with a pack of alphas.

I hear a hissed intake of breath before Ace appears in front of me.

"What are you doing?" He sounds confused.

He's confused? *I'm* confused. Do they not know the rules of the creed at all? I slide my eyes to Rogue in uncertainty, waiting for direction.

Sighing, he mutters to them. "I'll explain later. Just let it go for now. Gabe, head on up and she'll be right behind you."

Gabe hesitates, watching me on the floor with concern. "But…"

"*Now*, Gabe." The tone of Rogue's voice leaves no room for argument, and Gabe's shoulders slump as he turns away, heading out of the kitchen. I shuffle behind him to keep up, ignoring the sting of pain.

"What the fuck? And why is she wearing a *collar?*" I hear Ace's voice ring out from the kitchen, the murmur of their voices falling away as they head outside.

CHAPTER FOURTEEN
GABE

I move slowly towards the stairs, a mix of confusion and elation filling me. She's here. We actually have an omega female in our home and she's staying with us.

And she's fucking beautiful.

Wide amber eyes with long dark lashes remind me of falling leaves in autumn, my favorite time of year. Sculpted cheekbones sit high on her face, surrounded by waves of fire-red hair that fall down her back like a waterfall.

Something's off about this whole situation though. She's far too thin, for one, and her outfit can't even be called clothing. It's basically a camisole and a pair of panties.

When Rogue brought her into the kitchen after his vague explanation of the rules being stricter than he thought, I thought my heart would flip out of my chest. It was pounding so hard I expected the pack to pick up on it.

Devlin's acting weird too, which isn't a surprise. It was always going to be difficult given his background, but the omega's behavior tells me there's something else. There's also her appearance. She's stunning, but she's skin and bone and covered in bruises. The collar around her neck looks horrific. A growl runs through me at the thought of it, fingers twitching to pull it off her slender neck.

I know that there are strict laws governing alpha and omega relationships, but I've never really thought about it in detail before. I remember that Rogue mentioned a manual, and I make a mental note to look through it at the first chance I get.

The shuffling sound behind me makes my jaw grind. The sound of her crawling makes every alpha instinct I have howl in anger. *Shouldn't be kneeling*. Thinking of Rogue carrying her in, my heart stutters. Maybe she can't walk properly? *Carry her*, my instincts scream.

I spin around to face her, and she jerks.

"Can you walk?" I blurt out. Mortified, I screw my eyes tight for a moment. Way to go, Gabe. Just blurt it out.

Harper looks up at me, her flame hair falling around her face. "I...I'm not allowed to walk."

She's what? Harper clearly sees the confusion in my face.

"The Omega Creed?" she says hesitantly, watching my face. "It's the sixth commandment."

I haven't got any idea what she's talking about. I know of the creed, but I always thought it was more of a guiding principle than anything else, and I don't think I've ever actually looked at it.

"What does that mean?" I hate feeling like I'm looking down at her, so I drop down to my haunches.

"Omegas must kneel in the presence of an alpha."

My first instinct is to snort with amusement. Harper watches me steadily and I realise she's genuine. "Are you serious? That's bullshit. How does that even work?"

She shrugs, lightly, and leans back on her heels, gesturing between us. "Like this."

The amusement fades away and revulsion takes its place. "So... every time you're around an alpha, you're not allowed to walk? That's batshit."

Her lip twitches and she inclines her head in agreement. "It is, but it's the law. There are some exceptions, though."

I can't help myself, and I lean in closer to her. Her *scent*. It's autumn mornings, the sunset over a field. It's almost drugging in intensity. I inhale deeply, and she gasps lightly as my nose touches hers.

Pulling back, I give myself a shake. *She doesn't need you slobbering over her*, I chide myself. "Sorry, it's just… you smell amazing." Smooth, Gabe. Real smooth.

"So do you," she whispers. A surprised look comes over her face, as though she didn't mean for the words to slip out. We stare at each other for a moment until I remember exactly where we are.

Jumping up, I hold out my hand to her with a stern look that says I won't take no for an answer. Her throat works as she eyes it like it'll bite her. Glancing back towards the kitchen, she shakes her head at me, a tinge of sadness threading through her voice. "I can't."

"You can," I insist, keeping my hand out. "I'm not walking around while you crawl behind me. It's ridiculous."

Slowly, she reaches out and I grab her hand, pulling her up before she can change her mind. Her scent rises again as she falls into me, soft curves pressing against my chest as she relaxes. She's tiny, so thin that I could see her ribs poking through as she huddled on the kitchen chair. Protectiveness fills me, and I hold her close for a moment. Something's gone badly wrong with this omega, and I desperately want to make it better for her.

For starters, I'll get her some new fucking clothes. I don't know what happened at the omega compound, but her ridiculous outfit is almost translucent. Casually, I drop my hand down and pinch my thigh hard to try and stop the hardness I can feel in my trousers as my knot starts to swell. I start putting a list together in my head to distract myself from the feel of her in my arms. *I'm going to need those answers from Rogue.*

Reluctantly, I disentangle myself, taking a step away and giving her a rueful smile as I will my half-mast erection to stay down. "Sorry."

A glorious flush has crept over her cheeks, staining them a dark red. The alpha in me is delighted, noting that it covers her neck and down her chest too. Swallowing hard, I move my thoughts away before they get me into trouble.

A small, polite cough reminds me where we are, and I quickly turn and start moving up the wooden staircase. Her hand is still in mine, and I grasp it tightly.

Towing her down the hallway, I toss out vague directions, determined to get her into a warm bath and bed.

Not for that, Gabe. Don't be an asshole.

"So that's my room, Ace is over here, then we have Rogue's bedroom, a bathroom – we all have our own though, so we don't use it that much – and then this is Devlin's room." Stopping outside the guest room, I smile at her. "So, this will be your room. Sorry, you're next to Dev."

She smiles briefly but looks a little confused, so I elaborate. I won't share Dev's secrets without his permission, but I also don't want him to terrorize Harper on her first night with us – especially when it looks like she's been to hell and back already.

"He can be…loud at night. The noise might wake you up."

Her eyes widen and I belatedly realize what I've just insinuated. "No!" I yelp, ears burning. "Not that. He has… bad dreams, sometimes."

Her expression becomes drawn, shuttered. "I have bad dreams too," she murmurs.

Reaching out a hand, I gently push a tangle of red hair back from her face. The gold flecks in her eyes seem to flicker from dark to bright, and she watches me with just a hint of trepidation.

"Oh, love," I whisper. "What happened to you?"

It's a rhetorical question, and I regret it the moment her face closes over. Letting it pass for now, I push the door open and gesture for her to enter.

Looking around the slightly musty room, I realize that I haven't been in here for a while. There are some boxes pushed up against the back wall. The bed is made, although it's not fresh bedding, so I decide to change it while she uses the bathroom.

Harper's looking around, taking in the small room. I bite my lip in shame. She deserves a much nicer space than this.

"Sorry it's not much, but we'll get it fixed up for you."

"No," she rushes out. Her voice is quiet as she stares around. "This is lovely."

I point towards the adjoining bathroom. "There's a shower and bath in there. Do you want me to run a bath for you? I'll get you something to change into, although you might have to borrow something from us until we get you some new clothes. Unless… did you bring any with you?"

The barest shake of her head sends a thread of anger up my back. What the fuck are those dickheads at the compound playing at? Harper flinches next to me, and I realize that my scent has turned sharp, angry. It's not aimed at her, though. It's for her.

Oh boy. I'm in trouble.

I nudge her gently towards the other room. "Go and freshen up. There are clean towels on the side. I'll change the bedding, and I'll leave some clothes on the dresser. Get some rest and we can talk more in the morning."

She hesitates again, and I wait for her to speak up.

"I can't… sleep in the bed."

Um. What?

She sees the expression on my face and rushes out a hasty explanation, tripping over her words.

"I'm sorry. It looks really nice and soft and comfortable, I just… we're not allowed to use beds. Or bedding. It can trigger nesting instincts, so…"

She flounders as she tries to explain. What kind of bullshit have they been feeding everyone at the compound? It sounds more like a fucking cult than anything else. My brow creases. "But how do you sleep?"

She stares down at her feet, rubbing one foot against the other and I realize that it's embarrassment. "I have a cage," she whispers, the words barely audible on her pink lips.

I lock into a still position at her words. White-hot rage rushes up my throat, threatening to choke me. No. No fucking way am I allowing this bullshit. A fucking cage? Rogue and Dev's words come back to me from the kitchen, and I bite back a growl of disgust. This isn't even up for discussion, alpha lead or not. I'm not putting this girl inside a goddamn cage to sleep.

I'm snarling. Harper flinches away from my anger and drops back down to the floor, her instincts pushing her to submit. It makes me feel sick on the inside to see her like that.

"No, Harper," I drop down to meet her eyes, both of us on our knees. She keeps her head bent and I can scent the mortification coming off her. She's ashamed.

No one should *ever* be ashamed of who they are.

"No," I growl at her again, and her head snaps up at the sound of my alpha bark coming out. "I don't give a fuck about some omega creed. You are *not* sleeping in a fucking cage and you do *not* need to kneel in front of me."

Her eyes flicker across my face, uncertainty warring with hope within the deep pools of amber as she stares at me. I wonder what she sees when she looks at me. At my scar. She doesn't shy away from it, and her hand reaches up, trembling as she traces her fingers along the rough line gently. I exhale and a purr rolls out of me, making her shudder as her instincts kick in. She drops her hand to cover her stomach. A quiet moan makes me realize what I'm doing as she shifts her legs, and I catch a hint of honey as her body responds to me. It makes my mouth water. My instincts scream at me to *taste*.

God. I want her so badly. But I remind myself that she's not ready for that. We've only just met. And even if it suddenly feels like this girl holds a part of me, she needs care, and consideration, not an unfamiliar alpha taking advantage of her in a vulnerable position.

Breathing out deeply, I hold her eyes for a second longer before I break the connection.

"Go," I breathe. "Get cleaned up. And take the bed." She looks like she'll argue with me for a second, but her head drops slightly in submission, and she rises up. I look up at her as I stay where I am, an alpha on his knees in front of an omega. Something about it feels surprisingly natural. She moves slowly towards the bathroom, and I push myself to my feet, heading out to grab the bedding.

CHAPTER FIFTEEN
HARPER

losing the bathroom door gently behind me, I turn and put my back against it. Dropping my hands to my knees, I take a second to breathe in and out, fighting the temptation to go back out and pick up where we left off.

Oh gods. Thinking of him, so close to me, scent rising... a whimper breaks free, and I press my hand against my mouth.

How am I supposed to survive in this pack? I've only really met Gabe properly, and even Green – Rogue - and Devlin pulled a reaction from me that I've never felt before. If these feelings keep up, I'm doomed.

The words of my trainers at the compound echo around my head. Foreboding warnings about omegas who get too close to alpha packs fill my head, and I groan, ignoring the sound of my skull hitting the door as I drop it back. *I'm in so much effing trouble.* If the compound could see even a glimpse of what's happened this evening, I'd be back in intensive training in the snap of a finger.

Looking around, I see a beautiful copper claw-footed bath sitting proudly in the centre. It's crying out for candles, bubbles and hot water, and I step towards it, sorely tempted. I don't think Gabe would mind, given his reaction to the cage. Devlin's handsome scowl forces into my mind. I need to be careful, no matter how kind they seem right now. Reluctantly, I decide against it, moving over to the shower in the corner.

It's stunning, teal blue tiles edging down to remind me of a mermaid's tail. A large copper showerhead sits above it, and excitement threads into me at the thought of a hot shower.

If I can turn it on.

Frowning, I stare at the ridiculous number of buttons on the wall. How do I start it? Taking a guess, I press a few buttons at random and grin as water pours down from the ceiling. I haven't had a shower like this for years. Alone, undisturbed, no matrons watching me with beady eyes scanning over my body. I lift a hand to the heated towel rail, running my fingers over the fluffy white towel. It's so soft, and I shiver at the thought of wrapping it around me.

I might not be going for the bath, but I'm abso-fucking-lutely going to enjoy this moment while it lasts. Carefully, I twist the button until steam starts to fill the room and strip off my clothes, groaning in sheer delight as I step under the pouring heat.

This is heaven. I'm never leaving this shower. Just gonna stand under this and bask in the glorious warmth until I shrivel up like a raisin.

I twist to let the heat run down my back, sweeping my hair out and making sure it's saturated. Gods, I can't wait to be clean. Really, truly, squeaky clean. Grabbing one of the bottles littering the shelf next to me, I squeeze a dollop into my hand and rub it into my hair. The scent hits me just a second too late, undeniably Devlin. Frowning, I sniff my hair, the scent confirming that it's definitely something he uses. Shit. He's probably not gonna be happy with me. I debate using something else, but I'm nearly done and I don't want to be wasteful.

Lingering for a few moments more, I reluctantly press buttons until the shower turns off, yelping as the heat disappears and cold water drops down on me. *That's what you should have used*, the voice inside me whispers. It's true that we're not allowed to use hot water at the compound, but I just couldn't resist.

Stepping out, my toes twist into the soft mat. Grabbing the heavenly fluffy towel, I slowly pull the warm material around me, taking in every second. It feels amazing, soft and warm like the best kind of hug. I want to nuzzle into it, but force myself to stop at the last second. *You can't get used to this*, I tell myself sternly. *It's not going to last.*

Moving to the large sink, I find an unopened toothbrush in the cupboard above and scrub my teeth thoroughly, trying to wash away any remaining tastes of Jason and gulping water from the tap when I'm done. My hand swipes the mist from the mirror, and I take a good look at my face for the first time in weeks.

My hair is a jumble of knots, making me curse. Hopefully, I won't need to cut it, but it's been days since I've been in my little room at the compound and able to brush it through properly. My thoughts drift to Ava for a moment. She always used to brush my hair for me. We'd whisper to each other, sharing secrets and dreams that we both knew could never happen, but we still had hope. God, I hope she's okay.

Shaking off my dark thoughts, I gingerly listen at the bathroom door for any sign of Gabe. As much as I enjoyed his company, I really don't want to wander out in a towel, especially not with my scent as haywire as it is. Only silence greets me, and I open the door a crack to see the room is empty.

A small bundle of clothes sits on the dresser as promised, and I quickly pull on a pair of black shorts and a white shirt that swamps me completely, dropping almost to my knees. Sniffing it, my stomach flips at the hint of sea salt. This must belong to Ace. Continuing to inhale the shirt – I'm a creeper, but at least there's no one around to see – I turn to the bed and stare.

Gabe's changed the bedding, but he's also left a cream-colored blanket on top that's calling my name. It looks thick, and cozy, with a thin layer of grey fur. My eyes round and I dart forward before I can stop myself, grabbing it and quickly wrapping it around me. I let out a large moan at the sensation. Holy fuck. *Mine now.*

Ignoring the possessive thoughts invading my body, I hesitate for all of half a second before I dive into the bed, frantically rearranging the pillows and covers until I'm cocooned in the middle, the covers pulled over my head. It's dark, and quiet, and absolutely fucking blissful. Any remaining tension in my body slowly ebbs away at the feel of being surrounded. I don't remember ever feeling this content in the seven years since my awakening.

This feels like a *nest*. Even if it is a tiny one. This is everything I ever imagined. Soft blankets, cosy bedding, plump pillows, and an actual, proper bed. This is such a huge middle finger to the omega creed. If anyone from the compound saw me, I don't even want to think about the punishment. But Gabe said it would be okay, and I'm trusting him. At least for tonight.

As I curl up, thoughts of the last two weeks begin to creep in. Jason, leaning over me. The ice baths. His weight between my legs. The feel of the cane slapping my feet. Once, then again, then again. My breath starts to speed up at the memory, and I try to push it away as a tear trickles down my face.

You're safe, I tell myself firmly. I'm safe, and I'm warm, and I have my tiny nest. At least for tonight.

It's more than I ever thought I'd have.

CHAPTER SIXTEEN
ACE

"What the fuck? And why is she wearing a collar?" I hiss at Rogue and Dev. Rogue gestures for me to follow him outside. Devlin follows as I stomp after him, the wooden door swinging shut behind us.

Rogue stops by the truck and turns to me. "We'll talk properly when Gabe comes down. I don't want to run through it twice." A rough sound of agreement comes from Devlin.

Nodding slowly, I fight down the urge to argue. It won't do me any good, anyway. Rogue rarely changes his mind once it's made up. His normally unflappable attitude is what makes him such a strong pack leader. Especially for a bunch of misfits like us.

Devlin pulls the back doors of the truck open, reaching in and pulling out an actual goddamn metal cage with a grunt of effort. They weren't kidding. My breath fogs out in front of me, the chill reaching my bones as I eye it with distaste. It looks just like a dog cage, slightly bigger. My gut sours at the thought of our omega folding herself into this.

Shoving the cage into my arms, Dev snaps, "Take this inside. I'll bring the rest."

I lug the cage back in, dropping it in the corner of the kitchen. Stepping back, I look at it properly in the light. It's made up of thin metal bars and there's a sort of plastic mat at the bottom. Leaning down, I poke at it gingerly through the gap in the bars. It's solid as a rock, barely an inch thick if that.

She's supposed to sleep on this?

Dev follows me in, a box of items clunking down onto the table. Shifting over to him, I stick my arms in and start to pull things out, ignoring his irritated grumble. I pull out a thick beige manila folder, turning it over to see the words 'omega instruction manual' on the outside. Are they for real?

Pushing it to the side for now, I yank out what I belatedly realize are scraps of lingerie and hastily drop them. They float down on the table, little bits of lace and netting similar to what Harper was wearing earlier. "Where are her clothes?" I mutter to Dev.

He shrugs. "They're not allowed them."

His gaze is steady as he meets my eyes. He's serious.

"Well, that's fucked up," I say, leaning in to see what else is in the box. There's a smaller pack in there, and I lift it out to see.

"Artificial heat package." My lips curl in distaste and I bite back an angry growl. I've heard about artificial heats, and the whole thing rubs me up the wrong way. It's fucking insane, to be precise. I like my females mewling and dripping, begging and writhing underneath me as I fuck them, not unconscious and strapped down.

Devlin grabs it from me and opens one of the cupboards, chucking it in. I see the tension in his shoulders. He's not as cavalier as he's making out.

In my haste to see what other shit they've shoved in, I tip the box upside down and Dev swears at me. I can't help it, I'm an impatient fucker. We both look down at the contents in bemused silence. A pack of what looks like some sort of protein powder and a blue bag. I unzip it to reveal a toothbrush and ratty old hairbrush.

"That's it?" I ask, turning to Rogue who's entered the kitchen, locking up the door for the night. He stares at the stuff on the table but doesn't respond, instead pulling a bottle of scotch and some glasses down from the side. Collapsing into a chair, he groans, rubbing the back of his head.

"What a fucking day."

Gabe comes tripping into the room, and we all turn to stare at him. He's been gone for a few minutes – definitely longer than it takes to show someone to a bedroom. I cock a brow at him teasingly. "Been flirting with our little omega, G?"

He frowns at me and doesn't respond. That's enough to shut me up. My voice softens. "Hey, I was kidding." I hold my arm up in invitation, not expecting anything to come of it. My breath catches when he takes it, ducking underneath. I can feel his stress and try not to read into it. He just needs the touch. Hugging him to me, being careful not to overdo it, I look over at Rogue. "So, shoot. What's all this about?"

Dev pulls up a chair as Rogue launches into the whole story. By the time he finishes, Gabe is a vibrating ball of distress. Low growls rumble from his chest and his normally enticing scent is potent and sharp, hanging thickly in the air. More than once he's moved towards the door, and I've pulled him back. Not that I blame him. My own hormones are raging at the injustice Harper has suffered – and I strongly suspect that we don't know half of it. Pulling Gabe to the table, I nudge him into a seat and grab the manual I scoffed at earlier. Flicking through it, bile rises in my throat. "I'm not doing this shit."

Rogue shoots me a flat stare. "Kind of late to back out now. You want us to take her back to the compound?"

Mine and Gabe's protests erupt at the same time. Gabe sits

up quickly. "We don't have to follow what's in that book, though. We can just do our own thing. Who's going to know?"

"It says they *need* it," Dev cuts in, his voice a knife through Gabe's proposal.

When I slant my eyes to him, he's leaning back in his chair, balancing on two legs. His grip on his scotch is so tight I'm concerned he's going to crush it and cut his hand open.

"Apparently their biological systems work differently to ours. They need to *submit,* or it can damage their health. Badly." He spits the words out.

Gabe scoffs. "That's such bullshit. You saw her – do you really think not letting her look at us and making her crawl around is what she *needs for her fucking health*?" His voice rises at the end, frustration pulsing through him as Devlin looks away. I can't tell if he means what he's saying. He's locked the bond down tight, not letting anything slip through to us.

"None of us are disagreeing with you, Gabe," Rogue stares into his glass as he swirls the liquid around and Gabe frowns at Devlin.

"I don't want to put her in a cage or use a damn shock collar on her. But my father was clear before we left – people are going to be watching us, and we have to be seen to follow the rules. If they check up on us and anything seems off, she'll be dragged back to the OC and we'll never see her again."

Clearing my throat, I offer what seems to be an obvious solution. "So, we meet in the middle. We have enough security to know if anyone gets within a three-mile radius of this place. We can test different things, see how she responds and keep an eye on her. Your father can give us a heads up if the OC is planning to make a visit and we'll make sure we toe the line. Everyone's happy."

Gabe makes a sound of distress. "I don't want to do that to her, even if it's just for show."

"I think we're all agreed on that." I catch Dev's eye at his words, and he scowls at me. "What? I might not like omegas, but even I can see that this is beyond insane. She can't go back to that fucking place."

"What does she even eat?" I grab the pack that came with the box of bullshit and turn it over. "Er... so, beige sludge. Yum." Gabe pales even more and yanks the box of powder out of my hand, studying the back intently.

"I can't cook for her?" he sounds so horrified that a snort of amusement escapes me. Pressing my lips together to stop my snigger escaping, I catch Rogue's lip twitching. Not being able to ply someone with food is literally Gabe's worst nightmare.

Well, almost. Sobering, I ask, "So what now? How do we explain this?"

"We'll let her sleep for tonight and sit down with her in the morning. We find out what she absolutely has to do and what we can work with. She might feel more comfortable following some of the rules they've laid out. I think we need to offer her a choice as much as we can."

Gabe nods frantically in agreement at Rogue's words, staring longingly in the direction of the pantry.

I just know he's thinking of what to make for breakfast, and I send a silent thought of sympathy to the sleeping omega above us. She has no idea what's heading her way. Gabe in a feeding frenzy is scarier than meeting Devlin in a dark alley in the middle of the night. I make a mental note to stock up our walk-in freezer next time I'm in town.

"Well, I'm heading up." Dev stands, swiping the scotch as Rogue goes for a refill. Rogue curses and Devlin cocks a finger to his brow in a salute as he saunters out of the room, swinging the bottle between his fingers and leaving his glass on the table. I wonder what nightmares he'll have tonight.

Rogue looks at us both. "You should head up too."

Gabe points at him accusingly. "No working in the office tonight. We need you firing on all cylinders tomorrow."

Shrugging, Rogue brushes the concern off. "I just need to finish writing up the mission notes and then I'm for bed. See you in the morning."

"Do we need to do anything? What if Harper wakes up and wanders off in the night?" Gabe drums his fingers on the table in anxiety.

Rogue's frown pulls his eyebrows down. "She seemed pretty exhausted, but I'll make sure all the doors and windows are locked. She does have the collar on, so we can track her if needed. I don't think she'd get very far in her current state."

We all split up, heading to our respective areas, Gabe a step ahead of me as he takes the stairs, clearly going to check on Harper.

Rogue's shoulders are slumped as he moves away from us, down the corridor towards his office. Jogging after him, I grip his shoulder and he turns back to face me.

"Are you okay? Everything today with your dad must've been a headfuck." Rogue always tries to lock his emotions down, like he doesn't want us to see that our steady pack leader isn't made from stone. You have to push him.

Rogue grimaces. "A massive one. But I get the feeling there's something bigger going on with him. It wouldn't make sense for him to behave the way he did if there wasn't. Maybe it's just wishful thinking though."

He hesitates. "I hope… I hope he turns out to be the man I've always thought he was."

Clapping my shoulder, he hauls me into a brief hug. Surprise holds me tense for a moment until I wrap my arms around him. I can't remember the last time he initiated pack contact, but I'm not complaining. The bond hums happily, my pack bite mark buzzing slightly. Stepping back, he claps my shoulder and steps into the office.

Chapter Seventeen
Devlin

The next morning I'm in the kitchen making a coffee to chase away the pounding in my head when Ace stumbles through the door. His runs a hand through his messy, unkempt hair and grins with appreciation when I hold out a mug.

"Oh baby, I didn't know you cared," he coos at me in a truly fucking awful high-pitched tone.

I roll my eyes at him. "I'm just giving it to you so you don't steal mine," I say, hugging my own mug protectively. I need my coffee in the mornings.

"Thanks." Ace collapses into his chair with a smirk. "Any sign of our little omega?"

His possessive wording doesn't escape my notice, and I frown into my cup. Blowing across the hot coffee, I watch the steam dissolve and reform.

"Nope," I say, popping the 'p' sound. Honestly, I'm torn between making myself scarce before she appears and going up there to check on her myself. The thumping inside my skull reminds me that I made my way through the rest of the scotch before passing out.

"You need to talk to Pa? I can call him," Ace offers.

I appreciate it, but I don't need it today and shake my head.

I was trying to avoid any nightmares, figuring that our new guest wouldn't appreciate being woken up like that. But instead of my usual nightmares, last night I dreamed of… Harper.

I woke up to my cock in my hand and a stomach covered in sticky release.

My stomach flips as soft footsteps sound on the stairs, but it's only Gabe, yawning as he scratches his toned bare stomach above his sweats. Rogue appears behind him, impeccably dressed in a shirt and black jeans. I swear the man never actually sleeps, always last to bed and first to rise. His hair is slightly damp at the ends from the shower he takes after his morning workout.

We all settle quietly around the table, pretending to focus on our drinks. Rogue pulls the paper across to him, his eyes flicking too rapidly to be taking anything in. Ace is whistling, and the sound irritates my pounding head enough that I growl at him. Gabe fidgets restlessly.

The squeak of the guestroom door announces Harper's imminent arrival, and Gabe scrambles up, running the tap to look busy and washing his cup out repeatedly.

It takes a few minutes, but I finally hear a soft brushing that signals her coming through the door. Gabe turns, his mouth opening, but Ace beats him to it.

"Morning, little omega," he sings. Without asking, he just scoops her up off her knees and sets her on her feet. When she frowns at him, catching her balance, he bops her on the nose and her whiskey-colored eyes widen.

"No crawling allowed in this house, kitty cat, unless it's in the bedroom." Her eyes dilate, those pretty pink lips parting in a surprised 'o'.

She looks around uncertainly and Rogue smiles, pulling out a chair.

"I think we have some things to talk through. Would you like to sit down?"

She slowly sets herself on the offered seat. I can sense her discomfort at being surrounded by alphas, and I will my scent to tone down a notch. We're all staring at her like she's the second coming of Jesus, and as she glances around, Rogue's foot connects with my leg under the table.

"Shit," I curse, throwing Rogue a glower when Harper jumps a mile.

"It's alright," Rogue soothes her, his pheromones throwing off calming vibes.

Apprehension passes over her face, and my mouth dries up as she swings her gaze to mine. Those golden eyes are more of a dusky amber hue this morning, and it makes me wonder if she slept well. The circles under her eyes seem deeper than they did last night.

She tucks a lazy curl behind her ear, and my eyes follow the motion. A hint of a scent reaches me, and my nostrils flare, making me frown.

Is that my fucking shampoo?

Her eyes shutter at my expression, and she quickly turns away from me. Gabe touches her shoulder softly, and she offers him a real smile, lips moving up at the corners. "Morning, love," he says, offering her a cup. "Would you like a coffee?"

She stares at the cup for a moment before nodding. "Yes, please."

We're still watching as she takes her first sip of the black liquid, and I choke back a huff of laughter as her face changes. Wrinkling her nose, she stares at the coffee intently before taking another sip. Clearly, she's never had coffee before.

"Here, little omega," Ace slides a jug of cream and sugar over to her. "Have a play and see what you like. You can have sugar, right?"

Her mouth twitches at the corners. No poker face, this one.

"I'm not allowed to have it," she whispers, but I catch the longing in her voice.

"Actually, Harper," Rogue says, clearing his throat. "We wanted to talk to you about the instruction manual and how we might approach this arrangement."

Harper pales slightly and she nods, setting down the cup gently with a hint of sadness like she expects us to take it away from her. "Okay." Her forlorn expression tugs at me, and I force myself to turn away and grab the paper Rogue was reading. *Don't fall for it,* I tell myself. *Even if it seems real.* God knows someone has to keep their head around here. Gabe and Ace definitely aren't, and there's a softening in Rogue's face when he looks at our newest houseguest that concerns me.

Rogue hesitates, the pack bond sharing his nerves with us.

"We took some time to read through the instruction manual last night, and after... yesterday's events, we were hoping that we may be able to make our own arrangement. Something outside of the compound guidelines."

He sounds like someone's shoved a pompous stick up his ass. Harper starts to tremble, her scent hitting us like a fist in the stomach. Her fear fills the room and my body tenses.

"What is it?" Rogue asks her, a growl rumbling through his tone. Her panic sends tension rippling through us all, driving us to soothe her. I down the rest of my coffee abruptly. I don't need to be here for this.

"I'm not going to mate with you." Harper's voice rings strong and adamant, even though she's shaking like a leaf. Shock runs through the pack bond and I think back over Rogue's words, seeing the issue as he clearly puts two and two together.

"No, that's not what I meant," he protests rapidly, stumbling over his words. In any other circumstance, I'd be crowing over the dull flush making its way up to his neck, but Harper's distress is filling the room and it's a fucking siren call for us to resist. Ace's teeth are gritted as he holds tightly on to the table, and Gabe is leaning away, both trying to control their hormones before we panic her anymore. At Rogue's words, her fear ebbs slightly.

"What I mean to say is, er, things like the crawling, and the eye contact. As you can see, we're quite an informal pack, and it doesn't sit well with us to ask you to do that," Rogue continues in a firmer voice, obviously finding his footing. The distress finally disperses, and we all take a deep breath, Harper included.

"Sorry," she mutters, clearly aware of the strong cinnamon scent lingering around her. Gabe licks his lips, the same thoughts clearly running through his head as I shift awkwardly in my chair. *You don't like omegas,* I remind myself. *So back off.*

Rogue's face softens. "Don't be. I'm sorry for scaring you. I suppose what we're trying to ask is if there is anything within the guidelines that you absolutely need to stick to. For example, we're concerned that some foods may make you ill."

Gabe can't hang on anymore and interrupts. "Can you eat normal food? Please say you can!"

Harper seems startled, looking around us all carefully before landing on Gabe. "I… I can eat normal food," she murmurs. "But I've never really had much apart from really plain food, not since my awakening."

Ace asks a question I want to know. "How old were you when you awakened, little omega?" He winks at her when she looks over at him. "We're all curious to know more about you."

I'm trying damn hard not to be. I push my feet to move, but they're glued firmly to the floor and they ain't moving.

This is information we need to know, I tell myself.

"Fourteen." She smiles slightly at our aghast expressions. Fourteen is really young for an omega to awaken, and I want to demand more information. We don't even know how old she is, and a trace of panic rushes through me. Luckily, she carries on before I can make an ass of myself.

"My parents took me straight to the compound, and I've been there ever since, so... seven years? I think I'm 21 now."

Ace cocks his brow at her. "You think?"

Shrugging, she whispers, "We don't celebrate birthdays in the compound. I'm not really sure of the actual date."

Gabe's face falls at this new information. "It's November 12th."

"Oh. I'm twenty-two then. My birthday was October 31st." She sounds a little glum at the news, and I can't say I blame her. What's the harm in celebrating a birthday, for fuck's sake? Although I'm starting to understand that when it comes to the Omega Compound, we can't take anything for granted.

Rogue looks slightly relieved at this news. He's the oldest of the pack at thirty-one. I'm just behind him at thirty, Ace is twenty-seven and Gabe's the youngest at twenty-five.

I push down my own relief. It doesn't fucking matter how old she is, I'm still not going there.

"Can I ask why you haven't already been matched with a pack?" Ace asks quietly, ignoring Rogue's frown of disapproval at the personal question. "You don't have to answer if you don't want to. Curiosity is my biggest flaw, in case you hadn't guessed."

I find myself sitting forward, curious to hear the answer for myself. She's stunning. Any pack would snap her up in an instant.

Swallowing hard, she stares at her hands. "I'm not generally considered to be a *good* omega. My training didn't go very well, so they put me in extra training, then more on top. They were going to send me to a heat nest if I wasn't fit to be matched by my next birthday... I guess they changed their mind though. They put me in the project instead." Her voice trails to the barest whisper and her creamy skin pales.

A fucking heat nest.

Four snarls rip through the room, our scents bursting out of us in aggression as we all react to the thought of Harper in one of those foul buildings. I realize that where she's been is probably worse though, and just the thought makes me want to roar with fury.

Heat nests are the only way an alpha can access an omega if they're not considered rich enough, or connected enough, to qualify for a full match and bitemark. Which means that the majority of packs either go through the nests or choose a beta partner instead, given that you have to be both rich as fuck and close chums with the government to be matched. The only reason we got anywhere near Harper and the compound was through Rogue's connection with his dad.

There aren't enough omegas to go around, so the idea of the nests is that packs can share the benefits of an omega without the responsibility of having one full time. Basically, it's an artificial heat on steroids, with alphas paying for the privilege of bedding an omega. Any children from the matings are either given over to the pack if they can afford it, or farmed out for adoption. Beta males can't impregnate an omega, but there's a surrogacy program in place for beta couples to apply. To me it's a shitty excuse for asshole alphas to get their kicks with an omega without the tie of a bitemark.

Just the mention of the nests has us riled up. Rogue's fists are clenched as growls ripple through him, and he tries to pull himself together. I can see the struggle in his face. We've been walking a thin line in our pack for a while, and his instincts are riding him *hard*.

"Shit." I mutter. Harper stares between us all, her eyes wide.

If he flips, it could have a knock-on effect on all of us through the bond, and I can feel my hackles rising. Four angry alphas who've lost control and an omega in the same room is asking for fucking trouble. Harper could get hurt.

I'm halfway out of my seat when Harper stands, her hands shaking, and moves slowly over to Rogue. Hesitantly, she puts her slim hand on his back and gently strokes down it before dropping to her knees and placing her head on his thigh, leaving her neck open to his hands. The perfect act of submission. It catches my alpha in mid-snarl, Rogue's shock and sudden arousal echoing through the bond to pull us all away from the danger zone.

Damned omega instincts.

Of course, as an omega, she'll be able to sense and address our moods. It's like catnip to them. It's why we wanted her here in the first place. But all of that seems to pale into the background now compared to actually having her here in our home.

I've no idea why the OC didn't consider her to be a good omega. She's fucking perfect.

Rogue lifts his hand. Blowing out a breath, he pushes her hair away from her face gently and cups her neck with his hands, stroking his fingers down the pale column of her throat and avoiding the thick black collar that marks her as a possession of the Omega Compound. He doesn't look away from her, and there's a sudden tenderness in his expression that makes me twitch.

Ours. The declaration drops into my head suddenly, and I push it away.

She's not fucking ours.

Harper lets out a breathy moan, and the mood deepens. All four of us feel the tug of arousal, and Harper's borrowed sleep shorts do little to hide her honeyed scent from us. She can't see us from where she is, but I have a perfect view from my seat as her legs push together, surreptitiously trying to stop the ache between her legs.

"Air," Gabe gasps. "I need some air for a moment," He's

gone in a flash, Ace flying out of the kitchen door behind him. The cold winter air helps to clear out some of the heavy pheromones lingering around the room, and Rogue lifts Harper's chin up slowly.

"Good girl," he tells her, and a whimper falls from her lips at the praise. I suddenly want to take her into every room, scent mark every cushion and wall with cinnamon so we can't move without breathing her in.

My chair nearly tips over as I pelt after Gabe and Ace.

CHAPTER EIGHTEEN
HARPER

I freeze with my head pillowed on Rogue's thigh, his spring scent drenching me.

The movement was so instinctive that I didn't even hesitate. I could feel the anger pouring from the pack, their scents battering me from the inside out. I just reached for Rogue without thinking, and now I'm nuzzling his thigh like he's the blanket I wrapped myself in last night.

So much for my declaration that I wouldn't let them bite me. Right now, I'd bend over and call Rogue master if he asked me to. I think of presenting myself to him, and shiver at the thought.

His anger settles into a low thrum. The purring reverberates through me, forcing another pulse of slick from between my legs. I've never responded to any alphas like I do to this pack. I've never had these *feelings* before. I frantically rub my legs together, my body chasing something just out of reach. I'm so focused on what I'm doing that Rogue's voice makes me jump, the velvet tones drawing a low whimper from my throat.

"Sweetheart, we need to stop now."

I can't stop. Call it instinct, call it desire, call it whatever the hell you want, but the last thing I want is to stop. I shake my head, whimpering.

"Don't make me stop," I beg, staring up at Rogue's concerned face.

Devlin leaps up from the table with a curse, his rapidly retreating footsteps leaving me alone with an alpha and this clenching need low in my belly. I need more. I glance up at Rogue, his face full of pained need as he stares back at me.

Rogue's hand tangles into my hair, gently gripping it without hurting me, and his purring intensifies. Oh, dear god. The sound sizzles through my veins, a vibration moving straight towards my pussy. My hips start rocking, seeking something. There's a pushing in my abdomen, an edge of pain to the feelings running through me.

"Alpha, please," I moan. I feel *empty*. The feelings take on a sharpness. It doesn't hurt, but it feels like a warning. My body is telling me that it needs this. I sob when I push my legs together and it does nothing. I need an alpha.

In response, Rogue lifts me up so I'm suddenly straddling his thighs, my core pressed tight to the hardness in his jeans. *Yes*, the voice inside my head hisses. *This is what we need.* I start rocking mindlessly as he pulls my hair away from my face, forcing me to focus on him.

"Harper," he groans. "We definitely shouldn't be doing this."

I don't care. I've spent most of my life being told what I should do, what I need. I need *this*, and I'm taking it. I stare into his darkening emerald eyes, the scent of cut grass entwining with cinnamon around us. Whimpering, I move back and forth over his bulge as he clenches my hair in his fist a little tighter, the slight sting causing more wetness to flow from me. I lean back, placing my hands behind me to give myself extra pressure to rub against him, my hips circling frantically.

"Good girl," he whispers. "Take what you need."

His other hand drops to my hips and he thrusts himself up and into me, the feeling sending white-hot heat blazing down my spine.

"Fuck, yes," I'll beg. I *need* him. "Please, alpha, please,"

I'm moving faster, pleading for more. He pushes against me again and again as my cries get higher and more desperate, his brow creased as he focuses entirely on me. He slips his hand underneath the shorts Gabe lent me, cursing when I soak his hand. His fingers find my clit and rub, gentle circles and then harder, the sensation sending ripples of pleasure through me as my eyes roll back.

"Come, Harper," he barks, and he pinches my clit between his fingers.

I'm fucking flying.

The feel of Rogue's fingers, his heat pushing hard against my entrance, scoring me through the damp material is enough to tip me over the edge. Shuddering, I cry out in ecstasy, gripping his hair tightly as he buries his face in my neck, somehow avoiding my collar to draw rasping, long licks along my jawline, nipping at the underside of my chin. There are fireworks in my eyes and my vision stutters as the feeling rips through my body like I'm falling off a cliff. Rogue groans underneath me as he pushes up one more time, additional wetness coating me through his pants.

Panting, I let my head fall down, nuzzling his shoulder as my vision starts to clear. My body trembles with the aftershocks of what we've just experienced, little shivers up and down my spine. Rogue strokes me gently, murmuring soothing words in my ear as I pull myself together. Moving slightly, I become aware of the mess I've made on him and pull back in mortification.

"Oh, gods," I whisper. "I'm so sorry."

What the fuck was that? I just climbed my new alpha, who

I met *yesterday*, like a swing set. They're definitely going to send me back.

I try to pull away from Rogue, but his hand is still wound in my hair. He tugs it lightly, refusing to let me turn away and I lift my gaze up. He's going to be so angry with me.

"Why are you apologizing?" he asks ruefully. "I'm the one who lost control." He gestures with his free hand at the mess between us. Frowning, I look down.

"I didn't realise it would be…I've never…" I can feel my face flushing as his mouth opens slightly in surprise.

"You've never had an orgasm?" he asks me gently.

Shaking my head, I give up on trying to move away and instead hide my burning face in his shoulder, sucking in deep breaths of his fresh scent to try and clear my head. No, I've never had an orgasm. Omegas can't come on their own; we need an alpha for that.

My legs clench around him when he suddenly rises from his seat. I squeak in surprise as he strides out of the kitchen, taking me with him as he holds my legs wrapped around his waist, my arms tight around his neck. I glimpse an open plan living area with a large television and soft brown comfortable couches that I really want to curl up in before he pushes a door open and his scent fills my nose. This must be his bathroom.

I hold onto him tightly as he bends down, and I hear water running. My ass touches something, and I realize he's propped me up on a counter. He doesn't move away though, studying my face intently. Biting my lip, I glance up at him hesitantly, but I don't have anything to lose.

"Please don't send me back." It's a whisper.

A flash of shock flits across his emerald eyes and I brace myself for the worst. "We're not sending you back, sweetheart." His voice is firm, no hesitation, and a little thrill of happiness runs through me.

"You're not?" I ask hopefully.

He runs his hands gently through my hair and I lean into his touch. He makes me feel so safe. From the moment I met him. It feels like nothing can possibly hurt me with Rogue here.

"Definitely not," he says with a small groan. "But we do need to talk. I understand that your instincts will push you to respond to us in ways that seem strange. Ours are doing the same thing." He thinks for a moment, choosing his words carefully.

"The last thing that we want to do is to make you uncomfortable in any way. If you want something to happen, then that's fine. As long as it's something that *you* want."

His words warm me from the inside out. Consent is fucking sexy when you're an omega and at the mercy of your instincts.

I think I'd like to pretend that whatever the hell just happened definitely never ever happened. But also, it felt *amazing*. I want to do it again. Possibly a lot, so…

"Did you like it?" I ask him shyly. A smile pulls at my lips as his face transforms, a slow grin pulling across his features. "You're a temptress," he tells me sternly, but his eyes dance with laughter.

I decide to just go for it. "Can we do it again?"

He stares at me in shock for a moment before throwing his head back in a booming laugh. Rejection runs through me and I pull myself back. My lip trembles slightly and I bite it to stop the movement.

What are these fucking *feelings*? My emotions feel like a damned rollercoaster.

Rogue picks up on it immediately, his laughter cutting off.

"Hey. Slow down and wait a second." His tone is soothing as he rubs his cheek over mine, the slight stubble of his jawline rasping deliciously against my skin. I can't help but preen at the blatant scent marking.

"*Yes*, I want to do that again. In fact, I'd like to do that over and over again with you, and maybe some other things as well."

"Oh." I can feel the heat spreading up my face and probably coming out of my ears like steam, even as my core twitches in interest and my breathing speeds up slightly.

"However," he murmurs, running his nose along my cheek, "I don't want to take advantage, or make you feel that you have to do something that you're not comfortable with. So, let's take our time, okay? We still need to finish our discussion, and the others will want to spend time with you too."

A sudden image falls into my mind of me doing *that* with Devlin, Ace and Gabe watching me, and I whine again. Oh god.

Rogue breathes in deeply, and his brow twitches. "Let's just get you in the bath, love."

He steps away and my arms reach back out for him on instinct. I reign them in, thinking over what he's said. He's being considerate and I don't want to push my luck. I do really want to ask him if he'll get in the bath with me though. I want to see what he looks like under his fitted white shirt. My mouth waters and I distract myself by starting to pull down the sleep shorts. A bang and curse ring out and I look up to see Rogue rubbing his head.

"Walked into the door," he offers sheepishly. "I'll get you something clean. Take your time, and call out if you need anything." Backing out, he gently pulls the door shut. Stripping quickly out of the rest of my clothes, I tiptoe over to the steaming bath. He's even put bubbles in. I quickly poke my toes in, followed by the rest of me, and moan in delight at the feel of the hot water against my tense skin.

Heaven. This is heaven. Except it feels a little lonely without Rogue.

Yep. I am in so much trouble.

Chapter Nineteen
Rogue

H ot water pummels my back.

Pressing my hand against the tiled wall in Devlin's bathroom, I run the other over my face, trying to wash away the guilt. That was Harper's first orgasm, and she gave it to me because I couldn't control my own damn instincts.

My cock twitches and I close my eyes, moving my hand down as I remember her breathy moans and the feel of her wetness rubbing against me. She was bloody glorious, hair rippling down her back like fire, hips undulating as she moved over me to take what she needed. At that moment, I was her creature. She could have asked for my heart on a plate, and I would have ripped it from my chest in a heartbeat.

My instincts are riding me hard, telling me to get back to the other bathroom and make her scream out my name until she's limp with release. Groaning, I twist the shower temperature until the water turns ice cold. Hopefully, it'll get rid of my Harper issue.

When I'm dressed, I head back to the kitchen, stopping to drop a parcel of clothing outside the bathroom floor. Listening for a second, I can hear splashing and Harper humming. The sound echoes through me, a purr rising up. My instincts are pushing me to make sure she's cared for, and I'm tempted to head in just to make sure.

Shaking my head hard to dispel the image of a lithe, naked Harper rising from the bathwater, I nearly run into the kitchen. Dev, Gabe, and Ace are all stood with matching expressions, arms folded and eyebrows raised. Checking on the bond, I feel strands of jealousy rippling through with a definite tinge of arousal. I can still scent Harper's release in the air and clearly, so can they. They're all packing a serious erection.

"I hope that's for her and not me," I toss at them, heading to get a coffee refill. "You know I think you're all hot as fuck, but I don't swing that way."

Gabe's mouth falls open as he gapes at me. Ace stares. "Who are you, and what have you done with our serious pack leader?"

Shrugging, I sit back down, glancing towards the open door to see if Harper's coming back. I've given her my shirt this time, the possessive bastard in me wanting her smothered in my scent.

Ace snaps his fingers in front of my face, face twitching in amusement. "Focus, you horny motherfucker."

I growl at him just to remind him who's in charge around here, even as my lips twitch in amusement. He's not wrong. They all settle down, grumbling and shifting uncomfortably. Gabe fans the remaining scent towards the open door.

"I'm so jealous," he groans. "She smells…"

Staring at the pockmarked wood of our kitchen table, I press my finger into the grooves. "It was her first orgasm," I mutter, not looking at them.

The jealousy in the pack bond swells even more, and I swing up to glower at them. "Seriously?"

Ace shrugs. "We're alphas. And she's…"

"Amazing," Gabe practically has stars in his eyes as he stares longingly at the entrance to the corridor. Dev pokes him in the arm, hard, and he yelps, swatting at him. Jumping up, he heads to the pantry and starts pulling out ingredients.

"I'll make omelets," he says, frowning. "That's pretty basic, so we can try her with that and go from there."

"I like omelets," Harper says softly, and we all spin to face her in the doorway, Ace nearly falling off his chair. She's standing on one foot, the other rubbing up and down her calf. My shirt drowns her, and she's left a couple of buttons undone, showing more than a hint of her creamy skin. Her hair's been combed out, framing her face with wisps as it dries. She looks fucking edible. I grit my teeth as I scan over the bruises lining her body, a reminder for me to check her over for anything that might need treatment.

My pack clearly agrees as they're all staring at her like idiots. Even Dev isn't immune, mouth open as his eyes sweep over her bare legs.

Gabe recovers first, beckoning her in and pulling out a seat as Ace jumps up and gets her a fresh cup of coffee. She glances around at all of us shyly. "Thank you."

Smiling at her, I wait for Gabe to start on the food before picking up the conversation we dropped earlier.

"So, picking things back up," I murmur as she blushes, "We're really not formal, and we'd rather not stick to the instructions and do our own thing. This is only as long as you're comfortable, and you'll need to tell us if there's anything we should be aware of about what you need."

She nods, a look of relief pressing over her face, and relaxes back into her chair. Cautiously, she reaches out for the sugar and cream Ace gave her earlier, her eyes flicking to me. I nod encouragingly, and she starts experimenting with her cup. Taking a sip, her eyes widen in pleasure. My pulse jumps. "I like it this way," she offers Ace, who winks at her.

"I take mine black, personally."

"Like your soul," adds Gabe, as he starts putting plates down on the table. Ace acts wounded, and they start to bicker. It's more lighthearted than some of their recent arguments. The smell of the food fills my nose and glancing over at Harper, I can tell she's excited. Another punch to my stomach. When was the last time she had a proper meal?

Idiot. You should have fed her last night.

We need to do fucking better. I don't want her to ever go hungry again. Gabe stays close to her, watching her face intently as she daintily cuts into her food. The moan she lets out at the first taste sends a ripple across the pack, all of us immediately focusing on our own plates and trying to push our erections down. If she's always this vocal, we'll have permanent hard-ons at this rate.

Looking around, I take in the atmosphere. Even with the uncertainly, there's a *hopefulness* linking us together that I haven't felt before. Everyone is watching Harper whilst pretending not to as she scoffs down her food, and Gabe hums happily as he starts her a second omelet, muttering about adding cheese this time. Even Devlin can't stop shooting little glances at her, the harsh lines of his face softening slightly with every stolen glance.

She's been here for a matter of hours, and I can already feel the impact. Peace washes over me, and I push away intruding thoughts of the world outside. At least for today, we can enjoy getting to know her. Reality will intrude soon enough, but I plan to make the most of this time with my pack and try to rebuild some of the bonds that have been strained over the last year or so. Glancing at Dev, I see him staring at his plate with a frown. He's taken to Harper much better than I expected, but I can still feel his struggle. I push my concern down the bond, and he responds with a stoic flatness. He's okay, but I'll need to keep an eye on him.

Gabe, however, is another story. Our bruised alpha, who's hidden away from the world, is beaming as he cooks for Harper. I notice that he hasn't touched his scar once since we've been sat here, a nervous habit he picked up after the attack.

Ace seems much more relaxed too, his nervous energy toned down as he flicks balls of paper at Dev across the table, trying to make Harper laugh. Dev ignores him, but it just makes her smile harder until a bright giggle tumbles out into the air. Music and sunlight. I swallow down the urge to sweep her up and catch her laughter with my lips. Not yet.

After Harper's finished eating her fill, weakly protesting to Gabe that she'll be sick if she eats any more, I reach out and snag her hand, pulling her up.

"Where are we going?" Her fingers curling trustingly into mine makes my chest hurt. This girl is dangerous. We all know it, but I don't think any of us care, apart from maybe Devlin.

"I want to give you the full tour," I say, staring pointedly at the pack when they half-rise from their chairs to follow. Brow creasing in disappointment, Gabe flops back into his chair with a small huff. My stomach flips and I consider pulling him along, but I want some time to get to know Harper properly too. She's had time with Gabe and Rogue, and Dev hasn't pushed it, so I'm seizing the opportunity where I can.

Harper follows me closely as we head back down towards the living area. It's a huge, open plan room, a large hearth at one end offering a roaring fire on cold nights and the huge television set up for movies and gaming when we're in the mood.

"So, this is our main pack space. We call it the snug," I announce, pulling Harper to a stop in the middle of the room and gesturing around. She disentangles her hand and I push down my protest, following her as she moves towards the brown leather seating arranged in a semi-circle. Glancing at me, I realise she's waiting for permission and nudge her gently. "You don't have to ask. Make yourself comfortable."

She burrows down into the soft leather without another word, curling her legs up underneath her. It's a huge sofa, made to hold all of us, and she looks tiny huddled up in the corner.

"It's so *soft*," she whispers, running her hands gently across the surface. My heart clenches at the sheer enjoyment on her face, and I think of the section in the manual that talks about nesting. She's clearly never been allowed to make one. She's not even allowed a blanket.

Anger floods through me at the reminder of where she's come from, and I turn from her to give myself a moment to calm down, heading to the hearth. We'll probably come back in here later, so I drop down to get a fire going. After a minute, Harper's hand gently touches my shoulder. "What's the matter?"

There's no judgement in her husky words. Leaning back, I glance up at her where she stands, worrying her lip with her teeth. Reaching out, I gently pull it free. "Don't damage those beautiful lips, little omega."

A hint of cinnamon wraps around me, and my hand lingers against her mouth. I give in to temptation and sweep my finger against her softness, enjoying the way her mouth opens to me and her golden eyes darken. She's so beautifully responsive.

Before I lose control, I let her go and motion to the fireplace. "Have you ever set a fire before?"

She sinks down next to me gracefully, perching back on her heels in a clearly well-learned move. "No, but I'd like to learn. What do I do?"

I show her how to scrunch up the paper we keep in a basket next to the hearth, explaining where to position it and helping her choose blocks of wood to build the frame. She's a picture of concentration as she places them carefully down, the edges of her pink tongue just poking out of her lips. Temptation in one perfect package. I can barely pay attention to what we're doing, forcing myself to grab the long matches from the drawers in the coffee table.

She laughs in delight when the flames spring up. "I did it!"

She turns to me, the fire reflecting against her golden eyes. I swoop in without a second thought, grasping her face between my hands. The moment our lips meet, I'm lost. She's soft and pliant against me, her breasts pressing into my chest. Cinnamon and honey twists around us as her arousal makes itself known. A low whine builds in her throat as her mouth moves against me. I sip at those perfect lips, little nips that draw out the noises she's making and go straight to my cock. With a growl, I drag her into my lap, fully intending to replicate the noises I heard from the kitchen earlier. I want to see her come apart for me, crying my name as her body shakes and tips over the edge.

CHAPTER TWENTY-ONE
HARPER

I think I've turned into some sort of sex-crazed nympho.

That's the only explanation for the way I feel. Ace holds me tightly, his large hand spreading across my lower back as he lifts me onto him. My hips shift, seeking another release, and there's an embarrassing amount of wet flowing out of me as my slick releases in a wave of warmth. Ace's nostrils flare as he catches the scent, his piercing blue eyes running over my face like he can't decide where to look. "Ace," I moan.

These alphas are something else.

He lays me down, a soft fur rug meeting my back as he follows me, tucking himself between my legs. I tense instinctively as fear yanks me away from the warmth of the fire; the position so familiar to Jason pinning me down that my scent turns acrid with fear.

Ace pulls back immediately, sensing the change. "Harper?" he asks gently, and my eyes fill with tears as I wriggle out from underneath him. Covering my face with my hands, I let out a small sob.

First, I jumped Rogue, and now I've ruined this.

"I'm sorry," I gasp, and Ace lifts me into his arms, sitting down and rocking me lightly from side to side. I can't stop the wave of grief that comes over me. Sobbing, I bury my face in his shirt and he strokes my hair gently, letting me cry all over him. "It's not you," I hiccup, wanting him to know. He smiles sadly down at me, wiping away a tear. "I know. Let it all out, little omega."

It's all I need, and I huddle into him, crying softly. It's all so much. The last two weeks have finally caught up to me and all the worst parts are playing on a loop inside my head. I owe Ace an explanation, though.

"He tried to mate with me like that," I whisper, and Ace tenses under me.

"Who, love?" he asks quietly. His voice is pure ice.

"Jason," I force out. "He was the g-guard I was assigned to at the compound. They wanted to see if they could get more control over the omegas. I was in a fight in the dining hall so they told me that Jason would train me. He wanted me to submit to him, so he kept me in a room and hurt me over and over to try and make me. Yesterday, he would have. It was only because the Director called for us that he stopped."

It's hard to admit, but I was so close to giving into him. My mind and heart would have broken, but my body would have been his. A good little omega, just like they wanted me to be. An empty, pretty shell for him to rut on.

"But you didn't," Ace whispers gently. "You didn't give in. And if you had, then it wouldn't have been your fault."

"I nearly did," I admit. The confession hurts even more than I thought it would. "There were times when I *wanted* to."

It feels like I've failed, like I've given up something integral to who I am. Ace tucks me deeper into his side. "Harper, sweetheart, that bastard tortured you. Rogue told us a little last night and we barely know anything about what you've been through. You didn't break, and you're here, with us. That you can even function, even talk to us, let alone everything else, is a miracle, love."

I look into his soft eyes, searching for a pretty lie. But his eyes show only honesty, and sadness. He tucks some of my hair back behind my ear.

"I think you might be the bravest person I've ever met," he whispers.

"You do?" I stare up at him. Leaning down, he drops a gentle kiss on my forehead. "I really do."

We stay tucked together for a few more minutes, Ace humming quietly as he runs his hand slowly through my hair and I think over his words. I start to feel drowsy and as much as I don't want to, I shift around to let him know I'm going to get up. We can't stay here for hours with me curled up on his lap, even though at this moment there's nothing I'd like more.

"You feeling better, little omega?" He helps me sit up and I move to my knees, turning around to face him. "Thanks, Ace," I whisper, and before I can talk myself out of it, I lean forward to kiss him. His mouth parts in surprise at the contact, and he returns it gently. Some of the feelings from earlier start pulling at my core and I pull back with a rueful smile. "The others are probably wondering where we are."

"Gabe's probably pacing the floor waiting for lunch so he can feed you again," Ace teases, and I laugh quietly. I'm glad that my emotional avalanche hasn't stopped him from acting like this around me. I don't want a pity party. I want *them*, the family they've showed me so far. Even grumpy Devlin and his scowls.

This pack is so much more than I ever would have expected.

Please let this be real.

Ace jumps up and lifts me gently, holding my hips until I'm steady on my feet. The fire we made is flickering behind him, sending warm waves of heat out into the room. I glance towards the leather seats, wondering if he'd mind me staying in here for a while. I still feel a little tired.

"Why don't you settle in on the couch for a bit?" Ace suggests. The man is clearly a mind reader, and I smile at him before scrambling back to my corner. The leather's so soft and inviting. It feels like it's hugging my whole body. Relaxing into its embrace, I sigh with delight. Ace moves around me and starts to fiddle with the television. I haven't watched television for years, apart from some of the instructional films they showed us at the compound.

"What would you like to watch?" he asks, waving the remote at me.

A yawn slips out before I can stop it. "Anything. I don't mind", I mumble. I'm fighting to stay awake now. My fingers twitch and I wish that I had my blanket from upstairs.

Ace chooses a movie and hits the pause button. "I'll go and see if any of the guys want to watch with us. Will you be okay here for a second?"

"Sure," it's barely a word, my voice slurred as I doze. I feel Ace kiss my forehead and let me eyes flutter shut.

When I wake up, I'm surrounded by warmth. There are blankets piled on top of me, and my head is resting on something warm and firm. I sit up, for a second forgetting where I am, and relax as Gabe's face appears in front of me.

"Hey, sweetheart," he murmurs. "Do you feel better?" Nodding, I look behind me to where Ace is sitting, his legs sprawled lazily in front of him. I blush when I realize it was his thigh I was resting on, and he smirks at me. Reaching out, he gently tugs until I'm curled up against him, my head against his shoulder. Breathing in his salty scent, my muscles unclench.

We watch the film in silence for a few minutes. My attention keeps slipping to the bundle of blankets I pushed off me and onto the floor when I woke up. Something tugs me towards them, and I scramble off Ace and onto the floor. Gathering up the materials, I sit back down and get to work arranging them all in the right way, layering one on top of the other until I'm cocooned. The guys both watch me instead of the movie, amusement in their eyes as I fuss.

"You like blankets, then?" Gabe asks the question teasingly, and it pulls me from my work. Blankets. *Nesting instincts.* There's a pull in my chest at the thought. The interrogation unit would really lose their shit if they could see me now. I go to push the blankets away, but Gabe stops me, his hand reaching out to grasp mine.

"It's okay," he whispers. "We don't mind."

I slide my eyes across to Ace and he just smiles at me encouragingly. Slowly, I reach back out, my fingers grasping a fluffy cream comforter.

"Instincts," I say quietly.

I've never made a nest before, except for my tiny nest last night, and it doesn't really count. The OC was always very careful never to give us anything that could ever be called comfortable. Our bedding was sparse if any; to wash, we were only permitted a thin, scratchy towel and it was taken off us immediately when we were done. We weren't even given proper clothes. Having these blankets within reach is… irresistible.

It might not be a big deal to them, but to me…

Sadness fills me, and I fiddle with the top blanket, stroking my hand over its soft texture. How different would my life have been if I'd been matched with a pack earlier? Could I have had this all along, instead of pain and abuse with my instructors and Jason?

Even as the question runs through my mind, I know the answer. This pack is different. Any other alpha pack would have me on my knees, eyes to the ground, and following every instruction laid out by the compound. I shiver at the thought and Gabe runs a soothing hand down my arm. Shaking the bad thoughts off, I offer him a small smile. "Sorry. Got lost in my thoughts for a minute."

"Understandable." Gabe smiles back at me before he bounces off the couch, earning a short growl from Ace as I'm dislodged. "I just realized I left the snacks in the kitchen. We didn't want to eat them without you."

He disappears for a second and returns, balancing two bowls precariously in his arms. I jump up to help, and he laughs as he hands me one. "Thanks. That could've gone badly wrong." He waggles his eyebrows at me and I laugh at the fake tortured expression on his face.

"What is this?" I look down into the bowl and see– "Buttered popcorn?" My mouth floods at the memory. I love buttered popcorn, and– "M&Ms!" I clap my hand over my mouth, embarrassed at my outburst. But, I mean, it's chocolate. *Chocolate.*

I don't even realize I'm purring until Gabe's scent hits my nose. As I look up, his face is leaning in and he rubs his cheek against mine. I wrinkle my nose at the blatant scent marking and he shrugs, unrepentant. "Gotta get in wherever I can, love."

The three of us spend a blissful afternoon huddled together on the sofa, watching old films about a young wizard. I'm glued to the screen as I savor the taste of the food in front of me. Gabe and Ace are on either side of me, both of their legs pressing against mine. Their scents rise and fall with every sound I make, and their warmth sinks into me. As the third film finishes, I sigh in absolute bliss. "This is the best day ever."

Ace smiles at me, but there's a hint of sadness in it. "I'm glad you've enjoyed it, little omega." He bops my nose again and I laugh, batting him away. Gabe stretches, muttering about food as Rogue's voice comes through the open door.

Ace groans and pulls himself up. "Better see what the boss man wants."

CHAPTER TWENTY-TWO
ROGUE

A ce steals Harper away and the pack disperses. Dev points towards the gym.

"I'm heading down for a workout. Fancy it?"

I was in the gym at five a.m. this morning, working thoughts of Harper out of me until I was a sweating mess.

"Sure." Maybe it'll actually work this time.

We set up in silence, Dev heading over to the weight bench while I move over to the treadmill. Music blasts through the room, Dev cranking the volume up just the way he likes it.

I focus on the screen in front of me as my feet pound against the machine. Sweat pours off my face and I crank it up further, pushing the machine into an uphill incline. My legs burn as I push through the barrier. When the pace slows, I look around, confused. Dev stands next to the treadmill with his eyebrows raised. He waves the plug at me.

Throwing me a towel, he waits silently as I wipe over my face and neck. My heart is pounding, pulse thundering. Glancing back at the screen, I'm startled to see I've run the equivalent of a half marathon.

"Did it help?" Dev queries. He can see straight through me.

He's always been able to, ever since we were kids scrapping in the playground.

I shake my head and head over to the bench, sinking down with a groan to stretch out my exhausted muscles. Dev takes a seat next to me, dropping his head back against the wall with a soft thud.

"I just... I'm not sure what's happening here," I say, staring down at my legs with a frown.

Everything's moved so fast. It was only two nights ago that we were sitting around the table, the possibility of a female joining the pack a tentative future option. But here we are, less than forty-eight hours later with an omega of our own, working out ways to keep her safe from the reach of the omega compound.

My heart thuds as I think of Harper. The run didn't work. I just want more. More time, more conversation. More *Harper*.

I feel on edge when she's near me. My instincts go wild, insisting that I bite, claim, *mate*. Interestingly, I don't feel possessive over her with the pack, but the thought of her being with anyone else... my teeth snap together in agitation.

"It's been a lot to adjust to," Dev mutters, and I look over at him in concern. With everything snowballing the way it has, I've barely checked in on him, and a ball of guilt creeps into my stomach.

"How did you sleep last night?" It's no secret that Devlin has night terrors. We're all used to it, and I'd listened out for any activity last night in case it woke Harper.

Dev grimace, a hint of guilt crossing his face that confuses me. "Not bad, really. Finished the scotch and crashed pretty late. I probably got in a few hours."

"That's not a coping mechanism," I chide him mildly, leaning against his shoulder. We've been there before, with Dev using alcohol as a crutch to avoid his feelings, and it took a long time for him to come back to us.

He groans. "I know. It's just… she's inside my head, you know? Two days ago, I thought I hated all omegas without question. But seeing her there, and now she's here… part of me really wants to be involved with that, but there's a voice inside my head that's telling me to question everything."

"In what way?" I want to understand his concerns. Devlin rarely opens up like this.

"That this all feels really… convenient," he shrugs. "Since we were kids, we've been told that omegas are dangerous. That they use their influence to manipulate alphas and packs into difficult situations. She already has Ace and Gabe under her spell. I think Gabe would jump off a cliff if she asked nicely."

His tone is joking, but there's a thread of soberness in his voice. "What if there's a thread of truth in that? What if she doesn't even mean to do it, but she is? What does that mean for us?"

I think over his words for a few minutes as we sit quietly. As much as it feels like Harper has slotted in perfectly to our pack dynamics, I can't deny that his words have struck a chord. Have I been irresponsible?

Finally, I turn to him. "I'll be honest, I don't see that happening with Harper. I know what you mean – we've all fallen under her spell a little. But I genuinely don't think there's any manipulation happening here. If there's any, I think it's coming from my father and the OC."

Dev nods slowly, his mouth twisted as he considers my words.

"But," I continue, Dev's head snapping up towards me. "You're right. We don't know for certain, and maybe something could happen without her even being aware of it. I'll speak to Gabe and Ace and remind them that we need to be careful, maybe keep a little more distance until we're all more comfortable. We should be able to find a balance that works for everyone."

I don't miss his small sigh of relief, and his shoulders relax. He's clearly been worried about this. Leaning in, he rests against my arm, and I savor the contact with my packmate. My best friend.

"Thanks for not ignoring me," he mutters, and my heart twists. "Never," I swear, and it's a promise I intend to keep.

After we finish up in the gym I head back upstairs towards my office to get some work done. I call out to Ace as I pass the snug and he pulls himself up. Harper's head pops up and my heart does a flip in my chest. Her bright smile dims slightly when I only offer her a polite one in return, and I hate myself a little.

"Got a minute?" I ask Ace.

"Sure." He follows me into my office, and I close the door behind us.

"It won't take long. It's about Harper." Ace sharpens and he focuses on me.

Crossing my arms, I lean back slightly. "I know that she's settling in well, but it's still early days. We all need to be careful."

Ace's brow furrows. "What do you mean?"

"I mean that as much as we might like her, we also need to remember that the creed is in place for a reason. That means we need to be careful about how much we let her… influence our actions."

Ace swears. "That's bullshit. You know the Omega Creed is a pile of—"

"I *know*," I cut him off abruptly. "But regardless, whatever we think of the current set up, those rules were put in place to protect alphas and omegas, and I intend to make sure we do that, even if we're not following them to the letter. It's not just us I'm thinking of, Ace. It's her too. We don't have all of the information, so we need to tread carefully."

Frustration colors Ace's face, his lips pulled into a scowl.

"You're letting Dev get into your head." When I bristle, he backtracks. "I don't mean it in a bad way. I get what you're saying. But c'mon, Rogue, do you really think she's some sort of master manipulator?"

"No, I don't," I sigh. "But I need to protect our pack, Ace. And I need to protect her, too. I'm not saying you need to ignore her or avoid her necessarily. Just be careful."

He nods at me, and I ask him to send Gabe in. Gabe's face falls in disappointment when I tell him, but he doesn't argue. I watch him slide out the door, his shoulders slumped in disappointment.

This is the right decision for all of us. It's my responsibility as pack leader to make those tough calls. Even when my pack brothers don't necessarily agree with them.

When dinnertime arrives, Harper drops into her seat with a grin that tugs at my heart. I steel myself. I have to lead by example.

"Rogue, we watched movies today!" she beams at me, her eyes flashing a beautiful shade of sunshine yellow. Clearing my throat, I nod to her. "That's great."

"We had popcorn and chocolate too." She looks so excited as she tells me, but her words make me frown, a hint of worry running through me.

"Is that a good idea?" I ask gently. "We're already moving away from the compound foods. I don't want to push it too far."

Her smile falls away and she looks crestfallen, biting her lip. "Of course," she whispers. "I won't have it again."

My stomach swoops but I hold firm. It's true. I don't want to make her ill by feeding her too much sugar. If she's only eaten basic foods for years, then even just a little could make her unwell. Gabe and Ace exchange a loaded glance over her head. They clearly want to reach out to her, but I shoot them a warning look and they sink back in their seats with matching frowns.

Harper pushes her food around her plate, her shoulders pulled in tightly. Her happiness has completely drained out of her, and a pit of discomfort opens up in my stomach. I hate seeing the desolation on her face, especially after this morning. Devlin ignores us all, staring down at his food.

Christ, this is awkward.

Gabe pulls out a red velvet cake for dessert. Everyone declines, including Harper, who shoots a longing look at it before abruptly shaking her head. Gabe looks at me with accusation in his eyes, making me shift uncomfortably.

Muttering excuses, I disappear to my office. *This is for the best,* I tell myself.

So why does it feel like I've taken a wrong turn?

CHAPTER TWENTY-THREE
HARPER

I can feel Rogue's gaze on me, but I keep my eyes lowered. He gets up and heads out, not saying a word to anyone.

Gabe slides a slice of red velvet cake in front of me. My mouth waters. Red velvet cake is my absolute favourite food. I'm desperate to dig in, but now I keep hearing Rogue's voice echoing in my ear. I shake my head, gently pushing the plate away with a pang of regret. *One day*, I think mournfully.

"I'm full, thank you," I whisper. Gabe hovers over my shoulder, but he doesn't say anything, and the plate disappears. He starts to run the tap, washing dishes with a vigor that tells me he's not happy. I shrivel even more in my seat. Now I've upset Gabe too. I can't do anything right.

I don't know what I've done exactly, but there's definitely been a shift in how the pack are treating me. I wrack my brains trying to think of a reason, but the only one I can think of is that I've made myself too comfortable, pushed the rules too far. The day runs through my head and I cringe, thinking of the way I acted with Rogue this morning, and my time with Gabe and Ace this afternoon. They seemed fine at the time, but of course they're not. They were just being polite. Even to me, the omega.

That's fine. I'll keep to myself and stay quiet. A shiver of fear runs through me at the thought of being sent back to the OC. Jason will be there, waiting for me. I swallow back a whimper when I remember how angry he was when the Director sent him away.

Gabe curses, just as I hear the shatter of a broken plate. I jump at the unexpected noise, and I feel Devlin's eyes on me. When I chance a quick look, his perfect face is scowling again. Instinctively, I huddle into my chair, presenting a smaller target. He looks so *angry*. What did I do?

Misery surges through me at the thought that I've already managed to ruin things. Maybe the compound was right. I am a bad omega. I couldn't even manage one full day before everything's gone to shit.

I'm so full of tension that when Ace touches my shoulder unexpectedly, I flinch, a low whimper slipping out. Everyone stops and the atmosphere steps up a notch. Their scents swell up around me so quickly that it feels smothering for the first time, and I bite back a choke at the sensation. Devlin growls, and my eyes flick to him.

"Stop it," he demands, staring at me. I shrink back, not understanding what he means. Ace's hand closes gently over my shoulder, but he doesn't say anything. Devlin's glare moves to his hand, and I shrug it off quickly. I don't want to make things any worse.

"I'm sorry," I whisper. "I don't understand."

Devlin lets out an unmistakable snort of derision. "Are you sure?"

Behind me, Ace growls. Devlin's tone is mocking, and a lump springs up in my throat. What happened to the alpha who cradled me so carefully in the Director's office? I can't see any sign of him in the man in front of me.

The urge to run overwhelms me, and I jump out of my seat. It's too much, between the strong scents and Devlin's unmistakable anger. Slipping, I nearly fall before I gain purchase on my feet. I can hear Gabe and Ace's raised voices but I'm past rational thought. I just need to escape.

I fly up the stairs and into my room, pushing the door closed behind me. Slumping to the floor, I wrap my hands around my knees, trying to clear my head. A glint of metal catches my eye and my heart sinks. Someone brought up my cage.

I remember what Rogue said last night about sleeping in a bed. He said it was just for the night. I thought from our conversation this morning that things might be different, but I obviously misunderstood. A stab of sorrow runs through me at the thought.

I crawl forward, pausing to run my hand longingly over the soft cover hanging at the end of my bed. What I wouldn't give to hide underneath it now.

Turning, I back myself slowly through the cage door, wincing at the feel of the cold squeaky plastic underneath me. Pulling the wire door closed, I curl up, wrapping my arms around me to stay warm.

It's too exposed, too bright, too cold.

"Still better than the compound," I whisper, squeezing my eyes shut. *Still better than Jason.*

I need to see the positives. Today was… everything.

Omelets, and movies, chocolate and buttered popcorn. *Them.*

It's the best day I've had for years. I need to think of myself as lucky. I don't think they're going to hurt me. I just need to be a better omega.

My mind turns to the OC. I'm desperate to know how Ava is. Part of me is petrified that Jason's got hold of her. I start to shake at the thought, but Ava doesn't think she's twenty-one yet. Hopefully she'll be safe, at least for a few weeks longer.

I think about asking Rogue to look into it, but I dismiss it almost immediately. There's no way I can ask that of him. I need to be quiet and obedient. Asking for favors definitely doesn't fit the brief.

My back hits the cold metal and I hiss out a breath, shifting around to try and get comfortable. You think I'd be used to this by now. Jason would often make me sleep in here. It never really gets any easier, though.

Maybe tomorrow will be better.

"Do you want to be a good omega?" A reedy, high-pitched voice whispers nasally in my ear.

Whimpering, I nod.

It's dark. There are straps across my legs, my stomach, my throat. My ankles and wrists strain at the leather as it pulls tightly at my skin. It's getting hard to take a full breath.

"Please," I beg brokenly. "Please stop it."

Only silence greets me. I wait, maybe for hours. A small drop hits my forehead, the cold running down into my hairline. I pull frantically at my restraints but it's useless. I drop my arms back to the sides. My mind feels clouded, foggy, and I struggle to remember why I'm here.

"Do you want it to stop?" the voice whispers. The voice is my only companion in the dark. I try to remember what they want, straining my mind and my body. Something pops in my shoulder and I cry out.

"Tell me what you want," I'm crying, tears running down my face. "I'll do it. I'll do whatever you want."

"Master," the voice pushes. "Master," I wail. "Please, master."

A hand strokes over my hair and I whimper, straining towards the touch. "I'll be good, master," *I whimper. Maybe the voice will stop now.*

"A little more, I think."

"No!"

Hands shake me, a deep voice infiltrating my darkness.

"Harper!"

My eyes fly open as I'm pulled from my cage. I thrash, keening with terror and swiping at my forehead.

A hand touches me, and I throw myself down, putting my head to the floor. "I'm sorry, master. I'll be good. I don't need to be punished." Choking sobs stab my words.

"Jesus Christ." Hands lift me and I flail weakly. "Hush," the voice soothes. It sounds different. Deeper, rasping. "Stop, Harper. You're not there anymore."

Gasping, I open my eyes to Devlin staring down at me. His dark eyes scan my face, and I suck breaths in and out as I fight not to pass out, stars dancing across my vision. "Hurts," I groan. My body aches all over and I can't take a full breath.

"Breathe," Devlin barks, and his hand comes up to spread over my heart. "Now, Harper."

My body responds to his demand, and I wheeze with relief as I manage to get air into my lungs. Devlin lifts me effortlessly as he carries me across the room, and I curl myself into his warmth, sobs still falling from my lips.

It felt so real.

Leaning down, he pulls the covers back on the bed I slept in last night, and I start to wriggle uncomfortably in his arms. He pauses and I look up at him.

"Can't sleep there," I whisper, voice cracking. "Not allowed."

His brows fly up and he turns to look at the cage. Ignoring me, he settles me down into the softness and tugs the blankets over me. I burrow into them, pulling them over my head and breathing heavily.

I still feel too open, too exposed.

The panic starts to filter back in as Devlin starts to shift next to me as if he's going to leave. My hand slips out from the haphazard blanket nest I've created, and I grab his wrist as he tenses. His jaw works as he stares down at me, his dark eyes filled with pain.

We stare at each other for a moment. Something in his expression speaks to me. Two broken souls recognising each other.

"Please don't leave me," I whisper.

Devlin pulls his arm away. He won't stay. He hates me. Squeezing my eyes shut, I curl up into a ball, sobs wracking my body as I try to pull myself together.

The blankets shift as he slides in next to me, pulling me against him. It's not enough.

Whining in distress, I tug at him, until he lets me manoeuvre him so he's completely on top of me. His weight presses me down into the mattress, my nose buried in his throat as I breathe in his smoky leather scent. He's all around me, warmth and alpha and comfort. My whole body relaxes, softening into him.

This.

Devlin shifts awkwardly, and I wriggle underneath him. Hesitantly, he runs a warm hand down my arm. "Harper, this is—,"

"Safe," I murmur. "Feels safe."

If he speaks again, I don't remember it.

CHAPTER TWENTY-FOUR
DEVLIN

Awareness slowly filters in, and I stretch out, the movement eliciting a sleepy mewl. My eyes widen and I look down.

Harper lies nestled in my arms, her back pressed against my front and my leg slung over her hip. My dick is nestled in between the globes of her cheeks, and it stiffens as she pushes back against me with a low moan. I run my gaze over her, hunger pulling me to rock my hips gently. Her back arches lightly and her honey scent trickles into my nose. I want to roll her over and wake her up properly. I stifle a groan at the thought of licking into her dewy sweetness, her slick flowing into my mouth as I sip from her.

Guilt runs through me as I remember bursting in through the door last night. I hadn't been able to sleep, for once not worried about closing my eyes but running through the disastrous dinner with Harper. She'd looked so downtrodden when Rogue left, her eyes filled with tears as she stared down. There was no sign of the mischievous omega I'd seen glimpses of earlier in the day.

When she fled, Gabe and Ace had turned on me, a furious

argument taking place that ended with me storming out after I promised to apologize to Harper. I meant it, too. I was a prick to her.

And now… I'm here.

Finding her in the cage felt like I'd taken a knife to my chest. She'd clearly taken our words last night to mean that we were backtracking on what we said about bending the rules of the OC. Seeing her crying and shaking, her fear perfuming the air in a violent scent… it reminded me too much of myself. And as much as I'd wanted to be wary, knowing that I might have been responsible for her own night terrors didn't sit right with me. It felt like claws raking at my chest. *I did that to her.*

I blink rapidly as I realize that I slept through the whole night with her in my arms. That never happens, especially without the help of a bottle of scotch.

Harper shifts restlessly, her scent growing stronger as she moves her hips. Her legs rub against each other as she tries to get friction, a soft mewl of disappointment dropping into the air when she can't hit the spot.

Her eyes open sleepily, and she looks up at me where I hover over her.

I expect her to panic, to move away, but she surprises me. Shifting, she rolls to face me, her hips pressing into mine. I growl as my knot grows, blood rushing through my body at the silky soft feel of her.

We can't do this.

I move to shift off the bed, to end this before we do something I'll regret. Harper's whimper stops me. Her whiskey eyes are filling with tears.

"Harper, I…." I hesitate. I don't know what to say.

Apologize, idiot.

I was wrong to pull the pack back yesterday. I let old fears cloud my judgment.

"I'll get one of the others," I murmur. I'm probably the last person she wants to touch her right now.

She reaches out a hand and threads her fingers through mine.

"No," she whispers. "I need…need…"

Her hand drops to just above the line of her underwear and she rubs restlessly as her hips shift. It almost looks like she's in pain. Her scent turns acrid for a moment, the biting scent of her arousal drawing me in, instinct pushing me to ease her.

I shift towards her slowly, her eyes widening as I press back into her softness. She spreads her legs wider as I press my knot into her, and I can feel her slick even through my sweats and her underwear. I imagine sinking into her warm, wet heat, and Harper gasps as I swell even more. I thrust, experimenting, my mouth salivating at the way her eyes roll slightly.

"Better?" I ask, my voice a bare croak.

She nods, holding my gaze. "More, please." The sound is a whine.

Her begging flips something in me. I need to give her what she wants. My instincts are raking me down the insides, pushing me to pull her underwear down and sink into her. I can't take it that far, but I can take the edge off for her.

There's something I have to say first, though. I pull back slightly, forcing myself away from her so I can focus.

"I'm sorry, Harper," I breathe, staring into her amber eyes. There's no fear in them as she watches me, but the memory of her face won't leave me for a long time. "I was an asshole yesterday, and it wasn't your fault."

"Forgiven," she gasps, and she rocks towards me. I'm not sure she completely heard me. My instincts pull at me again, and I decide to repeat the apology later when we're both in a sound frame of mind. For now, though, there's something I dreamed about the other night that I want to try.

"Want to taste you," I growl at her, and she shivers at the sound. "Tell me now if you want me to stop."

When she shakes her head frantically and rubs against me, I could throw back my head and howl. Rolling her onto her back, I insert my hips between her thighs and drag my length slowly over her clit before pushing down, my hips moving in rapid circles. She cries out at the feel of me grinding into her, her legs opening further in invitation as she pushes herself against me, straining for release. I watch her closely for any sign of tension, ready to pull back if I need to.

She offers me her mouth and I take it, sucking on her lower lip and tugging it gently with my teeth, making her shudder. Leaning on my elbow, I wrap my hand around the back of her neck, dragging her in as I hitch her leg over my hip with the other. We move together, our hips in perfect sync, our scents thickening the air until it's ripe with lust and anticipation.

"Oh, gods," she whimpers as I break away, her mouth swollen red for me.

"Like seeing my mark on you," I grumble, taking advantage of her position and sweeping in to run my tongue up the side of her neck. I avoid her collar, the sight of it making me want to break something. Instead, I kiss my way down her body, pressing her arms to her sides gently and growling at her when she tries to move them. Her head thrashes as I move down. The t-shirt she's wearing smells like Gabe, and I grin savagely at her, sitting up as I release her hands and grip it, tearing down the middle. Her breasts bounce as she lands back with a gasp, a drawn-out moan cutting off with a choke as I seal my mouth over a perfect, cherry-colored nub and suck, my other hand palming her other breast and squeezing her nipple between my fingers.

My knot is swollen and I'm weeping from the tip, the scent of our fluids mixing together in the air and making me light-headed as she trembles underneath me.

"Devlin," she moans. The sound of my name on her lips untwists some of the ugliness inside me. This girl could be my own personal brand of scotch.

Her cries get louder, but I'm not ready for her to come yet. Releasing her with a soft pop, I admire the sight of her underneath me.

"Such a pretty omega," I murmur, tracing my hand between her tits and down to the soft thatch of copper curls at the apex of her thighs. Her keening cry is music to my ears as I spread her lips with my finger and gently scratch a nail down her swollen clitoris.

"Oh," she gasps, her head thrashing from side to side.

I'm aching to fill her up and pound her until she's begging for my knot. *Need.* Instead, I slide further down the bed. Yanking off her shorts, I push her thighs wider with my shoulders until she mewls at the slight burn.

She props herself up slightly on her elbows to watch, a scarlet flush painting her cheeks and creeping down her chest. I fight back the urge to flip her over and give her a spanking, see if her ass turns the same colour. *Another time*, I tell myself, and my cock jumps at the thought.

We lock gazes, her bright golden eyes misty with arousal as she breathes heavily. I turn and press a gentle, open-mouthed kiss to her soft thigh, enjoying the way her legs try to clench.

"You're gonna lie there like a good girl and take my mouth," I rumble. "Gonna suck you until your slick pours out of you."

Her eyes dilate and she nods breathlessly, throwing her head back with a moan when I bury my nose between her thighs. Honey and cinnamon and oranges. Fucking delectable.

I take my first long, slow lick up her center.

"Princess, you taste like sin," I growl.

Her back arches and she screams, trying to shift back, but my hands plant firmly on her hips, pinning her. I place little teasing licks around her clit as she begs and twists her hands into the bedding. Her thighs are shaking when I lean in and kiss the little nub gently before running my teeth over it.

"*Come*," I say roughly, and dart back in to suck, hard.

Her release sweeps over her like a wave and she thrashes under my grip, screaming my name into the house. I lick up every drop of her release as her honey-scented slick flows from her, grinding my hips urgently into the bedding as I feast.

For a moment I almost surge up, ready to sink into her but the tiny remaining rational part of my brain tells me she might be a virgin. I don't want to steal her first time from her, especially after last night. I have some making up to do. I come with a jerk, my fluids spurting into the bedding as I groan. It's easily the best orgasm I've ever had and I'm not even inside her. *What are you doing to me, princess?*

Her small hands grip at my shoulders and I follow her direction. She pulls me back over her body and I lean in, leaving small kisses over her shoulder and up her jawline as she catches her breath.

Her eyes meet mine with a slight amount of uncertainty. "Good girl," I purr, stroking my hand down her spine as I roll onto my back, taking her with me.

"I can taste your slick on my tongue, princess." Drawing her face to mine, I slip my tongue into her mouth, wanting to share the taste with her. Her eyes widen before she sucks it off me. Her obedience settles something inside me, and a twitch tells me that my body is more than up for a second round. I tug her down so her head rests on my shoulder and she takes slow, deep breaths, inhaling my scent.

She shifts, still wearing the remnants of Gabe's shirt. Looking down, I catch uncertainty in her expression. Time to revisit our earlier conversation.

"I'm sorry I spoke to you like that, princess," I whisper. Shame curls through me again at the memory.

She looks away from me. "It doesn't matter. If I did anything—"

"It does matter. You didn't do a single thing." My voice is firm. I won't let her think that anything about the way I've behaved is her fault. Blowing out a breath, I turn my gaze to the ceiling. I owe her an explanation.

"You know, I didn't want an omega here," I start, and I feel her flinch down to my bones.

Fuck. I'm already making a fucking mess of this.

I shift us both until we're facing each other. Her brow is creased, confusion in her whiskey eyes, but she holds my gaze steadily. Those eyes feel like they're looking through me to my damned soul.

"I'm no good at this shit, princess. I don't have the right words and I say things the wrong way. But yesterday wasn't about you. I've had this… thing, about omegas, since I was a kid. You just had the misfortune to be the first omega I've ever spent time with as an adult. I'm sorry I took it out on you. It wasn't fair."

She thinks over my words before she responds, her brows furrowed.

"Will you… will you tell me why you don't like omegas?"

Her voice wavers slightly, an edge of pain lining them. I pull her a little closer.

"When I was a kid, my father killed my mom. She was an omega."

She gasps, but I don't stop. I need to get this out before I lose my nerve.

"I was really close to them both. But then the war started. My mom gave up her job and stayed home with me a lot. I was just a five-year-old kid, though. I didn't know much about omegas, or alphas, except that I was one."

I swallow, pushing the memories back.

"This one night, my mom woke me up and put me in my

closet. She told me to stay there and be really quiet and she'd come back for me."

I stayed there for hours. Sat hugging my knees, trying not to cry.

"I didn't hear anything for a while. Then there was banging, and shouting, and screaming. I remember this snarling sound. It felt like the whole house was shaking around me."

Harper listens in silence, her hand reaching up to stroke my cheek. I grab her hand, anchoring her to me, turning my head to breathe her in.

"My dad ripped the closet door open, but his face was all *wrong*. It was twisted up and it was like he couldn't see *me*. Then he fell over, and he wasn't snarling anymore. But there was red all over his face."

I leave out the part where I wet my pants. My dad's face is the part that features most in my nightmares.

"What happened?" she whispers.

"These soldiers came and took me away, and they put me in a building with these other kids. They told me mom had been controlling my dad and it made him go crazy. He killed her, and they had to put him down. Like an animal."

They'd told me that on repeat. Over and over again until the message got through. Omegas were bad. Omegas took my parents away. My mom couldn't control her instincts, and it cost me them both.

Tears slip down Harper's face.

"I'm so sorry, Devlin," she breathes. She genuinely looks anguished, her face pale. "Where did you go?"

I clear my throat, swallowing the lump down. "They placed me with a beta couple. I was part of the early adoption program. There were a lot of kids in the same position then."

Trey and Alicia were nice people, but they weren't my mom and dad. And they didn't really know what to do with me, especially as I grew older. It was a miracle I had my pack around me. I check on them every so often, but we're not close.

"I didn't know that," she whispers. "That there were children left behind when everything happened."

I shrug. "Why would you?"

I mean it. She wasn't even born then, I guess. Then she would have been a kid, and then she awakened. And she had her own battles to fight.

I run my hand through her hair, admiring the glints of copper in the light.

"When you first got here, I was scared," I confess.

It's pulled from the deepest part of me. But she deserves to hear it.

"The moment I saw you in that office, I had this *feeling*. It was like I'd always known you, even though I'd never seen you before. It pulled up a lot of memories, but I should've handled them instead of taking them out on you."

I should have called Ezra straight away and talked it through. Ace's grandpa is a retired doctor, and he's been a huge support to me over the years.

"I understand, though," Harper whispers. Her shoulders slump. "How could you not feel that way about me, after what happened to your parents?"

She tries to pull away from me, but I hold onto her. "Wait, princess."

She stills, looking away. "Why do you call me that?"

My voice is hoarse when I reply. "Because you deserve to be fucking worshipped, Harper."

I've been an idiot, letting my past affect the way I feel about this girl. No more.

Her slim shoulders start to shake, and I pull her back to me. Fucking hell, I've made her cry again.

"I'm sorry," I say, trying to wipe away her tears. "I didn't mean to upset you."

She half-laughs, waving me off as she wipes her cheeks. "You really didn't. I think that's the nicest thing anyone's ever said to me."

"I think I have some work to do then." I'll tell her every day for as long as she'll have me. I pull her down next to me as she squeals slightly, the heaviness of our conversation passing and leaving me with… hope.

We lie peacefully for a few minutes. The way Harper nestles against me settles something in my chest. It feels… right. Her breathing calms and hot little breaths flutter against my skin as she gradually drifts back off to sleep.

I'm not far behind her, my thoughts slowing as I drift off. One final thought sneaks through, though.

Keeping Harper at a distance? Yeah. Not a fucking option.

CHAPTER TWENTY-FIVE
GABE

D evlin slips quietly out of Harper's room, his nostrils flaring when he catches the scent of three, very pissed-off alphas.

Rogue, Ace and I lean against the wall, arms crossed in identical expressions of annoyance. I mean, what the fuck?

Yesterday, he didn't want anything to do with Harper. He wanted *all* of us to have nothing to do with Harper. Then this morning, we all wake up to a house absolutely saturated with the intoxicating scent of an omega in full arousal. And Devlin? Right in the damned middle.

I've never been so hard in my life.

Rogue stalks towards Devlin with murder in his eyes. Dev at least has the good sense to back up, looking slightly sheepish. Dominance is flooding out of Rogue in waves, making me want to bare my throat. I'm not sure how Devlin is even still standing.

"What the fuck happened?" Rogue hisses, his hand shooting out and grabbing Dev around the neck. Dev snarls before he submits, his instincts clearly letting him know that he's not gonna win this fight. Rogue's been vibrating with tension the whole time we've been standing silently outside the door.

I idly wonder if us basically eavesdropping on them makes us creepy stalker alphas, and then shrug. Ah, well. To be fair, we would have picked up the scents even from outside the house, so it's not like we could have given them privacy even if we'd wanted to. Which I didn't particularly. Although I hope Harper won't be too upset when she realizes we overheard pretty much the whole thing.

Ace is palming his hand over his pants, clearly trying to rearrange the semi he's still sporting. I bite my lip as I stare and he catches me, letting out a low, inviting purr that goes straight to my fucking knot.

It can be hard for alphas to come together sexually, but it helps that my dominance levels are pretty low compared to Ace's. I blush at the mental image of Ace leaning over me, his hands on my hips as he presses me into a mattress, and quickly turn my face away.

Focus, I tell myself. I'm blaming the omega hormones for my randy thoughts.

Devlin and Rogue are both snarling at each other. "I know what I said," Dev snaps in a low voice. He shoots a look towards the door, clearly not wanting to wake Harper. "Things changed."

"In one night?" Rogue pushes back with an incredulous snarl. "What could possibly change in—"

"She had a *nightmare*," Devlin bites out the words, his eyes darkening. "Because I was a prick. I found her in the cage, crying out. I did that to her. *I did that.*"

Oh. Devlin's voice is hoarse, a slight tremble to the words. Oh, Harper. My heart breaks at the thought of her crawling back into that fucking cage to sleep.

Rogue takes a step back, releasing his hold on Dev's throat.

"I heard her, went in and pulled her out. I ended up

sleeping in with her. She didn't want me to leave. And then she woke up."

An uncharacteristic red blooms on Devlin's cheeks. "One thing led to another. We talked, and I apologized. She enjoyed it."

"Oh, we know," Ace chips in, and everyone throws him a glare. He raises his hands jokingly. "What? I'm just saying, we all heard it."

Rogue runs a hand over his eyes, his brow creasing with frustration. I feel a little sorry for him. Our pack's all over the place right now. The bonds must be running him ragged.

"Right," he grits out. "Can I assume that you're over any concerns you had?" he asks Devlin, an edge of sarcasm warring with genuine worry in his voice. Dev sends another look towards the door, something in his normally hard-as-nails expression softening.

"Yeah," he mutters, clearing his throat. "I'm in. Sorry. I'll try not to fuck it up again."

I sag in relief. Thank fuck for that. I don't want to go through a dinner as awkward as the one we had last night ever again.

The door creaks open. We all whip around in unison, our expressions a matching shade of guilty-as-hell. Harper blinks at us sleepily, her focus moving from one to the other. When she reaches Devlin, the corner of her mouth tips up, just a little. A wave of cinnamon hits me and I bite back a groan. Devlin, our hard-assed, grumpy, commitment-phobic alpha actually *melts*. Crossing over to her, he wraps his arms around her back and nuzzles her cheek, blatantly scent marking her. He whispers something and she laughs before shyly reaching up and kissing him gently on the mouth, giggling when he licks at her roughly. Devlin is *playing*.

I'm in too much shock to school my expression when he turns around, and he flicks me in the chin as he strolls past.

"Close your mouth, Gabe, you'll get flies in it." Snapping my mouth shut with a snap, we all watch him sauntering down the hallway. Smug bastard.

Harper is still standing with us, and she blushes when we all turn our awed expressions on her.

"You fixed Devlin," Ace whispers in exaggeration, his eyes wide as saucers. Harper frowns at him and crosses her arms.

"There was nothing wrong with him," she states, a small wobble in her voice. It's clear that she's still slightly uncomfortable around us, and I don't blame her. The mood swings in this house over the last few days have been enough to give anyone whiplash.

Rogue steps forward and gently wraps an arm around Harper, steering her down the hallway. I hear him apologising for his behavior last night.

"Family breakfast," he calls out to me, and I let out a small whoop in excitement. He's basically just given me permission to go full gung-ho – that means fry-up, pancakes, the works.

———

A bomb has hit my kitchen. An omega-shaped bomb.

There's pancake batter *everywhere*, flour is covering every surface and there's four pancakes of varying sizes stuck to the ceiling.

I don't give a fuck. Harper is glowing. When she said she'd never made pancakes before, I had her up and in front of the pan before she could do much more than blink. I thought it would be simple enough to walk her through.

Boy, was I wrong.

She's a walking disaster zone in the kitchen. I've never seen anything quite like it. She's dropped at least four eggs, knocked a pint of milk over, and she looks like some sort of weird ghost with a baking fetish with so much flour covering her.

Clearly, the rest of the pack have never seen anything like it either. Everyone is watching her with a mixture of amazement and arousal as she prepares her fifth flip, her little pink tongue slipping out to moisten her lips as she concentrates.

"You've got this, love," I encourage her, and the rest of the pack joins in. She was so disappointed after the last one. Fifth time *has* to be the charm. Right?

The pancake flies through the air and hits the ceiling with a slap. Damn. I really thought that would be it. I'm turning to Harper in commiseration when she gasps. Looking up, the pancake dislodges itself and drops to land perfectly in the center of Harper's skillet. Ace lets out a cheer and she stares at it, disbelieving.

"I did it!" she whoops, spinning to me with a heart-stopping grin.

I can't help it, I lean in and catch her mouth with mine, swallowing her gasp in a brief kiss. Devlin pulls her down into a chair and starts fussing over her, muttering about healthy choices and trying to feed her blueberries as she obediently nibbles them from his fingers.

The whole scene makes my heart hurt. This is all I've ever wanted for our pack. A home filled with laughter and affection.

My thoughts are interrupted by Ace. "Hey, Gabe," he whines. "there's something wrong with my hand."

"Where?" I jump to attention, grabbing for it just as it comes up and slaps me gently in the face. I blink, the whipped cream slowly sliding down my face and plopping down on the floor. The pack try valiantly to hide their snickers. Ace is howling. Right up until I throw a handful of flour in his face, and the food fight is *on*.

CHAPTER TWENTY-SIX
ROGUE

I stay well away from the danger zone as Ace and Gabe launch into a full-on food-fuelled assault. Snagging Harper out of the line of fire, I pull her into me, encircling her in my arms protectively. Devlin pierces me with a glare for stealing Harper away, but I just smirk at him, unrepentant after his behavior last night.

Harper wriggles in protest and I tap her on the nose. "Trust me, love, you don't want to get into the middle of this."

Harper turns pleading eyes on me. "But I've never been in a food fight before," she murmurs plaintively.

Fucking hell, she's pouting. Her plump lower lip pokes out provocatively, and I can't resist. I swoop in and nip it gently with my teeth, and Harper lets out a startled yelp.

"You... you bit me!"

"I did. You can't make that look around me and not expect a nip." No alpha could resist.

She stares up at me in a daze, raising her hand to her mouth. Taking my chance, I lean in and gently suck her abused lip into my mouth. She gasps and I surge in, slanting over her mouth and stealing a kiss. Gods, her *taste*. She softens immediately in my arms, pliant and curved into my body. My dick hardens and she inhales sharply at the feel of me pressing against her.

That's right, baby. Look what you made me do.

I thrust gently against her for a moment, looking for any hint of unease, but Harper surprises me. She wriggles back against me and brushes her hand against my length, shocking me into stillness.

"Sweetness," I warn with a low growl. "You're asking for trouble."

"Maybe I want trouble," she whispers. Her hand drops again and this time, she wraps her hand around the outline of my length and squeezes lightly. My vision short-circuits, and for a moment all I can think of is throwing her over my shoulder and heading to the nearest bed. Actually, the kitchen counter's closer.

I'm seriously considering it when something wet slaps me in the face. Harper's mouth drops open as something sticky and gooey oozes down my cheek, landing with a splat on my shirt.

I glare up at Gabe and Ace, both trying desperately to hide their laughter as they point to each other. Harper starts shaking underneath me. Even Devlin sniggers from the corner.

"You have a little something by here," Harper points delicately, her voice quivering. She touches her finger to my face and sucks the tip of it into her mouth.

Lifting my hand, I scrape it through the thick fluid clinging to my stubble and stare at my fingers.

Honey. My mouth pulls up into a smirk, and my arms tighten on Harper as I lift my hand threateningly. She starts fighting to get away, bursts of laughter falling out of her mouth, and I quickly rub my thumb down her jawline before leaning in and giving it a long, slow lick. My tongue rasps as I follow the line and Harper moans, her cinnamon scent entwining with the scent of her arousal and the sweet honey in my mouth. It makes my head spin. Playing with Harper is more fun than I've had for years.

That's it. Our omega shrieks as I lift her effortlessly. She lands over my shoulder, her ass in the perfect position next to me. I give it a gentle smack, testing the waters. The way her legs clench against me and her scent deepens suggests that Harper is definitely not against a spanking, and I grin. I catch Devlin's eye as he stares at us jealously, and slowly raise my middle finger to him as I stomp out of the room in search of a soft surface.

Gabe and Ace fall into hysterics and Harper whines on my shoulder. Her fingers clench against my ass and I smack hers again, a little harder this time, enjoying the mewl she lets out.

"Who's been a naughty omega?" I growl. She tenses, and I run my hand soothingly up the back of her legs, gentling her anxiety and running my hand across her cheeks.

Play with me, baby.

"Teasing me like that." A third smack makes her whine frustratedly as she tries to move, and her honeyed arousal rises like a mist around us.

I tut. "I think someone's in need of a spanking."

Harper's shorts dampen under my hands, letting me know exactly how much she likes that idea.

"Needy little omega," I growl.

She whines in agreement. "Please, Rogue,"

I slap her ass just a touch harder, her cry of arousal going straight to my cock. "Alpha," I demand. "You'll call me alpha while we're doing this."

"Yes, alpha," she moans, panting. The sounds coming out of her mouth stroke over me like a caress. I could come just listening to them. My office is closest, and I stroll through. The chair is big, comfortable, and more than enough for what I have in mind.

Taking a seat, I lower Harper carefully until she's facing the floor with her ass facing up as she lies across my legs. She's breathing heavily, honey and cinnamon pulsing from her skin as she stays still, her white shirt pulling against her back. I sit there for a moment, admiring her, before I reach forward and run my finger gently under the end of her shorts, along the curve where her ass cheek meets her thigh. When she tries to pull her legs up, she gets another tap, and stills.

"You look beautiful like this, love," I murmur. Running my hand back up her silky skin, I pull the edge of her shorts down slowly until her bare ass is revealed, creamy and smooth against my hand. She's wearing lace panties that arrived as part of her compound-approved kit, legs pressed together. My mouth waters at the urge to bite into that perfect skin. I trace her seam gently, dragging my finger down it as a purr erupts from me.

Harper shakes, letting out little trembles and moans as I explore every inch of her with my hand. When I can almost taste her slick on my tongue, I push my hand gently between her legs and she opens them immediately, enough for my hand to fit through.

"Good girl," I praise, and her back arches in response. Our little omega loves being praised. She opens up to it, like a sunflower when it grows towards the sun. I've always been highly dominant and Harper responds instinctively to it, a natural submissive that speaks to the alpha in me. I want her to submit to me, desperately. But on her own terms. I don't want to force it, and I need to be careful not to overwhelm her. It takes a huge amount of trust to submit to an alpha, and I silently make a promise as she lies trustingly in my arms.

I'll never betray your trust, love.

I gently rub two fingers against the soft, damp material at her entrance. Harper cries out as her hips move back and forth, seeking a harder touch. "Please, alpha," she keens. "Please touch me."

At her words, I slide aside the thin panties she's wearing, probing her entrance with my finger. "Fuck, love, you're so wet for me." Her honey drenches my hand, making it easy to slide a finger into her wet heat.

"Christ," I hiss. "You're so fucking tight, baby."

I slide it in and out, her walls clenching around me before replacing it with two fingers, slowly pumping them as Harper writhes underneath me.

"Please, Rogue. Alpha. *Harder*," she pleads. Wrapping my hand gently around the back of her neck, I urge her to stay still and my hand speeds up. Noises fill the air as she moves up and down against me. Her head tries to push up and I slide my fingers out of her and slap her pussy lightly, pressing the palm of my hand to her clit and rubbing hard.

"Oh, god!" her wrangled cry comes as her slick gushes over my hand, her whole body twitching as she comes with a scream. Fucking beautiful.

I flip her around and haul her into my arms, rubbing her arms gently to bring her around. She opens her eyes dazedly, legs still twitching. Smoothing her hair back, words of praise slip from my mouth.

"Such a good girl," I croon gently. "You're perfect, love." She buries her head into my shoulder for a moment, before pulling it back and rising up to take my face between her hands. I blink rapidly as her mouth descends on mine and she softly pushes her tongue in and out.

Sweet Jesus. I'm so hard I think I'm going to embarrass us both. My hips shift, the hardness catching Harper with a gasp. "Don't worry about that," I murmur, trying to pull her back to my face for more of those lazy, languid kisses.

Harper slides off my lap and onto her knees, dodging my arms. I stop breathing as she places her hand directly over me, rubbing in small circles.

"What are you doing, love?" This is the purest form of torture. I close my eyes with a groan.

They soon fly open when she starts tugging my zip down.

"Harper, you don't need to do that." I start to argue with her, but she pushes my hands away and stares up at me with a defiant frown on her face.

"But I *want* to," she purrs. "Want to taste you, alpha."

My eyes roll back when her soft mouth closes over my swollen head. She sucks gently, running her hands up and down my length as I fight to maintain control. I can't stop watching her, that glorious shade of red hair falling on either side as she sucks all my control from me, her head bobbing up and down. I thrust experimentally and she moans, the sound vibrating down my dick. It's heaven.

"Eyes on me, love," I growl. "Want to see those eyes as I fill your pretty mouth."

Harper obediently looks up at me as she sucks, hard, and it's too much. I shout as my release is pulled from me, streams of hot fluid spurting into Harper's throat. She swallows it down before pulling back and looking up at me, a small smile dancing at the corners of her lips as she licks away the last traces of her efforts. "Was it good?"

Jesus. "It was fucking perfection, sweetheart," I say hoarsely, tugging her into my arms.

Harper settles comfortably in my lap as I run my hands through her hair, petting her. Those amber eyes blink up at me lazily, full of warmth.

"I like this," she confesses, as she curls into me like a cat. Her face is open, vulnerable. Placing my hand against her cheek, I stroke my finger gently over her cheekbone. The barest edge of a bruise lingers there. I wish I could take away all of her bruises, all of her bad memories from that fucking place.

But all we can do is replace them with new ones.

"How can you trust us?" I ask softly. "When you've spent the last seven years with the OC?"

Even after everything she's been through, she still smiles, still laughs in a way that makes her whole damn face light up and shakes her entire body. Seven years of that place, but she's still so full of *fire*. So full of life.

That shining light could have been snuffed out by the grey walls of the Omega Compound. A thrum of relief pulses through me that we went to the OC that day.

If we hadn't, we might never have met her.

I pull her closer to me at the thought, a possessive rumble at the back of my throat.

Harper frowns, a crease between her eyes as she thinks over my question.

"I've spent a long time being told that a good omega is everything I need to be," she murmurs slowly. "There is nothing else for me. Just a pack, or the heat nests, children that won't be mine. And then I came here, and you were more than I ever expected."

She smiles at me. Guilt fills my stomach at our actions yesterday. Trying to keep our distance was a mistake I won't make a second time.

"You wouldn't even let me crawl to the car."

"Damned straight," I snap. "Your knees were cut up as it was."

She waves me off. "Nobody else would have *cared*, Rogue. They would have let me crawl. Put me in a cage, made me submit to them."

"But you didn't. You *asked* me what I wanted, and nobody has done that for me in a very long time. Even just now, you kept checking to make sure I was okay. It makes me feel…safe."

Tenderness fills my chest as we watch each other.

"I don't know what will happen," she continues. There's sadness in her voice. "I don't have any control over my future.

But I have control over my actions here. And that means a lot to me."

A fist squeezes my heart.

"You do," I swear, the words gruff and unyielding. "You have a choice for as long as you're here, love."

Which will be forever, if I have any say in it.

CHAPTER TWENTY-SEVEN
ACE

I snort as Gabe stares after Rogue and Harper with a look of longing on his face. It's been so long since we've all just let go and had fun like that. Running my hand through my hair, I dislodge flour that drifts around me like snow. Leaning into Gabe, I shake my hair like a dog and belly laugh as he dives out of the way.

Devlin watches from a safe distance, his usual moody frown swapped for a smirk. He's been lighter this morning than I've ever seen him. I'm glad that he's come around to Harper being here. *Because I wouldn't have let her go.*

My eyes drift to Gabe as he starts running the tap to clean up, catching on the slim muscles pulling under his shirt. He's been better with pack touch since Harper came to us. After the incident, he'd barely touch us unless he had to. I just didn't know how to reach him, but with Harper here, it seems effortless. I don't know why. She's not bitemarked, so she shouldn't be influencing our overall pack emotions to this extent. I'm not going to look a gift horse in the mouth though.

And she's definitely a fucking gift.

Swallowing, I look away from Gabe. I'm guessing that with

Harper here, our previous…relationship, is finished, once and for all. It feels like another barrier that we won't be able to overcome. Not that I feel that way about Harper. But Gabe's focus is on her, and I'm not sure there's any space for me.

I miss you.

Hesitantly, I move up to him. He's standing with his back to me, and when I reach out and touch his shoulder, he jumps like he's on fire.

"Shit, Ace," he groans. I follow his gaze down to where the water's soaked through his shirt, plastering to his skin. Stepping closer to him, I reach out slowly and give it a tug. Gabe's eyes dilate, a low rumble beginning in his throat. *Yes,* I urge him silently as his scent rises, entwining with mine. *Remember how good we were.*

Ignoring Devlin's gaze burning into my back, I take another step, testing. His breathing speeds up, and I dare to move closer still until I'm plastered up against him. Leaning in slowly, his eyes stare into mine until they blur out of focus. Inhaling his scent, I gently rub his cheek with my nose.

Gabe's low moan takes us both by surprise. He stiffens, cheeks flushing as he tries to turn away, but I pull him into me. This situation needs to be resolved. It's not good for either of us.

"Don't run from me," I plead, savoring the arousal and need on his face. "I've missed this, Gabe." I punctuate my words with a short thrust, both of us groaning at the sensation, my dick swelling uncomfortably behind my zip. I stare into his familiar face. "I've missed *us.*"

"I…I…" Gabe pulls back, running shaky hands over his hair. "I can't, Ace. We can't. Harper is here now, and things are different—"

"*Bullshit,*" I snap, a hint of a bark in my tone. His shoulders square and a low growl slips out, reminding us both that whilst it's nowhere near as prevalent as the rest of us, Gabe is still an alpha. I feel the second we lose the moment, and it's my fault.

"Don't pull that shit with me," he hisses, jabbing a finger into my chest. "I might bend over when it suits me, but I'm still an alpha too."

Hurt whips through me at the crudeness of his words and I pull my hand back. "I *know* you are," I whisper. *But it doesn't stop me wanting you.*

Gabe looks stricken. Maybe he's right. Doubt trickles into me as I think back on the times we've been together. It's always been Gabe submitting to me – never the other way around. I try to consider the alternative and a wave of uncontrolled anger comes over me at the thought, fists clenching.

I stare into his face, his brown eyes more familiar to me than my own. If that's what he wants, then he's right. We can't. I'll never be able to be that for him.

I turn my back on him, and head down to the basement. Maybe a workout will clear my head.

Hitting the weights, I try to find the positives.

We're all here. Our pack is still together even though there've been times when we've all doubted it will last. Harper is perfect for us, and she's already bringing us closer together. I make a note to myself to call my Pa and update him. He'll be delighted that we have an omega.

My lips twitch up into a reluctant smile remembering her pancake toss. Her golden eyes had lit up, the smile seeming to start with her mouth and slowly growing until I could have sworn she'd glowed with happiness.

Anger fills me as I remember Rogue telling us about what the guard said. *Jason.* My lip curls. *I'll be seeing you one day*, I silently promise. Harper deserves retribution for the shit he's done to her.

I mean – fucking water torture. My breath hitches at the thought, dread filling me. I've seen grown alphas tested like that during our training. They were screaming for their mamas after an hour. One of them lasted two hours before he experienced a full-on psychotic break and got pulled from the program altogether. None of us heard from him after that.

I can't believe they're pulling that sort of shit at the Omega Compound. People wouldn't support that kind of training if they knew. But then society has always been good at turning a blind eye for the common good, haven't they? And it's not exactly widely known. None of us even knew it was happening and Christian is Rogue's father, for fuck's sake.

Nobody truly has the faintest idea what goes on behind those metal walls, I realize. Betas stay far away from anything to do with alpha and omega politics unless it's the omega surrogacy program. They mock us and think we don't see it. *No more than animals*, they whisper behind their hands. *Beasts.* And that's just how they talk about alphas.

Omegas…. I blow out a breath. Omegas don't get talked about at all, and if they do then it's not in a good way. Betas believe that omegas are responsible for beta women not being able to carry children. All seems like a crock of voodoo bullshit if you ask me. But the consequence is that most betas are completely content with the aims of the Omega Compound, and the creed. A fitting response to a heinous crime, even if it's a blanket approach to a whole race.

And the alpha packs are almost as blind. Most toe the line and do exactly as they're told in the hope of being gifted an omega long-term. Even those who don't get the privilege keep their noses clean or they'll get banned from the heat nests.

If all omegas are like Harper, they should be fucking cherished. Not tortured. What's the fucking point?

They don't need a functioning mind to get pregnant, my subconscious offers. I slam the treadmill to a stop, swallowing down vomit. Just the thought is repugnant.

If half of what that asshole guard said is actually true, then our little omega is much stronger than any of us have really given her credit for. She hasn't spoken to us about what she went through, not since we built the fire. Then last night, Devlin said she had a nightmare. Concern fills me. I don't want her to hide her worries from us.

What if she tries to leave us? My heart seizes at the thought. What if she runs away, takes her chances on her own? I'm reminded of the collar, but the thought has hold of me and it won't let go. She's damned resourceful. Maybe she could get rid of it if she tried hard enough.

Devastation fills me at the idea of waking up one morning and Harper being gone. I need to speak to her. The urge to know exactly what's happened to her is beating through me like a drum, my hackles raising along with my scent. My instincts are overwhelming, fear and longing mixing into a dangerous potion and I roar, turning and hitting the mirror. It cracks, the long shards falling at my feet with a shatter as I catch glimpses of dozens of different versions of myself in the wreckage.

I need to know what demons she's facing.

So I can slay them myself.

CHAPTER TWENTY-EIGHT
HARPER

I step into the library, breathing in the scent of paper and ink. I used to love reading, although I haven't touched a book in years. My mom used to find me hidden away in corners, my nose forever buried in pages. Sometimes my father would tease me, joking that I should go out and get some fresh air, play with the other kids on our street. Mom would laugh and pull me close.

"You're a dreamer, Harper," she'd say, poking my nose gently. "You don't read because you don't have a life. You read because you choose to have many. And there's nothing wrong with that."

The spines of the books in front of me blur together as my eyes mist. I wonder where my parents are now. Are they still in our old home? Do they still sit at the same table, my father reading his paper, mom pulling her bakes from the oven, an empty seat where I used to be?

An awkward cough pulls me from my melancholy, and I smile at Ace as he loiters next to the door. He smiles at me, but it doesn't reach his eyes and a lump forms in my throat.

"What is it?" I ask. My heart feels like it's beating in my

throat. I'm certain that he's going to say the Omega Compound have called. Maybe I need to go back.

My legs start to shake when he hesitates. I won't go back to them. I can't. "Hey," he says finally, concern ringing in his voice. "Don't worry – everything's okay."

The relief almost takes me to my knees and Ace is beside me in an instant, steadying me with a hand under my elbow.

"Sorry," he says gently. "I didn't mean to scare you."

I breathe out with a small laugh. "I thought maybe it was something to do with the OC. I feel like an idiot now."

Ace shakes his head firmly, rubbing his hand up and down my arm. The motion calms my anxiety down. "You're not an idiot. I did want to talk to you, but I can come back. Is now a bad time?"

I lift my shoulder in a slight shrug. "It's probably a good time, actually. It'll stop me thinking of things I can't change."

"What kind of things?" he asks. Ace pulls me over to a small chaise lounge and settles us both down, his leg pressed against mine. It's comforting.

A blanket drops over me and I sigh. The feel of soft wool isn't something I can get used to after years of sparse conditions and harsh-smelling plastics at the compound. I burrow myself into it, gathering the ends between my fingers and twisting them.

"I was thinking about my parents," I admit. Ace says nothing, but he waits patiently while I weigh up my heavy thoughts.

"They just…left me," I murmur. I still sound bewildered even after all these years. "We were close. And then one day, my scent changed, and it was like I'd turned into a stranger. My father wouldn't even look at me. He told my mom that he'd wait in the car and left. Mom kept telling me that everything would be fine, and they were going to help me. She threw some of my things into a bag and then we were in the car, and they wouldn't speak to me at all after that. I didn't say my goodbyes, didn't see any of my friends, my grandparents."

I take a deep breath. "I just disappeared," I say quietly. "Like I'd never really been a part of their lives at all."

Tasting salt against my lip, I swipe my hand against the tear. Ace's hand comes up and he slowly wipes it away, rubbing his thumb across my cheek.

"People are always scared of what they don't know," he offers, but I shake my head.

"No," I tell him firmly. "I was part of their lives for fourteen years. They threw me at the compound guards like I was diseased."

I was, in their eyes. Hit with the dreaded omega stick.

Ace stares into the distance, his blue eyes stormy. "What then?" he asks quietly.

Turning to him, I note the tension in his posture. "I haven't heard from them since," I say, and he curses.

"We could track them down, you know," he offers. Sincerity rings through his voice, and his offer takes me by surprise.

"You would do that?"

"Of course I would." He says the words so easily, but I can feel the truth in them. His offer overwhelms me for a moment. I imagine knocking on the door, my mother pulling it open, tears gathering in her eyes as she pulls me close into a tight hug, her arms closing around me. Home.

Except it will never be home again.

"Thank you, but no," I whisper. Staring at my hands, I avoid Ace's gaze. "Maybe one day." One day, maybe I'll have the strength to demand the answers I need, although my gut tells me they won't be the answers I want. Ace squeezes my hand reassuringly.

This house, this pack, is starting to feel like home now. I still feel awkward, but it's not because of them. It's me. Everywhere I look, I see the shadows of the compound reaching out for me. The shadows under my eyes are deepening by the day.

Ace sucks in a breath and I glance at him. "Harper," he begins. "Did you…"

He cuts himself off and I watch him curiously. After a minute, he shakes his head with a wry smile. "Forget it. It's not important."

I squeal as the seat disappears underneath me, and I find myself deposited into Ace's lap. The thick muscles in his thighs offer plenty of room, and I lay my head against his shoulder with a contented sigh. Sea salt, driftwood and Ace. So much better than a chair.

"You can talk to me, little omega," the words tumble out of him, uncharacteristically serious, and I pull back my head to look at him. He gazes back at me steadily. I have the feeling that if I handed Ace my demons, he'd shield me with everything he has to keep me safe from them.

"You act the joker, but I see you, Ace Winter," I murmur. Our lips brush gently as I lean in, laying small kisses on his top lip, then the bottom. He tugs himself away with a grumble.

"I'm being serious," he scolds me. "I never, ever want you to feel that you can't trust me." He grabs my hand, holding it tightly.

"My shoulders are broad," he says softly. He wiggles them, wagging his eyebrows and making me snort a laugh. "I can carry some of that." He gently pokes my shoulder, and my heart clenches at the earnest expression on his face.

"Let me fight some of those monsters for you," he whispers, warm breath fanning across my face. His expression is pleading.

My eyes well up even as my chest grows warm.

I think Ace Winter just stole a piece of my heart.

Touching his cheek in thanks, I curl back up on his lap. He wraps his arms around me and we stay curled together in a corner of the library, a tenuous new bond between us.

I'm reading a book, Ace trailing his fingers up and down my arm, when Rogue's voice rouses us. He sits up slightly, not letting me go as he calls out.

Rogue appears at the door, his eyes moving between us as he shoots me a soft smile.

"You okay?" he asks.

"I am," I say, smiling.

It doesn't last for long, though.

"We've been summoned," Rogue says grimly, the smile sliding off his face. I flinch and Ace pulls me closer as he growls. "By the compound?"

"No," Rogue says as he throws himself into a chair opposite us. His normally pristine shirt is rumpled, and his hair is in disarray. He looks stressed. I've barely seen him since yesterday morning since he's been buried in his office.

"We've had an invite to the annual gala."

I stare at Rogue as Ace groans dramatically under me.

"What's the annual gala?" I ask.

"Hell," Ace mutters dramatically, his arm over his eyes. "Fucking hell."

Rogue rolls his eyes. "It's not that bad," he chides. Turning to me, he explains.

"The annual gala is a yearly event thrown by the company we work for. They're heavily linked to the government, so there'll be a lot of important people there." He hesitates. "Including some of the board members for the compound."

My heart sinks. "I don't have to go, right?" I ask, filling with dread when Rogue hesitates.

"The invite specifically mentions you." He hands me the piece of card and I stare down at the names. Even with the stress squeezing my stomach, I feel a small thrill at seeing my name entwined with the Winter pack.

At the bottom, there's a handwritten note.

I look forward to meeting your new pack member in person.

Ace reads the note over my shoulder. "Bloody Jackson." Picking up my worry, he starts to knead my shoulders gently. "Don't stress it, little omega. Jackson is our boss. He's an ass, but he's just being nosy."

"I agree, but it's not ideal. This is the first year they're allowing omegas. It will look suspicious if we don't attend." Rogue has that furrow between his eyes again. I want to rub it away with my finger.

"I'll go."

Both turn to me with matching stares of disbelief.

"You'll go?" Ace asks, clearly surprised.

Shrugging, I nod. "We have time to prepare, right? I'm assuming we'll need to be seen to be following the rules," I say to Rogue. He recovers quickly, grimacing.

"I'm afraid so. I'm so sorry, love. We could make an excuse and stay home, but they'd no doubt find a reason to come and visit. At least this way we have some control over the environment."

He shouts for Devlin and Gabe to come up as my mind twirls. A public event. With OC board members. I breathe in and out slowly. *You survived seven years*, I remind myself. One night is nothing in comparison.

And I'll have the pack with me. "You'll stay with me?" I ask Rogue. Uncertainty leaks into my tone. I can do this, as long as they're with me.

He opens his arms, a silent question in his eyes. I clamber off Ace, who relinquishes his grip with a rumble of disappointment, but he doesn't say anything as I move across to Rogue. I wrap myself around him, sliding my hand into the open v of his shirt. He purrs softly.

"I won't leave you for a second," he promises.

"None of us will," Gabe declares firmly as he wanders in. "What's all this about?"

Devlin follows in behind him and snarls as Rogue starts to explain.

"Absolutely not." He crosses his arms as my brows raise. Catching my eye, he explains, "It's a bad idea. These events are awful, princess. And I don't mean the shit food."

"Devlin is right, love," Rogue rumbles into my ear. "These people are not the type to forgive and forget if anything goes wrong."

They're all stressing, tension pulling around me like a scratch I need to itch. The feeling presses down on me, and I can't take it. I climb off Rogue's lap and turn to face them all, crossing my arms. They all look taken aback.

"How long was I at the compound?" I demand.

They trade uneasy glances, clearly picking up on my irritation.

"Seven years," Gabe offers hesitantly.

I point at him. "Right. Seven years. That means that I spent the best part of *seven years* on my knees for alphas." Four furious growls echo and my instincts scream at me to fall back, but I push back and straighten my spine.

"You've all been so good to me," I say quietly, searching for the words to help them understand. They all focus on me intently. It's a little overwhelming, actually. I try hard not to squirm. If they scent me then it'll throw my speech off.

"But," I say quietly. "You need to remember that I've been an omega since I was fourteen years old. I have been *this* since I was *fourteen*. That means that anything I need to do for one single evening is nothing that I haven't had to do a thousand times before."

Devlin leans forward, his brows creased in agitation and his russet hair falling into his face. He pushes it back carelessly.

"Princess, nobody is debating that. I saw you at the compound. I saw a little of what you had to deal with. I just don't think you should have to put up with that shit, even if it is just for one night."

"But it's not just for one night," Gabe interjects sadly, and my shoulders slump as he nods. Gabe gets it.

"No," I say quietly. "It's not."

The others look confused. Looking exasperated, Gabe snaps.

"Are we keeping Harper locked up here forever, then? Because at some point, we're going to need to leave the house. She's right – the location doesn't matter. This was always going to happen eventually."

"But the board—," Devlin interjects.

"The board will see a perfectly submissive omega. We will go to the gala, we'll stay as long as we need and then we'll come home. And you will stay with me. You will stand *next* to me. Because you won't be able to stand in front of me. Not for this."

My voice drops, but I remain firm. "I can do this, Devlin."

I look Devlin square in his beautiful dark brown eyes. My body is pushing me to drop, to submit. His dominance is pulsing out of him strongly with his agitation and I bite back a whimper.

Devlin takes a step forward and grabs my face between his hands. Pulling me in, he takes my mouth in a rough kiss, drawing a sigh from my throat.

He pulls away from me, resting his head against mine.

"I was wrong," he whispers. "You're not a princess after all. You're a fucking *queen*."

His words stab at my heart, flooding me with feelings.

"You're dangerous," he tells me, unhappy lines pulling his mouth down. "But you're right. I hate that you have to do this, but I'll be right there next to you."

He spins and walks out as I sway slightly, blinking.

"Holy shit," Ace mutters. "Call the body snatchers, they've taken Devlin and replaced him with someone agreeable."

Standing up, he moves to leave, Gabe doing the same. They catch each other's eye at the same time and I watch, fascinated by the flush rising on their cheeks. Ace pulls away and ducks in to kiss my forehead. "Proud of you, little omega," he whispers. I grin back at him as Gabe squeezes my hand. "I'll arrange an outfit for you," he tells me.

I groan slightly at the thought but nod. He's right. I'll need an OC-approved dress. As the door closes behind them, Rogue gets to his feet. "Are you sure about this, love?" he asks. His emerald eyes watch my face intently. "Nobody would blame you for not wanting to go. We can find another way."

"I know, but I need to." I do. I've been cowering behind the pack, waiting for a dreaded call from the compound or a knock on the door. This way, I feel a little more in control.

"I guess we'll see how well their training held up," I quip flippantly. A flash of fury crosses Rogue's face and I instinctively jump back, my eyes wide.

"Don't, love." His voice is so low I can barely hear it. "Don't make jokes about you in there."

I lean in and move his ruffled hair out of his eyes. They flash down at me, filled with worry.

"I'm sorry. We'll be fine, Rogue," I whisper.

I believe it. I believe in them.

CHAPTER TWENTY-NINE
HARPER

I hover in the doorway of the kitchen, skulking silently as I watch Gabe carefully measuring spices into a large pan. He reaches up to grab something from the cupboard and the line of his white shirt rises up, exposing tanned muscle.

I bite my lip as I stare at the dusting of gold hair reaching down past his waistband. Gabe is *edible*. He pushes his pale hair away from his face impatiently and curses as he stares at the mix.

I decide to stop lingering and make a point of dropping my feet heavily as I walk in. Gabe swings around and his look of frustration slips away, so quickly I nearly missed it.

"Hey, you," he says, his mouth curving up at the corners. "You hungry?"

I shake my head. Gabe is a *feeder*. He shovels food into people until they can't breathe. And since I arrived, he's made it his personal mission to get me to a healthy weight. Already I can feel it.

My shape is filling out, curves I've never felt thanks to the compound starting to appear. The pack has been noticing the changes too, and Gabe's ears flush a bright red as he quickly moves his gaze away from my body, even though I'm covered with another shirt.

This one belongs to Rogue. I've been keeping hold of the clothing they're lending me. I can't resist them. Their scents are intoxicating, but I have some new clothes arriving soon, so I won't have access to them forever. The thought of not being able to bury myself in the scent of their clothes makes a whine slip out before I can stop it, and Gabe stiffens.

He's halfway across the kitchen in the blink of an eye. "What's the matter?" he asks me urgently. His hand comes up and runs down my arm gently, and I lean into the gesture. It's not enough, so I step closer, hoping he takes the hint. When I glance up at him, our mouths are so close together I can scent the coffee he's been drinking.

His hazel eyes darken as we watch each other. I hold my breath, not sure what I'm waiting for. My heart pounds in my chest, so loud Gabe must be able to hear it.

Carefully, so carefully, he moves forward and presses his mouth gently against my lips. His scent invades my senses, baked bread and cinnamon and orange filling the kitchen with reminders of us. He raises his hands to cradle my face tenderly between his hands as his lips move over mine. A punch of *need* hits me right in the solar plexus, a twinge telling me that my pussy is well and truly on board if we want to take this further.

I gasp and Gabe seizes the opportunity. He sweeps in, claiming my mouth with his tongue as he explores me, his hands sliding around to the back of my head as a possessive grumble slides out of his mouth, sending shivers up my spine.

Gabe makes me feel *precious*.

He pulls back slowly, his hand cupping my cheek as he leans in and rubs his nose against mine. It's such an affectionate move that I can't help but smile, a curl of satisfaction taking place in my belly. That was exactly what I'd needed.

"Thank you," I breathe, and he smiles as he steps back.

"Don't thank me," he warns. "I'm really fighting not to drag you upstairs and lock us away for the rest of the day. And possibly tomorrow too."

I flush, my gaze dropping to the tent he's pitching in his trousers. Saliva fills my mouth as I imagine dropping to my knees for him, popping open his buttons and taking him into my hand like I did with Rogue. Hard, heavy, warm.

"Oh," I mumble dazedly in response. He smirks at me, and my mind clears enough to frown at him teasingly.

"Not fair," I complain, crossing my arms. "You scrambled my brain with your kisses."

"I did?" His eyes brighten, and he blushes lightly. He traces his finger across his scar. It's clearly a reflex.

I don't know enough about this pack. Who they are, their lives before me. How Gabe got that scar. I want to know. Possessiveness rises up in me, anger on behalf of a man who's treated me like a queen but clearly doesn't have a huge amount of self-worth if he's that surprised that I like his kisses.

"Gabe?" I ask. There must be something in my tone because he sighs and turns back to his pan. For a moment, I think he's ignoring me, and a pang of hurt flickers. Something inside me needs to understand his hurt. *You can't help him if you don't know*, my mind whispers.

A stab of surprise runs through me when he just turns off the heat. The resignation on his face tugs at my heart. He looks like he's bracing for bad news.

He catches my hand and tows me out of the kitchen, entwining our fingers together. I curl into his grip as he pulls me gently into the snug.

"Sit with me?" he asks uncertainly, and I drop down onto the leather loveseat beside him, curling up and resting my head on his shoulder.

We sit in silence for a few minutes, Gabe staring at the ceiling like he's searching for the right words. Guilt fills me. It's not my place to make him face his demons. God knows I have enough of my own.

"We don't have to talk about this." The words are a whisper, and he shakes his head softly, gripping my hand like a tether.

"I want to talk about it with you," he admits. "I should have already. I just didn't know where to start." He lifts our joined hands up. "I'm going to need to keep hold of this for a bit though." His forlorn expression just about breaks my heart.

"I won't let go." It's a small vow, but it makes him smile slightly.

CHAPTER THIRTY
GABE

I blow out a breath, gripping Harper's hand in mine. She deserves to hear this. For a brief, painful moment, I wish Ace was here. This story belongs to him, too.

To us.

I was sixteen years old when I finally understood that I was in love with my best friend.

All four of us were out exploring in the woods behind Rogue's house. Devlin and Rogue were arguing about whether we wanted to try and build a treehouse and if we actually knew how to do it.

Ace and I were messing around, chucking sticks at each other. He'd reached down, scooped up a handful of mud and advanced on me as I backed up.

"Don't even—"

The mud had hit me in the face before I could finish, the noisy splat as it hit my cheek sending Ace into hysterics. I'd retaliated, jumping on him and shoving the muck down the back of his shirt, and it had turned into war.

When we finally paused for breath, both of us rolling onto our backs, he'd casually reached out and linked our hands together, his pinky curling around mine. I'd stopped breathing altogether. I just felt… happy.

He'd turned his head to look at me, and I'd done the same. And our mouths met in an awkward, fierce clash of lips and teeth and anxiety and sheer fucking pleasure that made my eyes burn and my heart sing.

That was it. Devlin and Rogue didn't bat an eyelid – Devlin's raised brow told me that he might have suspected long before anything happened.

Society wasn't as kind. Male beta couples are a common sight, but two alphas? Alphas are supposed to be dominant, strong, male. Alphas are supposed to fuck females. And although I was definitely an alpha, I didn't have the same dominance as the rest of my future pack. I was slightly shorter, slightly slimmer. I didn't give a flying fuck, though. I was more than happy with who I was.

Whilst the guys threw themselves into special ops training as we grew older and formed our own official pack, I was happy to sit on the sidelines and cheer them on. I wasn't a total waste of space. I poured my energy into martial arts – Judo, Brazilian Jiu-Jitsu – there's nothing quite like that feeling of moving through a sequence. It's poetic, dance in combat form. I even mastered Krav Magra, so I could hold my own in a fight.

Ace and I were happy, and it was good for the pack bond to have a stable couple. But we knew that we had to think of the wider group too, and neither of us was averse to the idea of bringing in a female who could be someone for all four of us. Someone to sit at the very heart of our pack.

We decided to go straight for a beta. Ace met Elinor in a coffee shop one day, and she seemed…perfect. Pretty, intelligent, caring. She was also delighted at the idea of joining a pack, which we'd found difficult with other betas.

We made an agreement that she'd join the pack on a trial basis. Everything seemed perfect for a few weeks. And then the cracks started to show.

She avoided being alone with me. Any time I walked into a room, she'd make an excuse and slip right back out, claiming she'd forgotten something. If I suggested something, her nose would wrinkle, and she'd politely suggest something else.

But it was with Ace that I really saw it. We'd explained our situation and she'd told us she was fine, but she wasn't, really. She didn't like the idea of us having a relationship. Her lip would curl, just slightly, any time she saw us together. But the rest of the pack seemed to be adjusting well to having her around. None of them picked up any bad vibes from her. They could sense my unease through the bond, but I just laughed it off. I guess I just hoped that she'd adjust and see even if Ace and I had something, we wanted her to be at our center.

I started giving her as much space as I could, thinking that she might settle down and then we could take the time to get to know each other properly, and she would see that I wasn't a threat to her.

I thought things were getting better. She started to talk to me more, offer more casual touching and even some affection.

But then she saw Ace and I together one day, laughing as he pinned me to a tree in the garden and kissed me, breathlessly unbuckling my jeans. I caught her watching us. And I just knew from the look in her eyes that she *hated* the idea of us. Absolutely despised it.

I break off for a minute to collect my thoughts. The strain of our conversation is leaking into the pack bond, and I push away the questioning tugs from the others. I'm glad they're not here today.

"What did she do?" Harper whispers. She's curled into me like a cat, still holding tightly to my hand. She hasn't moved, didn't flinch even when I confessed the details of mine and Ace's relationship. Her warm eyes watch me, but I don't feel like I'm on show. I feel like she's waiting for me to fall so she can catch me.

"It was a few weeks later. Elinor asked if we could work together on a special dinner. It seemed like such a huge step forward. We spent an hour talking about it, and for the first time I felt like things were starting to fit together, that we were all finding our places in the new dynamic. She was coming to the end of her probation period, and the pack were talking about bringing her in permanently.

"So, I took the list she gave me, and I drove to the store she wanted a certain dessert from. She told me their apple pie was the best in the state and I had to try it.

"It was getting dark, and they caught me as I went to my car. The lighting was bad, and I was distracted. I didn't even hear them come up behind me."

A squeeze on my hand lets me know that Harper's still here with me. I glance over and see the tell-tale sheen of tears glistening in her eyes. "It's okay," she says when I pause. "Take your time."

"There were five of them. Her brothers, and a few friends. They had baseball bats and the first hit broke my hipbone. They kept joking about how I wouldn't be such a pretty alpha anymore by the time they were done. I was pretty sure I was dying. And then one of them leaned down with something in his hand. A knife."

I'll never forget the way it glinted in the dark. The searing burn as they carved a line down my face.

Harper cries quietly next to me, her head pressing into my shoulder and her leg lined up against mine.

"I woke up in the hospital. And I didn't have any sight left in my left eye."

I leave out the details of the therapy, the adjustment of learning to move and balance again without my sight. The pain the first time I tried to run through a Judo exercise and landed on my ass like a five-year-old.

"I want to kill that bitch. Where is she now?" Harper's fury takes me aback. She's… growling?

I pull her closer to me and lift her into my lap, wrapping my arms around her tightly. Closing my eyes, I breathe in her cinnamon scent, letting it ground me.

"She was gone, love," I breathe. "She didn't come to the hospital. When the pack came back home, she'd packed her shit and left. Nobody's seen her since."

Gone, but not forgotten. A rip down the very soul of our pack. The heartbreak of Devlin and Rogue that they hadn't picked up on it…

"And Ace?" Harper asks gently. It's clear that she understands.

Shaking my head, I press my lips together. "Ace nearly tore himself apart when he found out what had been happening. He went looking for the group on his own, came back covered in blood. He kept trying to talk to me, but I just… closed myself off. Locked myself into a cage inside my head and told myself that maybe this is what happens when alphas stray out of their lane."

"That's *bullshit*," Harper says, outraged. "Gabe. You can't think like that!"

She jumps up, escaping my arms and paces in front of me. I can't take my eyes off her, fierce and furious on my behalf. She's glorious. Her red hair flies out behind her as she stalks up and down, fists clenched.

She reels back to me. "Have you ever spoken to Ace properly about this?"

I shake my head, softly. "Love, the first time Ace and I have spent any kind of quality time in the same room since then has been in the last few days. Since you arrived."

She bites her lip, surprise flashing over her expression. "What difference have I made?"

Her question holds a tinge of self-disgust, and I sigh. What a pair we are.

"You didn't need to do anything but be yourself. Since you've arrived, I've seen more of my pack than I have in months. You make it so much easier to forget everything that's happened."

She sits back next to me and tugs my fingers away from my scar, replacing it with her palm. I watch her face as she gently strokes down the line, thirsty like a man seeking water in the desert. My mouth is parched for just a sip of Harper.

"This scar," she whispers, "is beautiful, Gabe."

I snort, about to deny it, and she puts her finger against my lips.

"I mean it." Strength rings through her voice. "Our scars show that we *survived*. That we're still here, still breathing, still fighting. But if you let your scars define your past, then they'll stop you from having a future."

She turns away from me and lifts her shirt.

I've never seen her bare back before.

Thin silver lines crisscross all over it, cutting into the smoothly elegant curve of her spine with vicious slashes. Dotted between the lines are thicker puckered areas that look like fucking burns.

My throat closes up in horror. Her skin is so smooth everywhere else, even down past her shoulders, but below that is a map of the horrors she's been through. There's so much that it's clearly happened over years.

Seven years. She was in that place for seven fucking years.

And I'm sat here whining about my face?

"Harper, love," I breathe out, my voice full of anguish. She drops her shirt, cutting off my line of sight and turns back to me. Her hands are shaking slightly, and I grab hold of them.

"You see?" she says quietly, searching my face. "We can't let them define who we continue to be, Gabe. That means that the bad guys win."

The way she looks at me. It's promises and passion and a possible future all wrapped up into one fiery red and amber package.

"You give me hope, you know," I whisper to her. The confession falls out of me, broken shards slipping from my lips, but it's true.

She makes me feel like anything is possible. That maybe, just maybe, Ace and I could fix what's been shattered. Maybe we could be something again. Something better than before. As long as she's with us, I feel fucking invincible.

I pull her close to me and we wrap ourselves around each other. The air feels emotionally charged, like we've stripped our souls bare and shown them to each other.

Look. This is who I really am.

And she's still here. She hasn't run.

I'm tracing my fingers up and down her bare arm as I think about her back. Anger fills me again and I swallow it down. There's no space in this moment for negativity. Harper is right.

I shift slightly and turn to her. "Can I see them again?"

Harper's shoulders bunch for a moment, before she nods. I gently position her so she's sat on the leather seat in front of me, between my legs.

Slowly, I slide my hands up her back, underneath the grey shirt that smells like woodsmoke and leather, lifting it up and off as Harper raises her arms obediently.

My hands gently trace over the ridges, a roadmap of indents and rough patches.

Harper sits quietly, her head bowed. I gently push the rest of her hair off her back and take in the full scale of the damage. It's fucking horrendous.

"Sweetheart," I whisper. "Does it hurt?"

She shrugs. "Sometimes. There are parts I can't feel at all, and a few areas where the skin can be really sensitive."

My hands move over her back, exploring every area. I soon realise where the sensitivity is highest, Harper's breathing patterns alerting me to the bigger areas as my hands move carefully along.

Carefully, so carefully, I lean in and press my lips to a particularly nasty scar. Deep purple in nature, it's undeniably a burn, about the size of two of my fingers.

A shiver ripples up Harper's spine and she inhales sharply. I move to pull back and her hand reaches back, pulling me closer.

"No, don't stop," she murmurs. "It feels… good."

A trickle of relief flows through me that I'm not hurting her.

"*Never want to hurt you.*" The words tumble from my lips, low and rough. I continue to move over the map of her back, tracing a delicate line with my tongue. She moans and I scent her sweet cinnamon as she presses her legs together. She shifts restlessly between my legs, and I pull my shirt off before carefully pressing my bare chest against her.

She fucking melts in my arms, the tension leaking out of her as she relaxes against me. I look down to where her head has fallen back, the contrast of her peaches and cream against my golden skin twisting my insides. I gently trace the graceful curve of her neck, hating the sight of the black collar.

I try to slide the edge of my finger underneath, but I can barely squeeze in the tip.

"Soon, we'll get this off," I promise. The OC will take it off if her move to our pack is approved permanently, but I don't want her wearing it for a second longer than she has to. I'd try and rip it off now if the OC wouldn't come down on us like a ton of bricks.

She turns her face in response, her lips seeking mine. I sip from her as her scent grows stronger, and I run the palm of my hand down and between her breasts. Her beath is coming faster now, ragged and broken as her scent turns sharp. Needing.

"Touch me." It's little more than a whispered plea as she shifts. "Please."

"Show me where," I tell her, and it comes out with the edge of a bark. Her hips lift off the leather and she grabs my hand, dragging it down and closing it over a perfectly shaped breast. I move my other hand down to match, and Harper groans as I massage them, the callouses on my fingers scraping over her pert nipples. She tries to tug my hand down, to where her slick is flowing freely. I can scent how much she wants this.

I stand in one quick motion, sweeping her up and moving over to the flickering fire in front of the hearth. Laying her reverently on the thick rug, mindful of her back, I sit back and drink the sight of her in.

"Fucking exquisite," I murmur, cupping her breast again and leaning in for a lazy lick.

My tongue rasps over the bud and she cries out as she tries to push her legs together for friction.

"Gabe," she moans. "Please. It hurts."

I won't leave our omega needing. I trace a line slowly down, taking in the golden-red patch of curls nestled between her thighs. I almost lose my breath at the vision she makes.

"Look at you, spread out for me like a buffet." Harper whimpers at my words, and I lick my lips as I lean down. *And I intend to feast.*

I drag my tongue through her honeyed folds, and she

screams out for me, lifting and twisting her hips as she seeks her release. Her pussy flutters, opening and closing as though it senses that my knot is full to bursting. I can feel it swelling, more than ready to sink into our omega and lock us together. It feels *primal.*

I hesitate for a moment. "Have you done this before, love?"

She shakes her head frantically. "No – but please, don't stop."

I close my eyes. I can't do this now. I start to pull back but Harper moans, her arousal replaced by distress.

"No," she gasps, and grabs my arm. "I *choose* this, Gabe," she says, meeting my eyes in a daze. "I choose this, with you. Don't take my choices away from me."

My heart shatters, and I know we're doing this. I won't deny her anything.

A choked sound makes mine and Harper's heads whip around. Ace is standing just inside the door, his eyes burning as they run over us, taking in every detail as I kneel over Harper with her spread before me like an offering.

His voice is strangled. "The bond – I felt…"

Shit. He felt all the repercussions of my discussion with Harper. I glance down at her, and her eyes are focused on me, even as she holds out a hand to Ace.

"Ace," she whispers. "Come here."

My heart jolts in my chest, a desperate longing filling me. Ace and I stare at each other, and it feels like all of my barriers have been stripped away, Harper's tearing them down like little more than feathers in the breeze as I stare into his blue eyes.

I miss you.

I'm sorry.

A soft mewl from Harper pulls our attention back, and there's a frown on her face that suggests she's hurting.

"Empty," she whimpers. She needs us.

"Shh, sweetheart," I soothe, rubbing my palm against her clit. "We'll fix it."

Thuds sound as Ace rips his shoes off, unbuckling his belt and stripping out of his clothes in seconds.

He moves towards Harper before spinning back and grabbing the back of my head, pulling me to him in a rough kiss and pressing his forehead against mine. I breathe in the scent of sea salt, driftwood and *Ace* for a moment, before nudging him towards Harper.

He gently lifts her up and slides in behind her. His brow creases as his fingers trace the ridges of her back, and he flicks a shocked glance at me. I nod, a silent agreement that we'll pick it up later. Right now, our omega needs us.

The sight of Harper's naked female body resting against Ace's alpha maleness sends every little bit of blood I had left straight to my cock, the rush of blood flow almost leaving me lightheaded and my knot swelling up in demand.

Ace kisses the side of Harper's head, moving his hands over her body and squeezing her breasts. Reaching down, he hooks his legs under each of her knees and spreads her wide open for me.

Fuck.

Her pretty pink pussy is dripping, the scent of cinnamon and oranges mixed with her honeyed arousal making my head sway. Ace drops his head to suckle against her neck, wherever he can reach with the collar in his way, his hands never leaving her breasts.

I shuffle up, palming my cock and running a finger over the moistness at my head. I lean forward, notching myself against her entrance and breathing in deeply as she moans at the sensation.

I brush back a lock of damp red hair, my eyes searching her face.

"Tell me yes, sweetheart," I have to ask one more time, careful to keep any trace of the bark out of my voice.

I need this to be her decision. Need her to choose me. Choose us.

Please, God, choose us.

I'm not sure our pack can survive without Harper, not now that we've had a taste of a life with her.

She cries out as I slide the head of my cock up and down her folds, her legs trembling in Ace's firm grip.

"Yes!" she cries out, her glazed eyes burning with the reflection of the fire as she watches me through dipped eyelashes.

"*Please*, alpha."

I grunt at her words, liking the sound of it on her lips. I'll be the best damn alpha for our omega, for as long as she'll have me.

Ace lets out a tortured groan, his eyes on our joining as I nudge gently into Harper's opening.

"Christ," he hisses. "You're so fucking beautiful, baby."

Harper mewls, her arm reaching up to clench into Ace's hair as I push a little further in, before crying out as I withdraw. I repeat the process several times until Harper is begging again, and then I thrust, hard.

Her scream of relief as I fill her completely locks my spine into place, Ace stiffening with a groan. I give her a moment to breathe and then my instincts overtake me.

I fuck her. Hard. Repeatedly.

Her eyes roll back into her head as my thrusts nudge the back of her womb, whines of pleasure dragged out of her with every push. Ace holds her steady, his hands never leaving her body. Sweat dampens our skin as we move together.

"Bite," she whimpers. "Bite."

She stretches her beautiful neck to me, and my eyes snag on the collar. Leaning in, I drop a kiss to her exposed skin.

"Not today, love." It comes out as a groan. I want nothing more than to mark her where everyone can see. Claim her as ours, the heart of the fucking Winter pack so everyone knows she belongs with us. But I won't put the future I can see ahead of us at risk.

One day, though. *Soon.*

Our bodies are undulating, and Ace is perfectly in sync, holding Harper steady for me against him. Our eyes meet as I thrust, and the heat in them promises more of this.

I could live the rest of my life like this, and I'd die a happy man.

Harper's warm heat, the scent of her slick – my knot tightens, and a flash of panic threatens. I've never knotted anyone before. But my instincts take over, and as my knot swells, I push forward one more time. Harper's legs shake as the knot slides into her opening, her body thrashing as she fights Ace's firm grip.

Ace leans in and hisses in her ear. "Come for us, little omega."

He pinches her clit as my knot notches into place and it sends us both over the edge. Harper clamps down on my knot like her body's sucking me dry as she screams incoherently, slick dripping down my cock.

My eyes roll back as I explode inside her with a bellow, my knot keeping my seed inside and shudders of pure ecstasy licking at the base of my back as she takes everything I have, draining me dry.

Satisfaction rumbles through me and I rock gently, murmuring hazy words of praise as Harper closes her eyes, small aftershocks of her orgasm rippling through her. Ace rubs gentle circles against her clit and she pushes back into him with a murmur.

"It'll help with the knotting," he whispers to me. We gently maneuver Harper between us until we're all lying on our sides. Me with my back to the fire, Harper secure on the end of my knot and her face buried into my neck as Ace's arms wrap over us both.

Fucking hell. That was... beyond anything I've ever felt. Ace's expression tells me he's feeling similar. Harper shifts gently, a purr slipping out as my knot nestles into her. I rock gently and she hums in satisfaction.

"Amazing," she sighs, a sleepy mumble to her voice.

Ace runs a hand over her hair gently. "Sleep, sweetheart. We've got you."

She turns her head blindly, eyes already drifting shut and I catch her lips in a soft kiss.

"You are exquisite, love," I whisper. A smile tips up the corner of her mouth as she dozes off in our arms. I feel my own eyes starting to close, my knot slipping free of Harper's body. Fingers link around mine, and my gaze flickers open to a familiar face. Ace curls his hand around mine, and I hold onto him tightly.

"Missed you," I whisper.

———

I whistle as I dart around the kitchen, putting together the final touches to dinner. I can't wait for Harper to try it. This afternoon was... it was everything.

I'm falling in love with her.

Ace slides in behind me, his warm breath ghosting over my neck and making me shiver.

"Hey," I breathe. Having him with us for Harper's first time was perfect.

"Just so you know," he whispers. "I'm not giving up on us."

A quiver runs through me at his words, my heart swelling. We have things that we need to talk through. But maybe, if he wants to chase – well, this time I might let him catch me.

Rogue and Devlin wander in, nostrils flaring immediately

at my scent. I haven't showered, not wanting to lose the traces of Harper embedded in my skin. I raise my chin and stand firm. A hint of envy floats through the bond. Rogue watches me carefully before he smiles.

"Is she okay?" he asks. I nod. He grabs some plates and carries them to the table as I wait for him to speak.

"You're not mad?" I ask, just to check.

Rogue laughs. "No, I'm not mad. I think she made exactly the right decision."

I beam at him as the door knocks. I feel like I'm floating on air.

"Delivery van," Devlin says. He has alerts sent to his phone from the cameras we have set up around our perimeter. "I'll get it."

He returns with a scowl on his face. He's pushing a huge square parcel almost as big as he is, and I jump across to help him.

"What's that?" Ace asks, confused.

"A gift from the fucking OC."

Chapter Thirty-One
Harper

I'm engrossed in a book Devlin left on my dresser for me. It's an old book, about an omega who hides her awakening from her alpha pack because of the way they treat her, even though they're fated mates. I don't know where he got it, but it's heart-breaking and addictive and most definitely illegal goods.

I'm enthralled by the idea of fated mates. I wish they existed. The idea of belonging to the Winter pack in that way... I would be theirs, and they would be mine too. The idea sends a chill racing up my spine.

That's not something that happens in real life, though. The most they can do is bitemark me, creating a link that will draw me to them. But I won't be able to bite them. I've never heard of an omega marking an alpha in that way.

Turning the page, I'm distracted by my stomach grumbling, and I glance outside at the darkening sky. It must be close to dinnertime, and I'm surprised that Gabe hasn't come to hunt me down so he can feed me some more.

Shutting the book carefully to save my space, I head down to the kitchen. The door is closed as I reach it, the mumbling of the pack coming through. Smiling, I reach out to open it, but my hand pauses against the wood as Devlin's voice comes through, angry in a way I haven't heard since I first arrived.

"So, we're supposed to inject her and then just tie her down?"

Devlin?

My hand drops like the door is burning me. Swallowing hard, I stare at the door. Gingerly, I lean forward to press my ear against it.

"Apparently," Rogue's gruff voice says. "It says here that it takes around an hour for them to pass out. The pheromones get stronger as the mix works through their system."

"There are metal chains on here." Ace's voice sounds weird.

My head is racing, dark thoughts running through my mind. They're talking about an artificial heat.

I know what happens. I've seen it.

Every omega in training has to watch a recording of an artificial heat. The image of the omega moaning, head lolling to the side, legs tied against the x-shaped cross as the males pump into her brings a wave of nausea to my throat, and my legs shake so badly I wonder if I'm going to collapse.

"Have they given us a timescale?" Gabe's voice chimes in with concern. My eyes squeeze shut, and a tear makes its way down my cheek.

Everything they've told me is a lie.

Backing away quietly from the door, I turn and pad softly up to my bedroom. As I push the door closed, a sob escapes, and then another, until I'm curled in a ball on the floor. Everything that's passed between me and the pack since I arrived here flashes through my mind.

Why did they lie to me? I would have preferred it if they'd kept to the rules instead of this. Do they think I'll just smile and offer my arm for the injection so they can get their seed into my belly? Waves of grief come over me as I think of my afternoon with Gabe and Ace, and I crawl to the bathroom, reaching the toilet just in time to lose everything in my stomach.

Lies. Beautiful, painful, dangerous lies.

I should have known better.

I'm not sure how much time passes. I'm sat with my back against the door, head on my arms when Gabe knocks. The sound makes me flinch. I can't face them.

"Harper, love? Are you coming down for dinner?"

He sounds so hopeful. Like he and his pack haven't just ripped my heart into two. I push my hand against my mouth to stop the cry, forcing it back down and croaking, "I don't feel great. I think I'm just going to go to bed early."

Gabe pauses before his voice comes through, filled with worry. "Are you alright? Do you need anything?"

Clearly, they're worried that their pet omega won't be up to performing. Bile fills my mouth at the thought.

"I'll be fine tomorrow. I think I just overdid it today." My croaky voice adds evidence to my story, and Gabe tells me he'll leave a tray of food outside my door in case I get hungry at all. He asks if he can come in, but I tell him I need some time to myself. His footsteps pause outside my door before he makes his way back downstairs.

Tears run down my face and I scrub them away, forcing myself to think clearly as I frantically think of my next steps.

I'll *never* submit to an artificial heat.

Shame fills me at the thought of me whining and begging for them, and all the while, they were planning to do this.

It makes sense now, why Gabe wouldn't bite me this afternoon. You don't need a bitemark for pregnancy. Just if you're planning to keep an omega around. And they're obviously not. Pain sears my chest at the realization that they've clearly never planned to keep me.

I stumble into the bathroom, staring at the collar around

my neck in the mirror. Leaning in, I try and get a closer look at it. The black plastic is thick, around an inch high, and there are three green lights on the side. I don't know what they mean apart from that they can track my movements. I try and push a finger through, but it's fixed so tightly to my neck that there's barely enough space for my little finger to squeeze in.

I briefly consider trying to force the collar from my neck, but I know that the trip switch will flip, and it'll shock me unconscious before I manage it. The compound will get an alert and they'll contact the pack. They'll know that I was trying to escape, and I'll be chained and in heat before I even wake up, probably. Tampering with your collar is a serious offense.

I have two options. I can take my chances and try and get the collar off. My thoughts go to Gabe's knife set in the kitchen. I could take one and run, hide somewhere close and try and cut it off. Maybe they wouldn't find me before I woke up.

Or I could just go along with it. Be the *good omega* I've been trained to be. I think of all of the moments I've shared with the pack. Rogue's stern face hiding his smile, Ace's devilish smirk, Gabe's heart-stopping grin, Devlin's hopeful expression. The choices they've given me.

All the glimpses of a future we'll never get to have. It hurts more than I ever thought was possible.

Maybe there's another explanation.

No. Resolution fills my heart and I shake my head at myself. There is no excuse for this. They haven't even spoken to me about it. *You haven't given them the chance*, a voice whispers in my head, but I brush it off.

I feel dazed, and I have to think clearly.

I don't have time to torture myself with what-ifs, and I can't ask them outright. If I do and they are planning to sedate me, it'll tip them off that I know.

I don't have any options.

I sit down on the floor, my head in my hands. Panic and blind, sheer terror fills me, my thoughts clouding over. The pain in my chest feels like I'm going to tear down the middle, white-hot agony splintering as I think of the four men downstairs. I thought I'd found something special. Something amazing.

A third option drifts into my mind. I try to push it away, but it grows, becoming more insistent until it's a beating drum pounding against my temples.

I won't be their toy. I can't. Pain lances through me at the thought, of lying there listlessly while they take what they need, fill me and leave me. My hands drop to my stomach and I think of the consequences of artificial heats. A child. They'd take my child away from me. And then I'll be given to another pack. And then another. Until I'm dried up. Or dead.

I won't let it happen.

There's one option in the back of my mind. The final choice I'll ever have.

I sit there for hours, staring at the floor, waiting for the noises that signal the pack going to bed, praying that tonight isn't the night they're planning on.

Ace and Gabe talk in the distance, a hint of slightly raised voices filtering through my door as they head into their rooms for the night. Then Devlin. His door opens and closes quietly, and I wonder vacantly if he'll try to come in tonight. Rogue is the only one left, and he stays up late.

A small jolt of surprise fills me when I hear his steady footsteps only a few minutes later. They pause outside my door, and I freeze, holding my breath.

He knocks lightly. "Harper?" his voice is quiet, worried. I stay still and silent on the floor, praying that he doesn't come in, that he thinks I'm sleeping. He stays outside my room for a few minutes more, slowly moving away. I hear his door close.

Wait. The minutes tick away as I stare at the clock next to my bed. The blankets call to me, their scents drifting over in comfort and temptation I desperately want. *Pretty lies and false promises.* I force myself to stay where I am for another hour before I ease myself up.

Slipping out of my door, I leave it open a crack, not wanting any of them to come and investigate the noise of it closing. I drift through the house, my bare feet tiptoeing silently until I reach the kitchen area. My hand trails over the knives softly, but it's not what I have in mind. My gaze snags on the door to the walk-in freezer, and a soft breath draws from my lungs.

That's it. I want to feel absolutely nothing. *Numb.* Just like I did in the ice baths.

Pushing the door open, I cringe slightly at the squeak, pausing for a minute as cold air sweeps over me. No footsteps sound overhead, so I slip inside, pulling the door closed behind me.

The ice claws at my veins as I pad over to the corner, my breaths puffing out in front of me like little clouds. My bare feet burn as I sink down, hiding from the view of anyone looking in. The cold is soothing, though. Drawing my knees up and hugging them tightly, I sit and wait.

This pain is familiar, more familiar than the rip in my soul.

Soon, I won't feel the cold at all. I won't feel the pain of their betrayal in my chest. I won't feel anything. I'll just... drift away. Like I was never really here in the first place. Just like what happened with my family.

Like I was never a part of the Winter pack.

CHAPTER THIRTY-TWO
ROGUE

I'm working at my desk when a light knock interrupts me. Gabe enters without waiting and plunks a mug of coffee in front of me.

"Is Harper down yet?" We were all worried when she told us she was unwell last night. Gabe immediately started panicking after their afternoon together.

His hair is rumpled and dark circles sit under his eyes, indicating that he hasn't slept well. I can sympathize. I feel on edge this morning and I can't pinpoint the reason why. There's an uncomfortable weight in my chest.

He shakes his head, looking despondent. "No. She didn't touch the tray I took up last night, either. I think she's still asleep."

I sit back in my chair, wondering if I should go and check on her. I don't want to disturb her, though. "Let's give it another hour or so," I tell him. "I'll go and check on her then."

Maybe her time at the omega compound is finally catching up with her. She's adjusted admirably well to the pack – to us – and even though she's seemed to be growing brighter every day, we all know that trauma can manifest itself in different ways.

Actually, it might help for her to talk to Ezra, and I glance at the phone. I'll call him today. It's something I should have done sooner.

"When are you back at work?" Gabe asks.

It's unusual for us all to be home for this long, but I was able to get us some compassionate leave after our last mission when I explained that our pack had been allocated an omega. We had a substantial amount of time off built up anyway, and I fully plan on making the most of this time with Harper as a pack before Ace, Devlin and I are pulled back out on active duty.

"Probably another two weeks or so," I say, drumming my fingers on the desk. "What will you do when we're out again?"

"Enjoy Harper all to myself," he smirks and waggles his eyebrows, and I throw a pen at him, laughing. It feels good to have this easy camaraderie between us again. After Gabe's attack, we all withdrew in different ways. Harper has brought this pack together again in ways she doesn't even realize.

Thinking of her, worry trickles through me, and I stand up. "Actually, I think I'm going to check on her now. If she's ill we might have to call the compound to send a doctor out, so we'll need to be prepared."

Gabe's face tightens at the mention of the compound, but he's right behind me as I head up to Harper's room. Her door is slightly ajar, and I look back at Gabe, who shrugs.

Pushing the door gently so it swings open, Gabe peeks over my shoulder as we see the empty room. Harper's blankets are crumpled, her book abandoned on the cover. The room feels... cold. Her bathroom door is open too, lights off. Frowning, I glance back at Gabe. "She must be downstairs after all."

Gabe checks the bathroom to be sure, and we both split up to head downstairs and look. The weight in my chest is getting heavier, telling me that something's wrong. Our agitation flickers in the bond, and Ace pops his head out of the snug doorway.

"Is Harper in there?" his eyes widen slightly at my bark. It's been a while since I snapped at them like that. "No, I thought she was still in bed. I haven't seen her since yesterday."

Gabe pelts up from the gym, Devlin close behind him in his gym kit, sweat dripping from his face.

"Where is she?" Dev asks, mouth twisting in concern. Ace looks between us, worry creasing his brow. "Is she not in her room?"

Gabe and I shake our heads in unison.

"Split up," I say urgently. The pack scatters and I start ripping open doors down the corridor, breathing deeply for any hint of Harper's cinnamon scent in the air. I check cupboards, behind doors, even in our airing cupboard, yanking blankets and bedding out in case she's managed to climb in, and there's no sign of her. The anxiety coming through the bond tells me that the others are having no luck, and we come together in the kitchen.

Ace is pacing, his hands locked behind his head, and Gabe wrings his hands frantically. Devlin's face is a mask, but the bond is screaming with his agitation. "We've looked everywhere in the house. Where could she be?"

I glance outside. "Maybe she went for a walk." Ace and Gabe immediately throw themselves out of the door, and I hear them calling out as they start to look around the house. Devlin's fingers tighten against the chair he's holding, and I hear a slight crack as the abused wood protests. "She can't be out there. Her collar won't allow her to get that far from the house."

"Unless she's taken it off." My mouth tightens at the thought. There's a shock trigger embedded, so if she's tried it…

Gabe and Ace reappear. "There's no scent out there at all. I don't think she's left the house," Ace mutters. Gabe is thinking, his face focused in intense concentration as he retraces Harper's steps.

"We've checked everywhere," Dev throws out, his voice a growl of concern. "Where else could she be?"

Gabe's head shoots up and he dives past us, pushing Devlin out of the way as he rips the door to the walk-in freezer open. He disappears inside as Dev shakes his head.

"There's no way," he begins, but his eyes widen. His snarl is low and furious, and he disappears after Gabe just as Ace and I catch it.

The smallest hint of cinnamon.

"Fuck," Ace snarls. I throw myself after them, praying that we've got it wrong, that Harper's not been stuck inside this freezing container for god knows how long.

I'm barely past the entrance when Gabe's howl of agony rips through the air. His emotions crash through the pack link and I stagger to the side, throwing my hands out to the wall. The ice burns and I rip my hand back as I move towards Gabe in the corner.

He's moaning wordlessly, pulling Harper into his arms. Her beautiful golden eyes are closed, her skin mottled with grey and her lips blue. Her bare feet dangle as he balances her, the redness of her skin screaming frostbite.

Dev is on his knees next to them, frantically feeling for a pulse. "I can't feel anything – fuck – princess, can you hear me?"

Ace pushes past me where I stand, frozen with indecision. I don't know what to do. I don't know how to fix this.

Ace bellows something at me, and I ignore him, staring at Harper's tiny body blankly. He shakes me, and sound filters back into my ears.

"What do we do? Rogue!" his tone is pleading, and I snap out of it.

I reach Gabe in a second, his howls not stopping as he

cradles her tenderly, pushing her hair away from her face. I lean down and pull her into my arms. Turning, I race for the exit, the warmth of the kitchen hitting me like a brick as I run through it and up the stairs, careful not to jostle Harper as I shout instructions over my shoulder.

"Call Ezra!"

Dev is quickest to recover and overtakes us, jumping the stairs two at a time. As I burst through Harper's bedroom door, he's already got the sheets ready, and I lay her down gently. Her head lolls to the side as I start CPR, counting the compressions and breathing gently into her ice-cold mouth, willing her chest to keep rising. Ace whimpers from the doorway, but when I turn he has his phone in his hand, hitting numbers and holding it to his ear.

Gabe is slumped against the doorway, his eyes on Harper's still frame.

"It's too late," he moans.

"Like fuck," I snap, beginning a second round of compressions. We need to warm her up. We might be able to save her. But I need help.

Come on, love. Stay with me.

"Rogue, the compound," Dev starts.

I cut him off abruptly. "We'll never see her again. They'll take her away."

Harper's chest rises slightly before falling, and I close my eyes briefly with a prayer of relief. Ace is rambling garbled information down the phone to his grandfather, and I grab it out of his hands, turning the speaker on. Ezra's voice rings out, his gruff tones snapping instructions rapidly.

"Get warm water and cloths — lots of them. You need to warm her middle first, if you start with her legs and arms then it could push blood back to her heart and stop it. Lots of blankets."

Dev is already running the bath in the next room, and I bark at Gabe to snap him out of his panic. "Get blankets!"

His hackles rise at my use of the alpha bark, but he doesn't resist. I hear him ripping things out of the airing cupboard. He skids back in, dropping a bundle at the foot of the bed and running back out to get more.

Noises come from the phone. "I'm on my way. How long was she there?"

My throat closes. "We don't know. Hours, maybe. Hurry, Ez."

"Shit. Get those warm cloths on her now. Remember what I said about starting from the middle. Neck, chest wall or groin only. Slow dabs, no massaging or rubbing or you could take her skin off." Gabe whimpers behind me as Dev bursts out of the bathroom. He grabs some bedding from the pile and starts ripping it into smaller pieces.

"I'm assuming she's beta?" Ezra asks.

"Omega. Does it matter?"

There's a split second of silence, Ezra's surprise palpable but he recovers quickly.

"Have you bitten her?" I growl lightly and he shushes me with the authority of an older alpha. "Quit with the posturing, boy, this is important."

"No," I force out. Regret runs through me. I wish we had. I wish I'd bitten her at the first opportunity we had, making it clear that she belongs to us.

Ezra curses and I hear the honk of his horn.

"That would help, but we'll make do. Forget what I said. She'll need your body heat, all of you. That means all four, assuming she's involved with the whole pack. Clothes off, cover her as much as you can, *gently*, and stay there. I'm about 10 minutes away. Leave the door open."

The line goes dead. I start shucking off my clothes, growling at Gabe to do the same. When he's slow to react, my scent rises in a dominating push, his eyes dilating as I shove my authority down the pack bond.

"Snap out of it, Gabe," I urge. I pull him to me briefly in a quick hug, anchoring him to the pack. Devlin and Ace are already naked, Dev crawling onto the other side of the bed. I growl at Ace when he tries to take Harper's other side and he shows me his throat, quickly dropping to the bottom of the bed. Gabe's weight presses down on the mattress as he follows. I can feel my dominance leaking out of me, covering the room in heavy pheromones.

"Cover her," I bark. They're quicker to respond this time. Carefully, so carefully, I turn Harper gently on her side and pull her to me, pressing my cheek to her face, her body plastered to mine. The cold runs through me like chalk on a blackboard but I ignore it. Dev is doing the same on my other side, his head gently nestled against her throat as he inhales deeply.

I feel Ace and Gabe arranging themselves, our legs entangling with each other as our breathing settles, the iciness of Harper's skin pushing deep into our bones. Glancing down at Harper, I see a slight tinge of color in her face.

"I think it's working," I say softly, and Ace lets out a whine of relief as Devlin shudders. We stay quiet for a few minutes as the cold slowly ebbs away and Harper's skin warms. Her heartbeat thuds against my chest, slow and sluggish, but *here*. We haven't lost her. I hear the door bang downstairs and footsteps running up, glancing over my shoulder as Ezra appears in the doorway, breathing hard with his medical bag in his hand.

CHAPTER THIRTY-THREE
ACE

I raise my head slightly to see my Pa standing at the door. Rogue turns too, hesitating for a moment and glancing down at Harper before he nods my grandfather in. His instincts are riding him hard. I wasn't sure if he'd get himself together downstairs. But he managed to pull himself back in time to take charge. Thank fuck he did, because none of the rest of us had been up to the task.

Ignoring my grandfather for the moment, I lay my cheek back down gently against Harper's leg. She still feels ice cold. Or maybe that's just me.

Her face, pale and lifeless, keeps coming back to the front of my mind no matter how hard I try to push it away. She must have been so fucking scared. I don't know how she managed to get herself stuck in the freezer, but she obviously couldn't find the release hatch to get out.

Gabe is almost catatonic next to me, guilt pulsing through the bond enough to make my hair stand on end. The freezer was his idea in the first place. He kept shouting that we didn't have enough space to feed four hungry alphas. We gave in when he started yelling at Rogue one time, asking him if we expected him to pull food out of his ass or spend his life at the grocery store. We knew he just didn't want to go back after the attack. He got his freezer.

Gently, I reach out, careful not to startle him, and carefully stroke my fingers through his hair. He turns his face to the side, ignoring me. I'll let it go for now, but not for long. He's made so much progress in the last few weeks, with Harper here. I won't let him withdraw into his shell again.

My eyes are pulled back to her like a magnet. She seems to have a little more color now, her chest slowly rising and falling, but she's still unconscious. My gaze flicks to Rogue as he sits up, keeping his arm over her and turning as if to shield her from my grandfather's gaze.

Ezra keeps his head turned, respecting the hormones that are clearly riding Rogue right now. He lifts his medical bag up, shaking it gently and murmuring to Rogue in a quiet, soothing tone. Rogue is tense but takes a step back to allow Pa to take a look at our girl.

I swallow, hard.

We failed you, little omega.

How the fuck did this happen?

Pa checks Harper over carefully, taking her pulse and pulling a cuff from his bag to measure her blood pressure. His fingers skip over her collar and he shoots a questioning look at Rogue.

Rogue shakes his head, whispering, "The compound." Pa rolls his eyes and continues with his slow examination. I mentally throw pushy vibes at him, needing him to hurry up and tell us what's wrong. He doesn't miss a beat before he snaps his teeth at me, and heat rises up my neck. I feel like an unruly teenager again. When Pa gets down to her legs, he frowns, pushing the mottled skin in and out. Her skin color hasn't returned to normal from her left knee down, and I'm petrified as to what it means.

His gaze collides with mine and softens as he reaches out a hand and moves it over my hair. I haven't seen him in a while, and guilt hits me as I realize what a shock this would have been to him when I called out of the blue like that. Pa brought me up, and we've always been close. But the last few weeks with Harper have felt like we're in our own bubble, hiding away from the world.

He looks over his shoulder at Rogue. "She seems to be out of the woods, but I need to hook her up to some fluids. I'll need you all to jump up now so I can get some blankets on her."

We all growl in unison, none of us liking the idea of leaving her side.

Pa just raises an eyebrow, and we all squirm, even Rogue.

"Come on now," he chides. "You want her to wake up, don't you?"

The thought causes me to spring from the bed, the thuds of Gabe and Dev jumping up a close echo. We all stand in a loose semi-circle as Pa pulls out a long thin needle and wraps a cord around Harper's slim arm to pop a vein. Rogue shifts uneasily as Pa inserts it, and he ignores the scents filling the room as he hooks a bag up, the fluid running down and into Harper.

She still hasn't moved at all. With her breath so slow, her skin so pale and those beautiful golden eyes closed to us... my heart clenches. She looks like a corpse. My instincts scratch at my nerves.

Pa gestures at the blankets and I start handing them to him as he layers them over her body, studiously ignoring her nudity. The second she's covered, my body relaxes slightly, the possessiveness draining out of me.

He fiddles for a few more minutes, checking her temperature and taking another look at her legs. We all sag with relief when he pulls the blankets back and her leg seems less mottled than it did before.

"There," Pa tucks the covers securely around her, before turning to us. "Now, I think we need to talk."

We all balk at the idea of leaving the room, but Pa ushers us towards the door. "She's going to be fine, but she needs fluids and *rest*. She won't get that with you all filling the room with alpha hormones. You're about as peaceful as a pack of charging rhinos. You can come and check on her in a while."

Slowly, we all filter out of the room. Gabe lingers reluctantly at the door until Dev pulls him away. We're a subdued bunch as we wander downstairs, turning towards the snug. None of us want to be anywhere near the kitchen right now.

When we're all settled, Dev and I on either side of Gabe and Rogue taking a seat in the armchair, Pa perches in the other. His gaze sweeps across us.

"Let's hear it, then. What's going on?"

Rogue launches into an explanation of the last few weeks, from their visit to the compound and Harper's arrival to today. As he reaches the moment we found her in the freezer, he trails off with a catch in his throat.

"We were nearly too late," his voice drops to a low growl. "I was going to make Gabe wait to check on her."

I can hear the pain in his voice, reflecting the pack bond in my chest. I reach up and rub over my heart to try and dispel some of the ache, but it runs deeper than that.

Pa studies us intently. He hasn't reacted much throughout Rogue's retelling, the odd question here and there and a growl when he heard about Harper's treatment at the compound.

Sighing, he looks around. "I want to tell you boys a story. Any chance of a drink?"

I glance at my pack, confusion filling me. What story? Devlin moves to the side, sloshing whiskey into glasses and handing one to each of us. I take a big swig from mine, welcoming the heat of it as it slides down my throat, and nudge Gabe to do the same when he stares into his glass forlornly.

Pa clears his throat.

"I haven't shared this with anyone for many years. You'll forgive an old man for collecting his thoughts." He raises his eyes to me. "And I hope you'll forgive me, son, for not sharing this sooner."

CHAPTER THIRTY-FOUR
DEVLIN

My thoughts stay with Harper upstairs as I settle back into my seat, sensing that Ezra is sharing something important with us. I hate to think of her lying there alone. We should be with her. I shift restlessly and Rogue gives me a look.

Ezra rests his head back against the armchair, his eyes unseeing as he thinks over his words.

"Fifty years ago, I met Ivy in a bar in downtown Chicago."

Ace jerks, his eyes now fixed firmly on his grandfather. Ezra has always been tight-lipped about Ace's grandmother and the rest of their family.

"I walked in and there she was, dancing around with her friends. It was an Irish bar, and they had a band playing."

Ezra hums a bar of a song before he trails off.

"She was everything I never knew I wanted. I fancied myself a bit of a man around town then. I used to get myself into trouble pretty much every night. Playing the big alpha. But it all stopped, the night I met her. One look and I just knew. And she felt the same way."

"We married quick, after a few weeks. Her folks were

furious – they had this beta doctor all lined up for her, but all we wanted was each other."

His lip twitches up at the corners.

"We were happy. We moved upstate and used everything we had to buy this little house with a porch. It was falling down around us, but Ivy just tied up her hair and we got to work. I managed to get on the medicine program at the college and we made friends in the neighborhood."

"It was around that time that the birth rates started dropping. Every day at the hospital we were seeing women losing their babies. Some days there'd even be queues of them outside because we didn't have space to hold them all. The grief was… indescribable. And then we discovered that it was all beta women."

Ezra takes a sip of his drink. The room is silent as we all listen.

"Public mood began to shift, looking for someone to blame. At first, it was just fringe conspiracy theorists. They whispered that the omegas were doing something to stop betas from carrying to term. It was ridiculous, of course. Omega biology doesn't work like that. They were just different. Different biologies, different hormones. The issues with the betas didn't affect them."

"But whatever the reason for the beta problems, after a year or so, it became obvious that omega pregnancies were going without a hitch. People started protesting outside the hospital, and even the staff started turning on them. Then people started sneaking in, trying to snatch the children. I saw two babies go missing. It was like anarchy. It got to the point where omegas stopped coming to the hospital for treatment, giving birth in back-alley rooms because they didn't trust their children not to disappear."

"That's horrific," Gabe mutters next to me.

Nausea swirls in my stomach at the thought. This is a side

of the omega war that we've never heard first-hand. These are the origins of my own life. The beginnings of the adoption program I was placed into when my parents died.

"It was," Ezra agrees grimly. He's a little pale, and Ace gets up to refill his glass.

Clearing his throat, Ezra continues.

"It only got worse from there. People we thought were friends turned their backs on us. I was still trying to keep up my work at the hospital, and Ivy started staying home. She didn't want to go out without me. It escalated. A brick through the window, groups watching our house. We decided to leave, to go into hiding like so many others had."

"A few days before we planned to leave, the government asked omegas to come forward for tests, to see if they could work out what the birth issue was by comparing them to betas. Very few came forward. By that point, they were too scared."

He swallows, looking down. "I encouraged Ivy to go. I thought it might prove that omegas had nothing to do with the birth problems. I saw it as a possible solution. And they had to stay in for the tests for a couple of weeks, so I thought she'd be safe, and we could make a decision when she came out. But she never came home."

His face is twisted in agony, and Ace lets out a whine of distress as Gabe leans against his shoulder, anchoring him with pack touch.

"What happened?" Rogue breaks the grim silence.

"The Government announced that all omegas would be placed into a mandatory protective program, effective immediately," Ezra says grimly. "If any omegas tried to hide, government lackeys hunted them down like dogs."

Snarls echo in unison, all of us unable to hold in our anger. There's a swoosh in my stomach, something telling me that this is important. I can't help but think of my mom and dad. Was this before or after the night they died?

"They just stole them away," Ezra continues. "Guards turned up at doors, dragging the omegas out if they didn't come willingly. The alphas were in a frenzy, so they'd hit 'em with tranquilizer darts so they couldn't fight back. They'd wake up and their omega would be gone. Bagged and tagged like an animal.

"Whole packs fell apart overnight, omegas ripped away from their mates. There was fighting in the streets, the government deployed troops and a curfew to keep order. It went on for months. People were mindless with grief. But they were ignored because most people had started believing the hype. They said it was the right thing to do. And there just weren't enough of us to turn the tide."

I feel sick to my stomach.

"Every day, I went to the compound they'd put them in," he murmurs. "I tried pleading, begging the guards to let me in, but they refused. There was too much unrest. They told me that any omega was now required to be part of this government program and I should just go home."

"I couldn't leave it, so I kept trying. I tried to force my way in, then climb over the fence. They had too many soldiers, too much security. Eventually, they told me that if they saw me again, they'd shoot me on sight."

"I was getting ready to go back," he says. Ace flinches. "I knew that I couldn't live without her. It had been six months and I'd hit my breaking point. But then I had a call to come to the compound. I've never moved so fast. But it wasn't for her. Instead, they handed me a baby. Just her, nothing else. Not even a note. They told me that Ivy had died in childbirth."

The whine slips out of me, and Ace slumps forward with his head in his hands.

"That was before the surrogacy program was implemented," Ezra continues. "I'd had no idea that Ivy was even pregnant when she went in."

"But I *knew* she wasn't dead. I would have felt it, you see. She wore my bond, and I wore hers. But there was so much uproar. It wasn't safe for the baby. There were gangs roaming the streets, looking for any excuse to cause trouble, and we didn't have a pack to help us. If anyone had seen us, they would have gone for Cora. So I packed up our things that night, and we left. I didn't even have a crib or a basket for her to sleep in. We moved upstate, where things were quieter. I told myself that I'd come back for Ivy as soon as Cora was a little older."

Cora. Ace's mom. She died in a car accident when Ace was a teenager, along with his dad. Ace's shoulders are shaking with emotion and Rogue gets up, striding over and wrapping his arms around him.

I can feel the heartbreak in the room, filling up my throat. I glance at Ezra, at his tear-stained face. I can't even comprehend the grief that he's silently endured all of these years.

"I was going to come back," his voice is almost a whisper now. "But then I felt the bond snap. And it was too late."

My head is spinning. This is so different from what I've been told all my life. From what I've seen with my own eyes. I turn Ezra's words over in my mind.

They'd wake up and their omega would be gone. Bagged and tagged like an animal. Whole packs fell apart overnight, omegas ripped away from their mates.

"But…" I choke out. Ezra looks at me, his blue eyes knowing.

Memories assault me. Soft singing in my ear. Screaming, the sound of broken glass. Growling, fighting. A woman pleading for mercy. Dull thuds. Wet across my face.

"They told me it was him." It sounds like a plea. My pack turns to me, realization settling over their faces. "That's why they killed him. They had to."

Ezra looks at me, his weathered face firm.

"I know what you think happened to your parents, Devlin.

But I swear to you, your father would never have hurt a hair on your mother's head. He wouldn't have been capable of hurting his bonded mate like that. He would have fought for her until the end. That's why the alphas fought like they did. It was never anything to do with mind control."

A growl curls up my throat, my body rejecting the idea that everything I've thought about my history for twenty years has been wrong. I've been told over and over that my mother had so much influence over my father that his mind couldn't handle it. That he'd snapped and killed her before being shot by government guards, put down like a rabid animal.

"There were a lot of incidents like that, you see," Ezra explains quietly, maintaining eye contact. "Gangs breaking in and trying to take omegas by force, or the soldiers getting trigger happy. The Government explained it away as omegas trying to manipulate pack bonds, that they were greedy, and it sent people twisted. We knew the truth, of course. It was them who'd twisted things. There just…wasn't enough of us to get people to listen. I'm sorry, son," he whispers. "I would have sat you down and explained this before, but I just didn't think you were ready to hear it."

I'm not ready now. I'm shaking badly at the realization that my father likely didn't hurt my mother. Instead, a faceless gang or even our own government, my fucking *employer*, tore our family apart. My mother… if this is true, then she might not be dead. Where is she now?

Without a word, I jump up and flee the room, ignoring Rogue's bark. He can't split himself between me and Ace, and he doesn't follow me as I head outside for some badly needed fresh air. I'm glad. I need a moment to myself.

Chapter Thirty-Five
Rogue

I can't breathe. There's so much emotion saturating the pack bond. Ace is hurting and Devlin – he suddenly snaps his bond down, effectively cutting himself off from his pack, and I growl in response. I'm not going to let him close himself off to us.

Not only that, but Gabe is an absolute mess too, his guilt soaking into me. And Harper is still upstairs, alone. We haven't even seen her open her eyes yet. I stare wildly around, not sure who to go to first. The caving in my chest urges me to split myself in every direction. It *hurts*.

Ezra snaps his fingers in front of me and I jump. Staring up at him, I can feel the glaze in my eyes as the bonds all fight for my attention. As pack alpha, I'm automatically drawn to soothe my packmates when they're in pain or distress. Having all of them batter me at once is an assault on my instincts.

Ezra places his hand on my shoulder. "Steady, Rogue." As a senior alpha himself, he can push some of his dominance into me. It's rarely done outside of packs, tending to cause more harm than it fixes, but in this situation, it's exactly what I need. I breathe in deeply, letting his support settle into me, and the overwhelming pull recedes slightly, clearing my head and letting me breathe. I nod at him in thanks.

Ezra looks down at his grandson, sorrow in his eyes. "Here, I'll take him, and Gabe. Go and find Devlin. There's more that needs to be said and we'll need to head upstairs soon."

Fucking hell. What more can we possibly say? Slightly dazed, I let him pull me up and he takes a seat, wrapping his arms around both Ace and Gabe. I look down at them for a moment, pack bonds urging me to stay and look after my brothers, but the bonds settle slightly in my chest as they soak in Ezra's calming dominance.

I run upstairs to check on Harper. She's still and silent, but her cheeks are slightly flushed from the warmth of the blankets and she seems to be sleeping normally, so I take that as a good sign. The relief nearly drags me to my knees.

Stepping into the garden, the winds curls around me, biting and nipping at my exposed arms. There's no sign of Devlin, but I know where he'll be. Circling around the house, I see his bent neck as he sits on the bench we placed on the porch when we first moved in.

We're both silent as I take a seat next to him. Slowly, I lean against him, letting him absorb some of my warmth. He doesn't pull away, which I take as a good sign, but the dullness of his pack bond prickles my senses.

"Ezra said he wanted to tell us something else," I say. Immediately, I want to punch myself in the face. It sounds so insensitive.

Dev doesn't bite, though. He just stays where he is, staring at the ground.

"You know," I say, clearing my throat. "I can speak to Christian about finding any updates on your mom."

Dev turns to me, clenched fists betraying his anger. His voice is still and expressionless. "She's probably dead by now."

"You don't know that," I urge. Dread prickles up my spine

at the thought. This is the one possible positive thing to come out of the conversation today. Dev's mom might still be out there. She might even be in the omega compound. We just don't know.

"If she's not, then she probably wishes she is." He swipes a hand over his face, exhaustion lining every feature. "I just left her, Rogue. I never questioned it. Just assumed that what they told me was true."

"You were a kid," I point out quietly. "What could you have done, Dev? Look at Ezra. He was a full-grown alpha and he couldn't get to Ivy. He nearly died trying."

"Doesn't matter," he says, shaking his head. "I haven't been a kid for a long time. I could've looked into this years ago."

Ezra's right, though. He hasn't been ready. It's Harper's influence that's softened Devlin's rough edges. Even a month ago he would never have sat through that conversation, would never have opened himself to the possibility that omegas might be the ultimate victims of the omega war, and not the ones who started it all.

I stand, brushing a leaf off my trousers and holding out my hand. "Come on. We need to hear what else he has to say."

"I think I've hit my quota of earth-shattering revelations today," Dev says, his face grim. He takes my hand though, the bond opening up just enough to let in a nudge of gratitude. I'll let the rest go for now.

Pulling him to me, I hold him tight until his arms come up around my back and he clutches me. We soak up the contact before stepping away and heading back in to hear what else Ezra has to tell us.

I feel down the bond for Ace and Gabe, relieved when they both send reassurance at me in response to my gentle tugging. Stepping into the room, I check over them both, and they both nod at me to let me know they're okay. Still, I tug Dev over to the couch and pull him down beside me as I sit next to Ace.

Leaning over, I touch Gabe's shoulder. His eyes are red-rimmed, but he glances at me with a small smile. It only lasts a second though, before his eyes flicker up to the ceiling.

"Ezra's gone up," he murmurs. "We thought we heard something. He asked us to stay down here." His head drops down again.

My immediate knee-jerk response is to jump up and sprint upstairs, check Harper over for myself to make sure she's alright. And possibly shake some sense into her for scaring us all like that.

On second thoughts, maybe it's good that Ezra has gone up. Even if my instincts are raking at my insides for letting an unfamiliar alpha near Harper when she's so vulnerable. I trust Ezra implicitly, though, so I nod at Gabe and stay put, forcing my leg not to judder in agitation as we wait quietly for an update.

CHAPTER THIRTY-SIX
HARPER

L ight pierces my eyes and makes my head hurt. I murmur sleepily in frustration and turn my face away, relieved when someone closes the curtains.

I try to turn over, but something tugs at my arm, and an ache shoots up my side. Drawing in a sharp breath, I try to feel what's sticking out of me, and a murmur cuts through my drowsiness.

"Harper? Can you hear me?"

My eyes fly open at the unfamiliar voice. I scramble backward, ripping the needle out of my arm. The sting is nothing compared to the panic coursing through me.

Oh gods. I'm back at the compound.

It comes back to me in a wave of horror. The words slipping through the door that I wasn't supposed to hear, the alphas I thought I could trust destroying me in a moment. The freezer. Pain rips into me, knives of agony stabbing into my chest.

I've clearly been unconscious, and the sight of the needle lying on the sheet in front of me sends terror through my veins. I whimper, wondering if it was all for nothing. Scrabbling, I reach down to touch myself down *there*, slightly reassured when I don't feel any soreness or swelling. They can't have triggered a heat.

A choked sound whips my attention to the alpha in front of me. I don't recognize him, and he's standing back, allowing me some space. That's not how alphas at the compound behave. With this realization, more awareness sinks in. Twisting my head slightly but keeping the alpha in the corner of my eye, I sweep my gaze across the room, confirming to myself that I'm still in the room that my pack gave me.

No. Pack Winter. Not my pack. Never mine.

I whimper, the pain of that thought making me double over. The strange alpha reaches his hand out in concern and I kick my leg out, sliding back as far as I can until the headboard meets my back and I can't go any further. A whine of fear pulls from me, and the alpha backs up again, his hands up. My eyes slide again to the needle, and he catches my look.

"Harper, this isn't what you think," he starts, a gentle, rumbling tone to his voice.

He has no idea what I think. I *know* what I heard. This is it. I grab my arm, staring down at the faint mark that shows where the needle went in, digging my nails in. How much did they give me before I pulled it out? How much time have I got?

My scent is rising along with my distress, sharp edges of cinnamon filling the space and making my eyes water as I let out a keen of anguish.

"Please," I whisper. "Please don't let them do this to me."

The alpha's brows fly up. "Do what, sweetheart?"

It hurts, to hear a name they've used for me on his lips, and I whimper again.

"Don't let them put me into heat," I beg. I feel too exposed, the urge to wrap myself in layers riding me hard. It's too bright, too open, too fucking much.

The growl that falls out of the alpha shocks us both, a loud rumble of pure anger that sends me scooting back again, agitation rolling up my spine.

"Nobody's puttin' you into heat," he says in a low, furious whisper. "What have they been saying to you?"

I eye him carefully, both of us in a tense standoff. I don't know whether to believe him. He looks truly shocked, though. Maybe they're not doing it right now. His expression gives me a small amount of reassurance.

Ignoring his question, I take a quick look at my bed. It's piled high with blankets, and something twists in my chest. I want them wrapped around me. The room is too big, the ceilings too high. The alpha doesn't miss a trick, though, and he gestures towards them slowly.

"Have at it," he says quietly. When he doesn't move, I reach out quickly and snag one of the blankets, wrapping it around me like a fort. I feel a small amount of relief, but it's not enough, and I cast a longing glance at the rest of the pile.

"I'm Ezra," the alpha offers, not moving from his spot. "Ace's grandpa."

I flinch when he mentions Ace. Ezra doesn't miss it, brows lowering slightly in confusion. Reassured that he's not going to pin me down and inject me with heat hormones – at least not yet – I take in his features. A shock of white hair sits over bushy grey brows, and blue eyes that I've only seen the shade of once before peer out at me. He's shorter than Ace and wider, his shoulders broad as he stands with his arms crossed.

My attention is distracted by the prickling running through my legs. It *hurts*. Ezra picks up on my wince.

"You've been through quite a lot in the last few hours," he offers, watching my face carefully. "The boys found you in the freezer downstairs. You were damn lucky not to lose a leg, or worse."

I cringe, looking down at my leg and touching it to reassure myself that it's still attached to me. "I didn't think about that."

"The pack was in a hell of a mess when I got here."

I moan in quiet misery, a tug of longing for them pulling at me. I have to be strong, though. I have to learn how to survive without them.

"Why were you in the freezer, Harper?" Ezra's question is quiet, but it holds an authority that makes me want to answer him. Ezra feels… not like the pack did, but soothing. Safe. Of course, I thought they were too. Before they broke me.

A tear gathers in my eye and trickles down my cheek, closely followed by another. I sink my face into my hands as sobs ripple through me. I can't breathe, my lungs gasping for air.

I feel Ezra moving closer until his hand lands gently on my shoulder. Part of me wants to push him off. *Not right*, I think. *Not mine*. But the bigger part of me really wants some affection right now. I nod slightly and he sits down on the bed, tentatively pulling me closer and letting me rest my head on his shoulder as I weep inconsolably.

He doesn't rush me and his hand doesn't move, aside from a gentle movement up and down my arm. That he doesn't try to take advantage makes me want to trust him more, and eventually, I pull back. He lets me go immediately and I give him a small smile.

"Thanks," I say, hiccupping. "Sorry about…that." I wave generally between us.

"Don't sweat it, sweetheart," he says kindly. "I don't know the details of what's happened here, but I'd sure like to hear it. If you're comfortable telling me?"

I hesitate, thinking it over, and nod. He either knows all of this already, in which case it doesn't matter if I tell him or not, or he doesn't know, and he might help me.

Slowly, the whole story spills out, right back from when I

first arrived. Ezra listens intently, nodding his head and cursing when I stutter through my explanation of what happened with Jason. I don't miss anything out and even talk through some of my life before the compound. I don't know why, but Ezra is really easy to talk to. Finally, we get to the conversation I heard through the door. A few more tears fall as I go through what I heard, and then I pause. I don't want to talk through what happened next.

"Oh, Harper," Ezra looks at me solemnly. "You didn't think you had a choice, did you, sweetheart?"

My lip trembles again and I look down at my hands. "It hurts, Ezra," I whisper. I don't mean my body, but he understands.

"I know, darlin'. I don't know what those boys were doing, but I swear to you, Harper," he says, placing his hand over mine. I grip it like a lifeline. "I *promise* you; those boys would rather cut their own arms off than do you any harm."

I so badly want to believe him, but I've had my hopes broken down so many times before that I don't think I've got any more of it left in me. "Why were they talking about…that, if they weren't going to do it?"

"Well truthfully, I don't know. But I know that pack, and I know my grandson. And I saw the way they reacted when you were hurt. They were devastated. Beyond devastated."

A small kindle of hope flickers to life inside my chest. Maybe… maybe I did have it wrong. Maybe there's a good explanation.

Ezra hesitates and I glance at him, tensing.

"When you were sleeping, I took the boys downstairs and explained something to them. I'd like to share the same thing with you, if you wouldn't mind."

A little confused, I just nod at him.

Ezra explains his history. His hand trembles slightly in mine, and I squeeze it a little tighter as he talks through his relationship with Ivy and the horrors that followed them. My heart hurts for him, and tears start falling again. At this rate, I won't have any left in me.

"I'm so sorry that happened to you, Ezra," I say softly. My heart is breaking all over again to imagine Ezra as a young alpha with a baby in his arms and no hope of seeing his wife again. And Ace. This was his grandmother.

Ezra clears his throat, wiping roughly at his eyes. "I know it's not the easiest to hear, and I'm sorry for it. It wasn't my intention to upset any of you, but I think it's important that you understand the context of your own circumstances, and I know the damn compound wouldn't have told you the truth." His mouth curls in derision.

My expression must show how confused I am. "Harper," Ezra explains, a hint of sympathy in his tone. "The way that you and the pack are both acting… you're forming a mating bond. A *true* mate bond, like Ivy and I had. A close one, too, from the state of you all."

I stare at him, uncomprehending. "A mating bond?" The words sound strange on my tongue. I don't know what a mating bond is. Is it like a bitemark?

Ezra nods. "I wanted to explain this to the boys, but there hasn't been time. Will you come downstairs with me so we can all talk it through together?" When I hesitate, looking at the door, he presses my hand between his. "I promise you, there's absolutely nothing to be concerned about. I'll stay with you the whole time if you want me to."

If I don't do this, then I won't know if I got it wrong. And I desperately want to see them. I want Rogue to wrap his arms around me and hold me tight, Dev to call me a princess in his gruff tone. I want Gabe to fuss around me and Ace to sit close to me, protecting me from the world. But I won't get that unless I pull myself together. Sucking in a breath for fortitude,

I climb off the bed. Ezra reaches out to catch me as I wobble and nearly fall.

"Careful, doll," he mutters. "You're gonna be weak for a little while. Let me help you, hmm?"

He carefully wraps an arm around me, and we slowly move out of the bedroom. Ezra checks on me every few steps to make sure I'm not about to pass out. Dread and anticipation are mixing up in my stomach. I twist my fingers uneasily in my pajamas as we head slowly downstairs and towards the snug, bracing myself. *Don't get too excited, Harper*, I tell myself. *This could be a trick.*

But I need to know.

CHAPTER THIRTY-SEVEN
GABE

My instincts are in a frenzy. They're clawing at my insides, demanding that I go to Harper now. I need to see her. I need to apologize. Get on my knees and fucking beg her to forgive me.

Guilt rears up again and Rogue pushes a wave of reassurance down the bond. Ace reaches over and squeezes my thigh gently. The touches are a comfort, but they don't take away the self-condemnation I feel.

If I hadn't insisted on having that fucking freezer installed. If I'd shown her how to use it. If I'd checked it sooner. If I'd checked on her last night instead of giving her the space she'd asked for, worried that we'd overwhelmed her.

I run my hands over my jeans, picking at a loose thread. This is my fault. I made the pack put that freezer in, so I didn't have to go out as much. We all knew it, as much as I pretended it was because we all eat so much and they pretended that yes, that was exactly the reason that we needed a massive freezer built with enough space to feed twenty people a day.

It was just…easier. It meant fewer trips into public, fewer expressions of pity, or the occasional gasp of horror at my scar.

Sure, you get used to it, but… you don't, really. Every time you feel like yourself again, a look or a word brings it straight back up again. Having the freezer meant I could stock us with enough food to last for months, the guys bringing any perishables home with them after work.

I'll never complain again, I promise to who knows who. *I'll own the scar and flip off anyone who looks at me twice. Just please let her forgive me.*

Shuffling footsteps reach my ears. We all spring up, looking frantically at each other. Rogue heads back to the armchair and Dev, Ace and I all sink back down, trying to look like we haven't all been sat here staring fixatedly at the ceiling for the past damn hour. I struggle with where to put my arms for a moment but give in the urge and sit forward, straining to catch a glimpse of Harper.

She slowly wobbles into view, Ezra with his arms wrapped around her for balance. Rogue smothers a growl and I resist the urge to rip her away from him. *Ours.*

I scan her, checking for myself that she's here. When I get to her face, I growl, the noise low and frantic. She looks scared out of her mind. Something scrambles in my brain at the sight and the noise from the others tell me that they've picked up on it too.

We all stand up, the sudden movement making Harper jump as Ezra tries to steady her. He shoots us a warning look as Harper shrinks back, a whimper coming from her throat.

Someone could slide a knife between my ribs, and it would hurt less. She's frightened. Of *us.*

I turn to look at the others. Rogue looks gutted, his face almost as pale as Harpers, while Devlin looks like he's ready to do murder. Ace's face is filled with pain as he watches her.

Ezra moves further into the room, almost dragging Harper with him as he whispers rapidly in her ear. She nods briefly and they move over to the other armchair, Harper wrapping her arms around herself as soon as she's settled. She's keeping her distance from us, and Ace lets out a rumble of distress. We all want desperately to hold her, our instincts dragging us towards her, but it's clear that she wouldn't welcome it right now.

Ezra stays close to her, and she throws him a grateful look.

"Let's get this out of the way," Ezra announces. "Did you or did you not discuss inducing an artificial heat without Harper's consent?"

Her face pales, changing to a look of betrayal as she gapes at Ezra in disbelief. The room is silent for a moment as we all digest the words.

"You what?"

"What the actual fuck?"

"Sweetheart—"

I stay silent. The look on her face is tearing me apart. She almost looks resigned, like she's waiting for us to admit something. An artificial heat? The thought of any fucking artificial heat is repugnant. The thought of *Harper* in that position makes me wish I had someone in front of me to shred. *Never.* It echoes through the bond, waves of affirmation from my pack confirming that we all feel abso-fucking-lutely the same way. *Ours to protect*, my mind hisses, and I'm only too happy to agree.

I can't hold myself back any longer, and my knees hit the floor with a thud. I shift closer to Harper, whining when she moves back away from me, her back hitting the chair. Her beautiful golden eyes are so dark that I can't see any sunshine in them at all, and the idea that we might have put those shadows there when she's already been through so much breaks me in a way I can't explain.

"Harper," I whisper, searching her face. "Baby, please… I'm so sorry, love. I would rip out my own heart before I hurt you."

It's true. Every single beat of my heart is for the woman in front of me. My sunshine. My everything. I feel dampness on my cheek, and I drop my head to her thigh. Harper sucks in her breath sharply as I offer her my throat. Sharp, potent cinnamon settles to a warm thrum around us, and then she's pushing me off. My heart shatters and swoops as she drops on her knees in front of me.

"Look at me," she pleads. "Gabe. Look at me, please."

"I can't," I admit, a catch in my voice. "I don't deserve to look at you." Every part of me feels shattered into a million pieces.

There are angry denials from my pack. A hand grips my shoulder, and Rogue's fresh scent and strength surrounds me. "This is not your fault, Gabe. We're all responsible."

Harper glances between us, her eyes wide. "Why do you think this is your fault?" she asks me, a hint of wariness in her tone.

I glance at her, just once, before looking away. "Because it's my fault you were in that freezer," I say, my voice breaking.

"Why?" Her voice is filled with pain. It tears at my insides.

"Because I never showed you. I never showed you the latch. I didn't even think about it. So when you were stuck in there, you couldn't get out. Because of *me*," I pause, my breathing heavy as I stare at the floor in defeat.

Her hands move into my vision, and she overturns my palm. "Gabe, I…"

When her voice trails off, I'm filled with utter hopelessness. This pack is better off without me. First, I pushed Ace away. Now this. If I wasn't here, maybe…

I push myself to my feet, shrugging Ace off as he grabs my arm when her small voice yanks me to a stop.

"I didn't look for the lever, Gabe."

My mind spins as I digest her words, and I turn to stare at her beautiful, broken expression. *Oh, love.* She's ripping my heart into tiny pieces. I think I understand what she means, although Rogue and Ace still look confused. Devlin growls out his anger at the words. Of course. He's walked in that darkness, too.

I just don't know *why*.

I'm back across the floor in an instant. "Harper," I breathe, my hand lifting up to her face. I stroke it gently, reverently. "Why didn't you look, honey?"

She stares down and I grasp her chin, gently, raising her up to face me. "*Harper,*" I growl when she shakes her head, and her eyes fly up to my face, widening. Yep, I can do the alpha thing when I want to.

She swallows hard. "I… I just wanted to be *free*." Her voice breaks on the word.

"I heard you talking and I thought – I thought you were going to…," My heart clenches as I realise just how close we came to losing her.

"You thought we were going to force you into heat," I finish hoarsely. Everything clicks together in my head, clarity I've been searching for ever since we found Harper in that damn freezer.

"I'm s-sorry. I won't live like that," Harper sobs, and I pull her into my arms. She's trembling, shivers rolling up and down her spine and I run my palm down it as she curls into me, her hands twisting in my jumper as she breaks apart.

"No, I'm sorry, love," I say, and I feel the pack surrounding us, adding their own apologies. They all look as devastated as I feel.

"I'm so sorry that we made you feel that way. I promise you, there was never a question of us triggering a heat." I rock her gently in my arms and a purr emerges from my throat, soothing her. She relaxes in my arms, turning to rub her cheek across my chest.

"It's not your fault. I got it wrong," she says quietly. "So, so wrong. I nearly…"

I pull her closer until there's no single space between us, pushing away thoughts of a world without Harper. The rest of the pack gathers around us, desperate to see her. I lean back to give them space and she looks up at Rogue. He's on one knee with his hand out, uncertainty and heartbreak in his eyes. She nuzzles me one last time before taking his hand and throwing her arms around his neck. Ace scoops her up next, whispering 'little omega' into her hair as he breathes her in deeply. Devlin stands uncertainly to the side as Harper turns, searching for him.

He still feels odd in the pack bond, muted, but there's a warmth there too. It grows a little more as Harper looks around, her eyes landing on him and beckoning. He goes, helpless to resist her. I know how he feels.

"Princess," he whispers. He shudders as she throws herself into him, his arms closing tightly around her back as she winds hers around his neck.

"No more doubts, little omega," Ace says firmly. We all turn to face him, Harper with a touch of surprise. Ace's face is filled with determination. "From now on, you talk to us if you're worried. Complete honesty."

Rogue nods in agreement. "We're all in, love. We're not walking away from this. If you'll have us."

"Yours," I growl. "We're yours."

Harper's scent washes over us, warm cinnamon and oranges wrapping around me like a gift. She buries her face in Devlin's shoulder for a moment before glancing back at us, a shy smile on her lips.

"Mine." It sounds like a vow. One I'll willingly swear to every day for the rest of my life. "And I'm yours."

Her words send a thrill through me, so strong I'm surprised I'm still standing. It's too much for Devlin and he sweeps in, claiming her lips in a long, lush kiss. I watch them both, slight envy wavering through the bond but mostly satisfaction. Harper moans as Devlin sucks on her bottom lip, and the scent of honey makes my cock come to attention. Before we can get too wound up, though, a voice interrupts us.

"Ahem. Sorry to interrupt, but…"

Harper blushes, realizing that Ezra is still here. I suppress a groan of frustration and palm my cock casually through my pants, rearranging myself so I don't give everyone a show. I catch Rogue doing the same and we exchange a wry grin.

Chapter Thirty-Eight
Harper

Happiness fills me as I stare around at my pack. *Mine.* I can't believe I got it so, so wrong. One look at the horror in their faces and I just knew.

Way to jump to fucking conclusions, Harper.

Rogue scoops me up and I laugh lightly, linking my arms around his neck. "Well, hello there," I tease, and his mouth quirks upwards at one side. I poke it gently.

He settles firmly in the chair with me tucked securely into his lap. I wish I had my blanket. This would be the perfect snuggle space. I've barely thought the words when Ace appears, a fluffy blanket in his hands. He winks at me as I pretty much snatch it from him. It must be his, and I breathe in his fresh sea salt and driftwood scent as I huddle into it. Between Ace's scent and Rogue's fresh grass, I feel cocooned. Ezra clears his throat again and I offer him an apologetic smile.

"I'm glad it was a misunderstanding," he whispers to me like we're the only two in the room, and I smile at him in thanks.

"Me too," I murmur back as Rogue runs his palm over my legs. He tickles lightly, and I kick out with a gasp of laughter.

"Sorry," he murmurs, kissing my forehead. "I just need to make sure you're alright."

My breath hitches and I turn my face to him, raising up for a kiss. His mouth meets mine carefully, gently pressing the top and then the bottom with soft touches. It sends warmth rushing through me and I hope it'll lead to more later. Way later. When Ezra isn't staring at us with exasperation.

He shakes his head, a grin lining his weathered face. "I forget how the mating process can get."

My head pops up as I nearly headbutt Rogue in the chin. Distractedly giving it an apologetic rub, I ask, "What do you mean?"

I have no idea what a mating process is, but I like the sound of it.

Ezra hums lightly as the guys settle down.

"A true mating bond is what Ivy and I had together."

A tear of sorrow rips through me at the reminder of his loss and I burrow my nose into Rogue's throat, breathing in his scent for reassurance as his hand tightens on me.

"I told you when the government ordered the forced detainment of omegas, many of the alpha packs went crazy. This was because a lot of these packs had true mating bonds with their omega."

Curiosity thrums through me as I remember his words upstairs. I know that the bitemark is a type of bonding. It forces the omega to bend completely to the will of the alpha, offering them greater leverage and control. This doesn't sound like that though. I notice the pack sitting up straighter and listening intently.

"A mating bond develops over time. It can't be forced, and it doesn't happen for every pack. There is no clear checklist of what you do to induce a mating bond, although there are some typical steps that you might expect. It just…happens. It starts with being drawn to each other, and if given the attention it needs, then a true bond will form. Call it, love, fate, whatever you like." Ezra smiles, a touch of sadness in his expression.

"As the bond develops, the omega and alphas involved start to exhibit certain behaviors. Alphas become more prone to aggression outside of the pack, highly protective of their potential mate and very alert to their needs."

I meet Ace's wide-eyed glance and we both look down at the blanket.

Ezra continues. "Omegas, on the other hand, can see quite dramatic developments. Their scent deepens and they become very prone to nesting, wanting quiet, contained spaces. This becomes a crucial omega need when they move into a natural heat." I flinch and Ezra shakes his head, answering the question that sits on the edge of my tongue.

"Not an artificial heat," he clarifies softly, and my pack growls in unison at the reminder. "A natural heat is just that – completely natural. Omegas used to have heats fairly regularly, normally a few times a year, but only when the mating bond was complete. This would normally be when pregnancy would occur. The final step of establishing the mating bond is a mutual bite during heat. Alphas place their bites on their omega, and the omega places their bite on the alpha, creating the final strand of the bond and linking the two together."

My eyes widen as I imagine my pack wearing my bite. *I want that.*

"The bond also causes changes to hormone levels for both alpha and omega. They can find themselves acting irrationally, to say the least. You must remember that omega biology is different to a beta. They *need* to connect with their alphas. If this need is not met, it can cause physical pain and damage to an omega. It can be incredibly dangerous, particularly during a heat."

I sink back against Rogue, thinking over this new information. Devlin leans forward. "Ezra, how does the creed fit into this?" I flinch slightly at the mention.

Ezra grimaces, his hands tightening on the arm of the chair. "The government took everything that was pure and natural about the mating bond and bastardized it. The rules of the creed take their origins from the true bonding process. Any mention of the mating bonds was wiped out after the omega war. It didn't fit their narrative."

I imagine omegas stolen from their homes and forced into compounds, ripped from their children and families, and forced to obey a set of rules that made a mockery of everything they lived for. "That's so cruel," I breathe, and Ezra nods in agreement.

"The omega creed was the final nail in the coffin for mating bonds," he says softly. "It made it almost impossible for any bond to take root and grow. How could it, when the omegas were being abused so badly? Bonds need affection, love and support to grow. It relies on the alpha meeting the needs of the omega. The creed stripped all of that away. Of course, that was the whole point. It allowed the Government to share omegas as they pleased, either through gifting them to packs or through the heat nests. So much easier for them without angry packs and bond mates coming after them."

Ace shifts. "Ivy – my grandmother. You were bonded mates."

"We were," Ezra says. "When the bond was complete, I felt her inside me every day we were apart. We could push emotion to each other in much a similar way as you can through your pack bond." Ace nods.

"It also meant that I knew the moment she was no longer on this earth. There is no pain like it," he finishes quietly.

We fall into silence for a few minutes, each of us deep in thought. Desperation pulses through me at the thought of a bond like the one Ezra has described. I want to be joined to this pack in that way.

"And you think that this might be on the cards for us?" Gabe asks.

Ezra peers around at us in surprise. "On the cards?" he says. "You're already well on the way. It's quite clear from your behaviors."

CHAPTER THIRTY-NINE
HARPER

A *mating bond.* My hand slips down to my chest as the pack lets out simultaneous expressions of shock and surprise.

I should be shocked, but I'm not. This feels…right. Like it was always meant to be. I glance around at them and see everybody looking at me.

"I… this doesn't feel like a bad thing to me." My voice comes out too high. Maybe it does to them? A spike of fear stabs into my heart. Maybe they don't want a mating bond with me.

I suddenly feel like I'm trapping them. My eyes drop to the ground, emotion creating a lump in my throat. Tears spring to my eyes and I let out a sniffle. Knees appear in front of me and I glance up at Devlin as he slides his arms around me. "What is it, princess?" he asks urgently, searching my face worriedly. "Do you not want this?" Rogue growls behind me.

"I do," I whisper, staring at him. "I want this, Devlin. With you. With all of you." Devlin's finger catches a tear from my cheek. "Then why the tears?"

"It's so much to ask," I say quietly. His brows lower in

confusion, so I explain. "You've already done so much for me. With the compound, and the creed. This just seems like it's too much to wish for."

Dev's arms tighten around me, and he growls. My back snaps straight as he barks at me, my eyes flying wide. Devlin is *pissed*.

"Now, you listen to me," he growls. "I don't care about the creed or the damned Omega Compound. We can move away if we need to, somewhere they'll never find us. The only thing we care about is you."

He leans in, nuzzling my cheek and I choke back a hiccup, hope filling me.

"The only thing this pack needs is you, princess," he whispers in my ear. "Everything else is just background noise."

I bury my face in my hands as the sob slips out. His words settle my anxiety in a way that makes me realize I've been hiding how much this has bothered me. I've flipped this pack's lives upside down and they're risking everything, just so I can have a normal life. If the government found out about our relationship, I'd be taken away and they would be imprisoned, or worse, for breaking the creed.

Rogue releases me to Devlin and he sits down with me in his lap, holding me tightly and running his hand up and down my back. Gabe throws himself down next to me, hesitantly reaching out his hand and beaming at me when I grab it, holding it tightly. Ace and Rogue look like they want in, too, but this couch really isn't big enough for all five of us.

Ezra watches us with interest. "Harper, I think that the bond may be affecting your hormone levels."

Realization hits me and I nod. "I've been more emotional lately, quicker to react to things badly." My thoughts briefly touch on the freezer and I shudder, Devlin tightening his grip on me.

"The bond would certainly explain it." Ezra thinks for a

second. "During the mating process, omegas need to feel safe, and secure. This applies both physically and emotionally. Harper, do you have a nest?"

My mind short-circuits. "No," I breathe softly as Devlin tenses beneath me.

I think back to my conversation with Ace and Gabe. I suddenly want a nest, a proper nest, more than I've ever wanted anything in my life.

"I've been feeling more sensitive towards bright lights and large spaces. And I've been sort of… collecting… blankets. And bedding. And, um, clothes?"

All four men turn towards me.

"Is that where my shirts have been disappearing to?" Rogue asks.

"And my jumpers?" Gabe quirks a brow at me.

Ace hums. "I'm missing quite a few pairs of boxers…"

My cheeks flame and I squeal, "that wasn't me!"

Ace grins and I notice Gabe blushing a furious shade of scarlet next to me. Hmm… interesting. Reminding myself to have a little chat with him later, I decide that this conversation has gotten way out of hand.

"So, I could maybe have a real nest?" I ask hopefully. *Say yes. Please say yes.* Rogue's head turns towards me.

"Sweetheart, you can have anything you want," he says, chiding me. "Why didn't you tell us you wanted a nest?"

I shrug, avoiding his eyes. Truthfully, I didn't even think about it. Nests are so frowned upon for omegas, I genuinely didn't think it was an option.

Legally, I'm not even allowed to own a blanket. I mean, Jeez. What does the government think we're gonna do, take over the world, one soft furnishing at a time?

Rogue frowns at me, that delicious crease telling me I'm in for a world of trouble later. Maybe we'll repeat the spanking. I close my legs quickly before any of them can catch my scent.

"So, nesting," Gabe nods, rubbing my hand. "We can do that. What else?"

"Gifts," Ezra says firmly, and my ears prick up. What's this now?

"Gifts?" Devlin says, straightening and pulling me with him. He sounds slightly befuddled.

"It means that omegas need to feel cherished. Adored. Courting gifts are an important part of the process." I squeak a little at this, a warm feeling sending tingles down my arms. I'm *really* liking the sound of this.

Rogue frowns and turns to me. "We really haven't been good alphas to you, have we, love?" I immediately protest. I don't think that. I don't want them to think that. My whole life has changed since I came here. This pack is absolutely everything to me.

"I don't need fancy presents and nests to feel wanted, Rogue." I mean it, but a small lump appears in my throat, my body protesting. I bite my lip, torn. Ezra leans forward, a knowing smile on his face as he picks up on my discomfort.

"I understand that you mean that, Harper, but there are certain things that your physiology demands. As an omega, you *need* your alphas to show that they can provide for you. It builds a feeling of safety, security. They'll have similar feelings too. This is just part of the process, but it certainly doesn't replace the relationships you've built."

Okay. I can work with that.

CHAPTER FORTY
ACE

Harper lets out an oomph as she crashes down to the floor, my punch catching her in the stomach.

"Shit!" My heart jumps into my throat and I rush forward. She's already pulling herself up, eyes blazing with determination as she backs away from me.

"Again."

Demanding little omega. Her kitten-clawed attitude makes me want to bite. Preferably without any clothes on.

I hold up a hand to stop her before she tries to dropkick me.

"Sweetheart, give me a second. I literally just punched you in the stomach." *I* need a fucking second. Trying to teach Harper self-defense is harder than I thought it would be.

Having Harper here, her delicately spiced scent filling the room, is playing fucking havoc on my instincts. I want to push her down to the mat and cover her, sliding my hand down to feel the slick between her thighs. My knot is pulsing, uncomfortably thick in my workout sweats. It goes against every instinct I have to put her in any position where she has to defend herself. Devlin came to our first session, and I kicked him out after ten minutes. I thought he was going to rip my throat out.

Her eyes, deep pools of amber in the afternoon light, darken even more and I scent honey on my tongue. Our girl's getting wound up.

Scoffing at me, she says, "Don't be such a baby. You barely touched me." I bite back a growl, loving how she's opened up enough to play with us like this. She tries to rush me again and wobbles, overestimating her steps. I easily hook her ankle as she careens past me and flip us both down, cushioning her fall with my body. She lands with her knees astride my hips, plump lips pursed in a shocked 'o'.

I smirk at her. "I win. What do I get?"

I thrust my hips up, groaning as my knot swells, begging to be locked into her honeyed warmth. Harper shudders and her eyes roll back slightly as her hips undulate. She's a fucking goddess, hair blazing down her back in a tight braid, face raised to the sunshine. She's starting to fill out with the help of some proper meals, and her curves make my mouth water. I want to worship at her goddamned temple. Lay everything I have at her feet in sacrifice.

The last few weeks have been… blissful. We closed the world out and spent time getting to know each other properly. It was fucking hard at first. Like really awkward family therapy. But we talked it out. Harper walked us through everything she'd heard that night, and we showed her the wooden cross that the compound had sent. My fists clench as I remember the look on her face when she saw it. Like it was her worst nightmare come to life.

So we handed her an axe and helped her burn it to fucking cinders in the garden.

Watching her then as the firelight shimmered in her eyes – it was like we'd handed her something precious. A weight lifted off her shoulders.

She told us how worried she was about artificial heats. Now that we know, we'll be even more careful with our words in future. Harper has enough worries, without that one eating at her as well.

Talking of worries… I reach up and push back a lock of damp hair from her forehead. Seeing the expression on my face, she grimaces.

"It's not time yet," she argues. The soft whine in her voice makes me pull her hips down, and we both moan as I thrust into her softness.

"It is," I croak. Clearing my voice, I sit up, pulling her to me for a deep kiss with my hand locked around the back of her neck. Breaking away, I push our foreheads together, breathing in her scent. Letting it ground me.

Because tonight is the gala, and it's going to be fucking horrendous. Fear twists in my stomach at the thought of Harper being anywhere near the board members of the Omega Compound.

"We don't have to, little omega," I whisper.

"Yes, we do," she whispers back to me. Her voice shakes slightly, and I run my hands up and down her back in firm strokes until she softens.

I know why we're going. But I don't fucking like it.

We all clearly feel the same. We're all dressed and waiting at the bottom of the stairs. Tension drenches the walls with our scents, sharp and acidic. Rogue is pacing, Devlin is casually sliding so many weapons into place that I'm not sure how he's even going to walk, and Gabe is stressing.

"I should go and help her," he starts, and I grab his hand.

"No. She said she wanted to do it."

His hand feels warm in mine and my fingers gently trace

his callouses. I've missed these hands so much over the past few months. He might be a little more scarred, but my Gabe is definitely coming back. And it's all down to our little omega.

Rogue turns to face the staircase and we all follow suit.

All of us stop short. Devlin curses. My mouth dries as Harper elegantly makes her way downstairs.

She's a fucking vision.

Her hair is braided back into a low crown, the intricate weaving dotted with small flowers. Red curls fall around her face, framing it perfectly, and she's lined her eyes with black kohl, giving her a distinctively feline look. I inhale sharply as I take in her dress. Emerald green works perfectly with the fire in her hair, two large slits running up either side. It's pretty clear that she's not wearing any underwear.

Matching growls rumble through the pack as our agitation snaps the air with sharp scents. Devlin shoulders his way forward, scowling.

"You are *not* wearing that," he barks. When Harper takes a step back, responding to the dominance in his tone, we all turn our disapproval on him, and he crosses his arms defensively.

"I am not taking her into that wolves den wearing *that*," he hisses to us. "We'll be fucking overrun before we even get to our table."

Harper matches his firm expression, crossing her arms back and fixing him with a scowl.

"I *have* to wear this," she snaps. "It's the dress provided by the compound. I'd draw far more attention if I didn't wear it."

Devlin's shoulders slump, and he steps up to her. He holds out his arms and Harper darts into them, burrowing her face into his shirt.

"It's just a few hours, Dev," she whispers. "In and out, right?"

"I don't like it," he grumbles. "Something feels off."

"Like what?" I ask. I've learned too many times not to doubt Devlin's instincts.

"I don't know, but it's putting me on edge. We need to be tight and stay together."

Rogue nods determinedly and extracts Harper, tucking her under his arm protectively.

"Let's go over it one more time before we go. From the top."

CHAPTER FORTY-ONE
ROGUE

I step out of the truck and throw my keys at the valet.

"We won't be staying long," I tell him, and he nods as the rest of the pack exits, slamming doors. Devlin moves past me, his vacant mask back in place as he pushes down the anger I can feel, swelling the bond from four directions. Popping open the boot, he helps Harper get out of her cage.

I press my lips together. We can't afford for anything to go wrong tonight. All of us have to play our part.

And Harper has to play the biggest part of all.

She elegantly sinks to her knees at the end of the red carpet, arranging the slits in her emerald dress so she can move as much as she can. Reaching into my pocket, my hands grasp the chain tightly. Breathing in and out, I count to five and shove my feelings back down. It goes against every instinct I have to move over to her and clip the chain to her collar. She doesn't look up at me, doesn't speak, keeping her head down obediently. It grates at me, even though this is what we agreed.

One hour, I tell myself. Two, max. And then we can get her away from here.

Ace and Gabe move ahead of us. Gabe pauses, hesitation

making him turn back before Ace grabs his hand and tows him forward.

I loop the leather strap around my wrist loosely as Dev takes up his position next to me. Glancing down at Harper, her vulnerable nape and scars revealed with her hair up, I clench my teeth.

"We can do this," I whisper. Devlin nods next to me.

"Let's get on with it."

The ballroom is a heaving mass of activity. An orchestra plays an instrumental waltz from a raised platform. Only a handful of couples are on the dancefloor though. Tonight is about alliances, relationships, and power. The majority of guests flit from candlelit table to table, kissing cheeks perfunctorily and murmuring empty platitudes.

Ace and Gabe finish examining the table arrangements and head across the room, frustration lining their shoulders. I bite down a curse as Dev hisses.

"This is intentional," he mutters as we move slowly to a brightly lit table in the center of the room, where we'll be seen from every angle. There's nowhere for us to hide.

Harper shuffles obediently just behind my right leg, keeping close. As we reach our arranged seats, a wave of juniper sweeps over us, announcing the arrival of a tall, broad-shouldered alpha with a mischievous grin.

"Rogue," Jackson acknowledges, a twinkle in his eye. I can feel his curiosity as he glances down to Harper, silent and perfectly positioned at my side.

"Jack," Devlin barks, the barest civility in his voice. "Do we have you to thank for this?"

Dev gestures at the table and Jackson belts out a laugh, the loudness turning several couples towards us nearby.

"Well, we couldn't have the Winter pack here and not include your new addition, could we?" Jack smirks at Devlin, who ignores him and turns to me.

"I'll get drinks," he bites, and strides off to the bar. Ace and Gabe move in closer, surreptitiously placing themselves behind Harper in practiced nonchalance.

Jackson leans into me, and I resist the urge to curl my lip as he invades my space. Our boss has always liked to press our buttons. He calls it character-building. We call it general assholery.

I've never considered him sleazy, but then, I've never seen him around women. My hand tightens on Harper's leash as he looks down at her, a lecherous glaze entering his eye as he licks his lips.

"I understand the radio silence now," he murmurs. "Quite the catch, your new omega. She smells… edible. You'll let me know if you plan to share?"

Three matching growls slip out at his words. Harper keeps her head down, but the chain shakes lightly in my hand, her scent shifting to the sour tang of fear.

I know some alphas rent their omegas out for extra funds. Many will pay handsomely for the chance to knot an omega. Bile rises, and I force it down as Jackson raises a brow at our dominant display.

"I'm afraid we won't be looking at that just yet," I force out, the words feeling like razors in my throat. I push out a smirk to add to the lie. "We're only just breaking her in, after all."

The words taste like ash on my tongue. But Jackson sniggers, taking the bait.

"I can understand that." He casts a last look at Harper, eyes zoning in on the scars on her back. They're on full display, her dress backless.

He claps me on the shoulder. "I like to play with broken things. Let me know when you change your mind."

With a nod to Ace and ignoring Gabe altogether, he takes his leave.

I run my hand gently over Harper's head, just once. A noise slips out of her and as I take my seat, she shuffles closer, leaning in to place her head on my thigh.

Devlin reappears, drinks in his hands. He passes them out with a glare on his face. "Omegas aren't permitted to drink here." He spits the words out and I push calming vibes at him down the bond, wordlessly warning him to be careful. I'm a little concerned at the tension thrumming through him. We're all on edge this evening though.

We all take our seats. Jackson is just the first visitor. A steady stream of alphas visit our table, empty words on their lips and lustful eyes planted firmly on Harper. We receive several offers, including one tall, older alpha who offers to swap Harper with his own omega, a shaking black-haired girl with shackles on her ankles and fear staining her bruised face. I let Devlin see that one off.

Harper stiffens, a whine of pure fear drawing from her and making us all stand as we scan for the threat. The scent of bitter citrus reaches my nose and Devlin's anger level ratchets up, making us all vibrate with tension.

This fucking asshole.

Jason pushes his way between two alphas who snap at him for his rudeness. He ignores them, a smirk on his face as he beelines towards us. Fucking hell. If I'd known he'd be here, I would have rejected the invite and fuck the consequences.

Harper pushes her face into my leg as she fights down her panic, and I stroke my hand over her soothingly as Jason stares at her with beady eyes. Her scent pulses, a burst of strong cinnamon that surprises me in its intensity. It's like a punch to my stomach, and my nostrils flare. I pray that she'll keep it together. This asshole would love nothing more than to drag her back to the clutches of the compound.

"Well, hello there," he smirks at us all. He's either brazen as fuck or just plain stupid, because the vibes coming off our table are very much *take-another-step-and-we'll-rip-your-fucking-throat-out.*

"We've met previously," he holds out a hand to Devlin, who ignores it completely. "I'm Jason Harding."

"We know who you are," I cut in before Devlin can blow it. "What do you want?"

A snarl accompanies the end of my words, and the smirk slips off Jason's face. He holds up his hands placatingly.

"Well now, fellas, no need for all of this posturing. I was just coming along to see how 792 is settling into her new arrangements. I hope that her training has been a… benefit… to you?"

His eyes slide to Harper, her face nestled into my leg.

"Well, I'm not sure," I remark, choosing my words carefully. "We wanted a functional omega. The water torture may have been a tad overkill."

Jason opens his mouth to respond, a sour look on his face, but I cut him off.

"Nevertheless, she's obedient and well-behaved. We're quite pleased."

Jason nods, his eyes still on Harper. There's a glint in his eye that I don't like. What's this fucker's angle?

"You won't mind if I just check, will you? Professional pride and all that."

The fuck? Before I can respond, he snaps a word and our whole plan falls completely to shit.

"*Present*," he snaps, and Harper's fear rips into our pack like a bomb.

I'm too shocked to stop Devlin as he flies out of his seat, his fist landing in Jason's face. Screams and shouts ring out from across the ballroom as they both fly back, crashing into another table and sending glass and tableware flying. Devlin rips Jason off and drags him to the floor, locking his hands around Jason's neck as he wheezes.

"*Ours,*" Devlin snarls. Ace throws himself across to rip Devlin away, my hands tied with Harper at my side. I entangle my hands quickly, passing the leash to Gabe and diving into the melee.

Fuck, this is bad. Everybody is watching us make a show over our omega. This is attention we absolutely didn't need.

Grabbing Devlin by the hair, I twist to pull him away. He turns on me, snarling, but I push a wave of dominance down the bond and meet his eyes steadily at the same time.

"Submit," I order, my voice a whip. Dev fights it for a moment before he sags, showing me his throat. I can feel him shaking, realization setting in. I'm not entirely sure it's his fault though. We've all been feeling on edge thanks to the mating bond.

Jason wheezes out a laugh as he crawls away.

"Interesting response to your omega. Been getting a little closer than you should have been?" His words are taunting, and I grab Devlin's chin, keeping his eyes on me as tension ripples through him. I force down the urge to rip that fucker's head off.

I have to stay calm.

Turning, I fix my gaze on Jason, raising my voice so the tables around us can hear. Damage control.

"You taunt a dominant alpha, you deserve everything you get."

Jason splutters, but there are a few agreeing nods from around us. More than one table is watching us with pursed lips and suspicion though.

Turning to check on Harper, I see Gabe standing in a defensive position, with the leash dangling loosely from his hand. I follow his eyes down, and my heart breaks. I want to turn around and let Devlin loose, join with him in ripping Jason to pieces so no part of him can touch our girl again.

Harper's face is pressed into the ground, her elegant hair tumbling loosely from its position, flowers scattered on the ground. Her arms are stretched out in front of her, white knuckles clutching at the carpet, and her ass is up as she presents herself exactly how Jason demanded. The fear running through her makes her tremble, the echo running through her whole body. Her scent hits me like a hammer, and I curse, my steps faltering as I try to reach her. It's so strong that alphas are circling, sniffing hungrily at the air.

A dangerous tension crackles, the threat of alphas who want to *rut*.

Her scent is spiking, sharp waves of cinnamon and orange sweeping over us. My heart climbs up my throat as she whines, the sound low, pained and needing.

It's a fucking heat spike, just like Ezra warned us.

We have to leave. *Now.*

I keep a tight hold on Devlin, dragging him over to them, Ace following behind. Growls ripple as they both catch the full impact of Harper's spike, and Devlin darts ahead of me, trying to get past Gabe as he nudges Harper behind him. Devlin isn't acting rationally right now.

"Enough," I hiss as I reach them. Gabe looks lust-drunk but steady enough, and I motion for him to stay close to Harper. Grabbing Devlin by the shoulders, I redirect him to face the silent room, full of alphas inching closer to us with lust in their eyes.

"Clear a path," I say urgently. The haze seems to clear as he shakes himself free, jaw clenching as he takes in the danger we're in with a nod.

With Devlin making space, I try to get Gabe and Harper moving, keeping my hands free in case we need to fight. Gabe gently tugs on the leash, but Harper doesn't move. Her fear has her frozen to the ground, and the rippling need of her scent is growing by the second.

"Omega," I bark, hating that I have to use it. Her spine straightens with a snap and I scent arousal trickling from her as she whines.

"Follow Gabe."

An alpha snarls at Dev, trying to edge around him. We'll be surrounded if we don't get clear now, and then we'll have to fight our way out. Making a snap decision, I scoop Harper up into my arms and start shouldering through the crowd. Ace follows, snarling at anyone who reaches out.

We push our way out of the ballroom, and I break into a run. The valet I handed my keys to stares at us as we burst through the doors, retracing our steps.

"Where's our truck?" I bark at him. He raises a trembling hand, pointing to the parking area as Ace rips the keys from his fingers.

His half-hearted offer to go and get it falls away as we sprint into the darkened lot. Ace hits the button and the truck lights up.

We throw ourselves in, Ace sliding into the driving seat as I pull myself into the backseat, Harper breaking apart in my arms.

"Go!" I order and our tires spin as Ace shoots out of the lot like the hounds of hell are after him.

Harper's scent fills the space around us and I curse. She's incoherent, moans falling from her lips as she throws her head back, hips pumping.

Her need calls to all of us, and Ace curses as the van swerves slightly.

"Keep it together," I snap hoarsely.

Christ, it's so fucking strong. Is this a full heat? My mind becomes clouded as her need claws at my insides, raking up and down. My cock is rock hard and leaking pre-cum in a steady flow, my trousers dampening as we speed towards the house. We're a good twenty minutes away still, and Harper whines, an edge of pain in her throat. She needs soothing now.

"Fuck." I pull her up onto my lap. "Devlin," I snap. He's clutching the arm of his seat, fists clenching so hard the plastic is cracking. His head snaps up to me before moving to Harper and softening. He slides off his seat, pulling himself forward and starting to undo his trousers.

Gabe's eyes widen. "But—," he starts.

"She's in pain," I whip back at him, yanking Harper's dress up until her bare pussy gleams in the moonlight through the window. She moans again and her slick pours from her. Dev inhales, his nostrils flaring and a growl pulled from deep in his chest. *"Need."*

"Now, Devlin," I snap. I'd do it in a heartbeat, but I need to try and keep it together for the pack.

Using my knees, I push her legs wider and Dev buries his head between her creamy thighs. Harper cries out at his touch, her spicy scent deepening as she bucks her hips wildly. Devlin grabs her hands and holds her still as he lashes her frantically with his tongue, dipping in and out of her clenching core until she trembles and comes in a gush. Dev pulls back, his face glistening with her juices and his face ravaged with want as we wait to see if she's eased.

Within seconds, she's struggling in my arms again. Her eyes flicker open and she searches wildly until I turn her head and her eyes land on me. Her pupils are so wide I can barely see any amber at all.

"It hurts," she whimpers. "Help me."

"We've got you, love."

Devlin has his cock in his hand, smearing fluids as he jerks it up and down. Grabbing Harper behind her knees, he slides her body forward and impales her with one thrust as she throws her head back in a needy wail. Her head lands between my thighs and I reach down, stroking her cheeks gently as Devlin pumps into her with a frantic rhythm.

Wordless cries of pleasure fall from her lips. Her hand grabs onto my thigh and she buries her face in it as Devlin rocks, not slowing his pace.

"So, fucking, tight," he curses. "Clenching me like a fucking glove, princess."

Harper whines at his words. Gabe leans in from my other side and puts his fingers to her clit, rubbing it in fast circles as Harper screams out in pleasure.

"That's it, sweetheart," Gabe murmurs to her. "Doing so good. Such a good omega."

Devlin shouts as Harper twists, slick flowing out of her as she whimpers through a second orgasm. Pushing forward, Devlin's knot slides into her, the wet sound sending waves of need down my spine as they lock into place, bodies completely connected. I swallow, hard.

Ace is holding up like a trooper in the front, breaking all kinds of speed limits as he whips the van through our gates and pulls to a stop outside. He throws the door open, chucking himself out. I can hear him breathing heavily as he inhales deep gulps of fresh air.

Harper's scent finally starts to soften, and we all slump with relief. Carefully, I lift her shoulders and Dev wraps his arms around her, dragging her so her front is pressed against his chest. Her head lolls sleepily as she murmurs his name, nuzzling into his neck.

Dev carefully climbs down, Harper wrapped around him like a bow with his knot still deep inside her. He slowly moves to the door, Ace unlocking it and flicking lights on.

Gabe moves past me and shoots straight to Ace, locking him into a deep kiss as he presses his lower half into him. They stumble back and disappear.

Sighing, I throw my head back against the car seat.

What a fucking shit show.

Heading into the house, I'm greeted with a mixture of arousal and frustration. I can hear Gabe and Ace going at it from here, Gabe's moans punctuated with short sharp gasps as they work the need out of their bodies.

There's nothing from Harper and Devlin, and I assume he's taken them both off to bed until the knot settles and Harper comes around.

Locking the main door, I move around and check all the locks before sliding into the office. I have a feeling we might get a visit from the compound, thanks to our little stunt this evening. I try to call my father, but he doesn't pick up. I spoke to him yesterday and he told me he was arranging the paperwork to sign Harper over to us permanently, but he's refused to give me any more information about his strange bahavior at the compound. He did promise to look out for Gabrielle and Molly, though.

A distinctly feminine moan reaches my ears, and I clench my fists. My erection is still nudging me insistently, ripples of need urging me to go up and sink myself into the soft omega upstairs. I want her all to myself when I finally take her, though.

Instead, I head to the shower and turn it on. *Cold.*

CHAPTER FORTY-TWO

HARPER

My eyes flicker up and down, drowsiness threatening to close them again. I'm so warm. Turning, a male grumble tugs at me and arms wrap me in a smoky-scented embrace. Devlin. I smile, rubbing my face against his chest.

Something nudges at my consciousness. Something important.

Last night. The gala.

"Devlin!" I gasp, my eyes flying open. He's alert in an instant, pulling me against him as he sits up. "Fuck, princess," he says, searching my face. "Are you ok?"

"I'm fine," I say, but there's a tremble in my voice. I wiggle out of his warmth and throw myself out of bed, searching for clothes. Finding Dev's shirt thrown on the floor carelessly, I shrug it on, and my eyes roll back slightly at the scent coming off it. Oh yeah. I definitely heat spiked. Warmth fills my belly at the thought, but the gut-wrenching need from last night has definitely passed.

"We need to get the others," Dev says, clearly sensing my panic. I nod, frantically doing up the buttons.

"Jason will report us," my voice shakes as we lock eyes. "The Compound will come for me."

Devlin follows my lead, grabbing jeans and tugging them on. We burst out of the room and Dev bangs on Rogue's door while I tap on Ace's. A rumpled Ace opens it, lips curling in a grin when he sees me.

"Little omega," he says, a rough purr in his voice that makes me lean towards him. "Are you feeling better?"

Gabe appears behind him, yawning, and a smile spreads over my face despite the worry in my chest. He blushes when I catch his eye.

Rogue calls from down the hallway. "We need to speak to my father. Harper is worried about the compound pulling us in for last night. Time for damage control."

Gabe and Ace straighten immediately, tension locking their spines.

"Like fuck are they taking you anywhere," Gabe snaps, stepping forward and running his hands up and down my arms soothingly.

"Don't worry," he whispers, tugging me into an embrace. "Rogue will be able to sort it with Christian."

My stomach is churning, nausea rising up as I remember the carnage. Jason won't let the humiliation go. Not a chance in hell.

We pile down into the kitchen, Ace pulling me onto his lap while Gabe puts the coffee on. I start to feel a little foolish as I look around at them all.

"Sorry," I whisper, and they all turn to look at me in surprise. "I woke up and just panicked."

Ace rubs my back in soothing circles. "Don't stress, little omega. You might be right, but it's nothing we won't be able to sort out, I'm sure."

"I'll call my father now." Rogue pulls out his phone and

starts to dial, but there's a tap on the door. Devlin pales, searching for his phone.

"I didn't set the perimeter alarms last night," he whispers. Because of my heat spike.

We all tense. Fear forms a lump in my stomach, and I look around. Rogue and Devlin exchange a look.

"I'll get it," Rogue says, standing up. He comes over to me and kisses the top of my head, his hand cupping my cheek gently.

"Better get down, sweetheart, just in case."

I nod and slide off Ace's lap, dropping to my knees next to his chair. Panic sends shivers down my limbs but I bite it back. The pack are right. If there are any issues, Rogue's father will hopefully help us sort them out.

Devlin gets up, yanking open drawers and pulling out a gun. He throws one to Ace, who checks it and slots in the cartridge Dev tosses. Devlin looks at Gabe, who shrugs and points a finger at the knife set.

Rogue's mouth tightens, but he doesn't say anything.

We all listen as he moves out to the hallway, pulling open the main door. There's a buzz of male voices, and I whimper. Ace strokes my hair gently, the movement soothing the buzz in my veins, but the ball of fear in my stomach is telling me that something is very wrong.

Rogue's voice rises. "Is this really necessary, gentlemen?"

Devlin cocks his head, listening. "It's a full check," he whispers. There's a hint of fear in his voice and we lock eyes.

The bedding. The clothes. Everything *reeks* of me, especially after last night. Devlin realizes at the same time and pales as Ace curses. I close my eyes.

They'll take me back.

Rogue steps into the kitchen, features masked with bored indifference, but his green eyes glitter with anger and worry.

"The compound is carrying out a check on the property," he announces. "We've had no notice, and I'll be calling my father to confirm," he says, swinging his gaze to the large male who's walked in behind him.

"You can do that," the guard agrees. "In the meantime, I'll need you all to exit the house whilst we conduct our checks."

"Seems a bit overkill," Ace mutters. None of the pack argues, and we all head outside. I shuffle on my knees, ignoring the sting of the gravel. Rogue can't carry me today.

I'm looking at the floor, so Devlin's startled shout makes me jump. My eyes shoot up and I see Rogue on his knees directly ahead of me. He's swaying, shaking his head frantically as he tries to shake off whatever they've hit him with.

Male grunts and thuds sound around me, and forgetting any notion of keeping my head down, I swing around in horror. Gabe and Ace have collapsed. There are *needles* sticking out of their necks.

Devlin staggers towards me, his face filled with horror. "Harper," he wheezes. He drops down to one knee as he reaches out to me. "Run," he breathes. "*Run*, princess."

He barks out the last part before he drops.

I don't think. I don't breathe.

I *run*.

Scrambling to my feet, I ignore the shouts and take off. Feet flying, I head straight for the forest, zig-zagging in case they decide to shoot at me.

They pull themselves together, shouts indicating that at least a few are following me, but I'm fast.

My feet run over twigs, stones, thorns catching my legs. All I have is Devlin's shirt. My eyes blur and tears fall as I crash through the bushes.

Devlin. Rogue. Ace. Gabe. I moan, the tugging inside me begging me to stop, to turn around.

Devlin's bark keeps me running until eventually, I have to stop. I drop my hands to my knees as I gasp for breath. Pain radiating up my legs tells me my feet are badly cut up, and I shiver at the cold.

I don't know what to do. I don't know where to go.

If I can hide long enough, I could try and make it back to the house. I could call Ezra.

The half-baked plan makes me feel a little better, and I look around for a good hiding place. I can't run much further. The heat-spike from last night is still filtering out of my system, making me even weaker than I normally would be.

Spotting a tree with a small hole at the base, I head over to it and try to squeeze myself inside, wincing as the bark scrapes along my arms. It's tight, but I manage it. Scrabbling at the dirt with my hand, I try to rub as much as I can over myself. Devlin's white shirt will stand out like a sore thumb if anyone comes this way. I do the same with my hair and tuck it into the back of the shirt, before curling up.

I bury my face in my hands and finally let the fear in. What have they done to my pack?

I hope it's just a tranquilizer, but what if it's something else? What if one of them reacts badly?

My body shakes with the urge to crawl out of my space and go right back to them. I need to make sure they're okay. The urges batter at my body and my scent rises up, acrid with fear and longing.

Shit. My scent.

What if they're tracking it?

Just as the thought crosses my mind, there's a shuffling sound. I stay completely still, praying that the mud and my small hole is enough to hide me. I bite my lip until I taste blood, forcing the fear down.

Don't find me. Please don't find me.

I fight to keep my breathing even.

The sounds move away, and I close my eyes in relief.

A snout pushes into the hole, scrabbling paws trying to squeeze through. Outside, a chorus of howls rise up into the air.

They've found me.

I press myself back against the wood. There's no way I can get out of here. The dogs will track me if they don't go for me first.

I frantically look around, but I'm trapped.

The minutes tick by, the dogs circling outside with excited yips, occasionally trying to wrestle their way in.

I have no weapons. No alphas. No shoes.

When a hand eventually reaches in, I sink my teeth into it. The man pulls it back with a shout of anger and I fling myself out of the small space, muscles aching from being folded in for too long.

I don't make it three steps before I'm tackled, my chin smashing into the ground as I cry out in pain. A familiar scent buries through my brain, and my terror shoots up.

Bitter, bitter lemon.

"Hello, 792," Jason whispers, nuzzling my neck. "You've been *such* a bad girl."

My body thrashes frantically as I try to get away, but one bark from him and I relax, my bones unclenching as I sink into the dirt.

He pulls me up, grabbing my collar.

"Just like old times," he smirks. He's still wearing the clothes he wore to the gala last night.

I rear back and spit as hard as I can. My saliva hits his cheek. The smirk slides off his face.

"Stupid bitch," he hisses. "Stupid little omega."

I hiss at him. "Don't fucking call me that."

He drags me back towards the house as I wrap my hands around his fingers on my collar, trying to pry them loose as I call him every name under the sun, turning the air blue as I curse him out.

It's no use, though. I can't get away from him, and the guard whose hand I bit is following behind us, shooting me filthy looks. I have no choice but to keep up, stones and sticks embedding themselves into my battered feet. If I fall, he'll only carry on and drag me by my neck.

The house comes back into sight, a black SUV parked up next to our truck. I cry out as I see my pack scattered, lifeless, on the ground. Exactly where I left them.

"Ace! Gabe!" I shriek their names, yanking my neck against Jason's punishing grip.

I need to go to them. When Jason tries to pull me away, I snarl at him, ripping my neck out of his hands. I run, landing beside Devlin and dropping to my knees as I check frantically for a pulse.

"Please, please…" I beg, my heartbeat thundering in my ears. He's breathing, but he doesn't respond to me at all, and Jason catches up with me, yanking me back by the hair as I scream for them.

Jason and I tussle as he drags me over the ground, stones cutting open my skin. I fight like a banshee to try to reach them.

Devlin, Gabe, Ace, Rogue. All of them still, all of them silent.

I grab hold of Rogue's boot as Jason drags me past, one last-ditch attempt.

"Wake up," I beg, a keen in my throat and tears streaming down my face. "Wake up, Rogue. *Please.*"

Jason rips me away and throws me into the back of their truck. I grab for the handle but there's a guard there, waiting, with a cloth in his hand.

I try to hold my breath, scratching at him with my nails until he swears, forcing my head back. Grubby fingers press over my nose until I have no choice but to open my mouth. My head swims as the chemicals filter into my bloodstream.

Please. Please let them wake up, is my last thought, before I succumb to unconsciousness.

CHAPTER FORTY-THREE
DEVLIN

There's a foul metallic taste in my mouth.

Groaning, I try to roll over, the light burning my eyes. Sharp rocks dig into my arm.

Someone is shaking me, shouting. My eyes feel blurry and gritty as I stare up at them.

A pungent scent waves under my nose, and my mind sharpens. *Fuck. Fucking hell.*

Princess.

I sit up, head pounding, and Ezra's face swims into view, filled with horror. He takes a step back, tucking a bottle into his pocket.

Pushing him aside, I stumble to my feet.

"Princess!" I bellow. I remember her turning to run as my legs collapsed under me.

Please tell me she got away.

I shout her name again, desperate for her to appear. "Harper!"

Nothing. My knees threaten to buckle underneath me.

"Devlin," Ezra snaps, shaking my shoulder. I run my hands over my face and nod.

"I'm okay," I tell him hoarsely. "Need to find Harper."

He studies my face and heads over to Gabe. Ace and Rogue are both up, pale-faced and unsteady on their feet.

"What the fuck," Ace mutters, cheeks tinged with green as he battles not to vomit, "was that?" He drops to his knees next to Ezra as Gabe stirs.

I'm as stunned as they are. When the guard told us to move outside, something told me that things weren't right. I thought I'd been prepared, but I hadn't seen the tranquilizer coming.

What the fuck is the compound playing at? And where have they taken Harper?

If they've touched a hair on her fucking head, I'll torch the compound and dance on their ashes.

Rogue has his phone up to his ear.

"Dad," he says roughly. Christian's voice echoes through the phone, and Rogue explains. I motion and he hits the speaker button so we can all hear.

"I haven't authorized any extraction," Christian says urgently. "Whoever this was, it wasn't us."

Ice steels up my spine as Gabe moans in distress. Ace's jaw clenches and Rogue stares at the screen.

"Are you sure?" he asks urgently. "Can they do it without you?"

"No," Christian answers firmly. "In fact, I signed your release papers yesterday. Harper has effectively been released from the compound and is now a permanent part of your pack."

"So if it wasn't the compound…," Gabe mutters, swaying beside me as Ace wraps an arm around him. I think back to the moments I remember before passing out.

"Fucking Jason," I growl, and everyone turns to me. "He was inside the vehicle. I saw him before they got me."

Christian swears colorfully. "I fired him weeks ago. Straight after you left with Harper. If it's him, he's not doing this as part of the OC. But his father has his own money."

Everyone growls, and fury comes over me at the idea of that asshole being anywhere near Harper.

"Can you track her collar?" Rogue asks.

"Give me ten minutes." Christian hangs up the phone and we stare at each other.

"Let's suit up," Rogue orders grimly. We all head into the house, pulling on our combat uniforms and boots. When I duck back into the kitchen, Gabe is sliding knives into a holster on his leg.

He looks at me, his hazel eyes filled with defiant challenge.

"I'm going," he says firmly. Ace stands behind him, arms crossed. I nod and start stocking up my own weapons silently.

I force my mind away from images of what could be happening to Harper. I have to focus.

Rogue sweeps into the kitchen, dominance bleeding off him. Ezra follows behind him, concern in his eyes. I wonder what he sees. If this is history repeating itself.

I clench my jaw, staring down at the gun in front of me. I won't let that happen. None of us will.

Rogue spreads a map out on the table, circling a location. "We have a lead. The collar is heading in this direction." He points at a route leading out of the city.

We can assume the collar is still on since the compound has a special tool to remove it without hurting the omega. I doubt Jason has access.

"How long were we out?" I ask, staring at the dot.

"Around two hours," Ace answers. His voice is pure ice, the shadow taking over.

That means they have a two-hour head start on us.

"Let's go," Rogue orders. Ezra follows us out.

"You'll get her back," he says, conviction in his voice. Ace grabs his shoulder tightly, squeezing, before throwing himself into the back of the truck.

I duck into the passenger seat, biting back a curse at the scent of our previous evening hanging strongly in the air. Gabe chokes, and Ace tucks him under his arm.

Rogue slides into the driving seat. His nostrils flare but otherwise, he doesn't respond, in full-on mission mode. "We ready?" he asks gruffly. His eyes slide across us, assessing.

He doesn't wait for a response before he pulls out.

I'm coming, Princess, I promise her. *We're all coming.*

I pray to the fucking gods that we'll get there in time.

Chapter Forty-Four
Harper

*S*o cold.

My teeth chatter as I squint at the bright light shining in my face. When I raise my arm to block it out, my wrists pull tight against metal.

I tug. I'm on some sort of metal table. The cold soaks into my bones and I shake, realizing that I'm not wearing any clothes.

Rogue. Gabe. Ace. Devlin.

My whimper sounds like a gunshot in the silence. I want to see where I am, but the light is too bright and I close my eyes, frustrated.

It suddenly shuts off and I open them a crack, trying to push past the white blotches flickering across my vision.

The clomping of heavy boots sounds from a distance, moving closer. I pull again at my wrists, but the burn tells me they're not going to give way.

A hand lands on my leg, tracing upwards. Horror fills me as I realize they can see everything, my legs strapped open. I make a noise, a sound of protest, and the hand stops.

"Please," I whisper. A tear slips from my eye.

"Please, what, 792?" Jason's nasally sound echoes through the room, and I sob. Anyone but him.

"Let me go," I plead. "I haven't done anything wrong. The compound—,"

"Oh, you're not at the compound, 792." His voice is gleeful.

Shock laces through me. If I'm not at the compound, where am I? I wrestle more frantically with my restraints, yanking at them desperately.

"Stop," Jason barks, and I freeze.

He puts his hand back on my leg and runs it up my body. Turning my head to the side, I try to ignore him.

He pinches my nipple hard, and I cry out.

"Oh, 792." His face appears into view, yellowed teeth breathing sour breath into my face. I try to move back as much as I can and he grabs my chin roughly, nails digging in.

"This is your fault," he hisses. My brows crinkle in confusion.

"I don't understand."

"*Did I say you could fucking speak?*" he bellows. Flecks of spit land on my face as I flinch.

Pressing my lips together, I watch him. His tuxedo is wrinkled and unkempt, his hair greasy. He looks unhinged. Spinning, he jabs his finger at me.

"I lost my job because of you, bitch," he seethes. "My father cut me off. Says I embarrassed him."

I didn't know the director fired him. I feel a small twinge of pleasure at the thought, and my lips twitch. It's no more than the fucker deserves.

The slap catches me by surprise, my head whipping to the side as my lip splits. Woozily, I roll my head to stare back at Jason.

"Now look what you made me do," he mutters. He strolls

down to the edge of the table and adjusts something. With a stab of horror, I realize that it's a camera.

"I have to thank you, though," he says casually, like he hasn't just split the side of my face apart. "Your little display last night worked perfectly, although I had to move up my plan somewhat."

I stay silent, burning to ask what he means.

He adjusts the camera so it's pointing directly at me.

"The show will start soon," he says with a sadistic grin. "You're going to make me a rich man, 792."

My heart hammers in my chest as my fear spikes.

He turns away and pushes a small trolley up towards me. Dread twists in my gut as I see the needle laid out.

No.

I start to twist frenziedly, tugging my restraints furiously. I know what that needle is.

I'd rather die before putting that in me. I start screaming, spitting, cursing at Jason. He casually pulls a rag from the tray and stuffs it into my mouth as furious tears stream down my face. The dirty material nudges the back of my throat and I fight not to throw up.

"Now, now," he says chidingly. "That's not the sort of language our buyers want to hear."

His words sink in. Buyers.

He's *selling* me.

"There we go," he says soothingly, as I run out of energy and my body collapses back onto the metal.

He wraps a cuff around my arm and it squeezes tightly, making my veins pop out. He casually traces his finger down one, humming to himself, and pins my arm as he inserts the needle in. He covers it with tape to keep it in place and hooks a bag of liquid up next to me. I feel numb, and we both watch as the first drops roll down and into my arm.

"Alright, then," he says. He cups me down there and I

moan through my gag, my distress scenting the air with burnt cinnamon.

"You'll soon be begging for it," he murmurs as he rubs his hand back and forth. I try in vain to push my legs closed, the feel of his hands on me curdling my stomach.

"The auction will begin soon, but we'll give them a little taste, shall we?"

He flicks a switch on the camera and a red light flickers on. My skin crawls, bile shooting up my throat at the idea of random alphas watching me, greedy eyes staring at my body.

It takes a few minutes before I feel anything, and I keep twisting, trying to break free. I don't know what I'll be able to do even if I manage it, but maybe I could keep Jason at bay long enough for my pack to find me. I whine at the thought of them, and a sudden wave of *need* clenches in my belly. It's much stronger than last night and I instinctively try to curl up, shuddering as it licks down my spine and makes my toes curl. The table holds me, though, and I stay where I am, my body locked into place.

Jason reappears, a mask over his face as he laughs.

"Here it comes, 792. Hope you're ready to be fucked. I've had a *very* generous offer, and he'll be here shortly. He's going to remove your collar, too. Then we'll run the auction for what's left of you."

A groan slides out of me. I lick feverishly at my lips, which suddenly feel dry. Need is starting to claw at my insides now, as the artificial heat begins to take over. Heat flushes over me, waves of warmth pulsing from my stomach to my clit and making me cry out. It grows until it starts to burn and I keen as the pain overwhelms me, rocking up in waves that never seem to end. I glance feverishly at the bag and it's only a third of the way in. I can feel slick seeping out of me and my core clenches around nothing, searching for a knot as my hips twist.

The pain grows, a mindless scream pulled from my lips as

my back arches. *This* is why they sedate omegas during artificial heats.

When the bag is empty… I'll beg for their knots. If the pain doesn't kill me first.

Jason steps up next to my face, staring down at me with pleasure dancing in his eyes.

He pushes my hair back and I turn my face away.

"Oh, and by the way," he whispers. "Your little pack won't be coming, I'm afraid. They're dead."

My eyes flash to his, triumphant and glittering with excitement.

A howl tears from my throat, terror, need, lust and horror mixed into a horrific concoction. *Dead.*

I feel the moment that my soul rips. Irreversible, incomparable pain fills me from my fingers to my toes, a knife stabbing straight through my heart. *They're dead. Because of me.*

And then the heat serum pulls me under.

CHAPTER FORTY-FIVE
GABE

We're about ten minutes away from the warehouse we've tracked Harper's collar to, and I'm battling back the waves of fear threatening to overwhelm me. It's been hours. She's been gone for fucking *hours*.

Focus, I tell myself. *You need to focus.*

Beside me, Ace studies the blueprints he's managed to get hold of. The warehouse is relatively small, tucked away between taller buildings used for storage. The collar is still transmitting, meaning that they haven't broken it off her.

I never thought I'd be so grateful for that fucking piece of plastic around her neck.

I run my finger over the knives in my holster, soothing myself with the cool metal.

We pull to a stop around a block away. Rogue's fingers flex on the steering wheel. Our bond is full of fear and determination. It must be hitting him like a freight train.

Devlin passes me a pair of infrared goggles, and I slip them over my ears, flicking the switch. The three men around me flash green.

Rogue's cell rings, and he presses the button to answer.

"We're here."

Christian's furious voice echoes through. "We've picked up potential activity around an omega in heat in the area you're heading to. Apparently, there's an illegal auction running."

Horror seizes my throat. *An auction. Harper.*

"Be careful," Christian continues. "Call me when you can."

Rogue stabs the phone to end the call and sits for a moment, his hands flexing on the wheel of the van as he bows his head. The waves of dominance pulsing from him are so strong that I push myself back, battling the urge to bare my throat.

"Right," he says after a minute. "We need to focus. We have a plan, we will execute the plan and we will *bring her home.*"

This is our pack leader. His voice is pure ice, his face expressionless as he throws instructions to Dev and Ace. He softens slightly when he reaches me and touches me on the shoulder.

"Stay safe," he orders, and I nod. I'm not planning on being a hero. I just want to bring our girl home. And I'll happily kill anyone who stands in my way.

We edge closer to the building, all of us with our goggles on as we scan for any guards. Rogue holds up his hand and we pause. He motions to Ace and he slinks past us, disappearing into the shadows.

I spot two guards at the entrance of the warehouse. They're not paying attention, chatting casually with their arms crossed, guns slung over their shoulders.

Serious fucking error of judgment, assholes.

Ace explodes out of the shadows behind them. He's at the second before the first can even raise a hand to his throat, gurgling as the blood slips out and he drops to his knees. Guard two gets the same treatment and Ace scans his perimeter before giving us a thumbs up.

"Go," Rogue says, and Devlin moves ahead, scope up as he checks for threats.

Ace pauses at the doors of the warehouse, listening for any activity. He shakes his head as we edge up to him, his eyes darting to me. "Nothing," he murmurs, shooting a look at Rogue for orders.

Rogue takes a second to consider as Devlin keeps his scope up, scanning for any further guard activity.

"Go," he says, and Ace cracks open the door. We all rock back at the punch of cinnamon and orange. It's bitter and twisted, the scent twisting my insides in a sharp snap of want. Devlin growls behind me and my heart clenches in fear as my knees threaten to buckle. *We're coming, love. Just hold on.*

I try to avoid breathing deeply, forcing the stiffness in my pants away as we head in. The warehouse is empty, freezing cold air causing my breath to puff out in front of me. Harper's scent is raking my stomach with needy claws, but I force myself to focus. I won't be the weak link on this mission.

There's a tugging in my stomach urging me to the end of the warehouse, and I motion to Rogue, pointing in the direction I want to go. He nods, and I wonder if he feels the same pull.

We all move in as the scent grows stronger. I list slightly at the sheer bombardment, shaking my head to clear it.

Then something shatters the silence.

A low keen echoes through the doorway. It's undeniably Harper, and it's filled with so much agony that it pulls an answering moan from my own throat. My heart jumps, and then we're all sprinting.

She needs us.

Rogue reaches the door first and yanks it open. The scent was strong before but that was *nothing* to how it feels now. Harper's heat is a knife to my solar plexus, a compulsion that demands I go to her. Twisted, burning pain.

Needs me.

My eyes glaze over as the urge to rut threatens to over-whelm me.

A whine breaks the silence, and our heads whip to the center of the room. Fucking *gods.*

My heart shatters as I stare at her, any thoughts of rutting vanishing from my mind.

Harper's naked body is twisted, shackles binding her to a metal table. Sweat beads on her body as she writhes, an odd shape to her left shoulder that tells me it's popped out of the socket.

Her panting is punctuated by tiny hoarse moans. They sound deeper, broken, as if she's torn her vocal chords.

I choke, white hot rage running through me. Beside me, Devlin roars with anguish.

Her lower body is bare, her thighs glistening with juices. The alpha standing next to the bed calmly zips up his trousers and turns to face us.

"Sorry, gents," Jackson smirks. "No harm, no foul, eh? I couldn't resist when Jason contacted me. I'm sure you can understand. She's quite the tasty piece."

Rogue snarls, but says nothing as he cocks his gun. Jackson loses his cocky grin, taking a step backwards and raising his hands.

"Now then, no need to be hasty. Perhaps you misunder-stood me. Things didn't get that far. Let's just take a step back, shall we? We don't need to fall out over an *omega.*"

His lip twists cruelly as he says it. Like omegas are somehow less than the piece of shit we're looking at.

"You," I say. I don't even spare him a glance, my eyes fixed on our beautiful, broken mate. "You are *everything* that is fucking wrong with this world."

Rogue pulls the trigger without another word.

I'm at Harper's side in a flash, running my hands over her.

She's unconscious, her body rippling even as her eyes remain closed. "Ace," I call, my voice breaking. He appears next to me, his breath ragged as we look down.

"Get the restraints," I rasp, and he moves to assess the straps keeping Harper tied to the table. I touch the bag of artificial heat enhancement. There are only a few drops left.

I close my eyes for a moment, agony threatening to pull me under. *I'm so sorry, baby.*

Gently, I extract the needle from her arm, peeling off the tape as softly as I can. I move my hands over her as gently as I can, checking for further injuries. Rogue's hand reaches out as I move towards her shoulder, stopping me. His face is tortured.

"I'll do it," he says hoarsely, and I nod. I don't think I can. I grit my teeth at the sound of her shoulder popping back into place, and Harper lets out a tortured scream, arching before her body flops back onto the table.

There's a scuffling sound from behind me, and I turn as Devlin storms through the door. He has Jason's throat clasped in his hand, his feet dangling pathetically in mid-air. My fists flex and I move across to them. I can scent his fucking blood in the air, and it's *mine*.

He throws Jason to the ground, and the weasel tries to crawl away from us. He raises his head to show me his beaten face as he dares to glance at Harper.

I kick him hard in the face and he howls. "Don't you *fucking* look at her," I snarl. Devlin moves to stand at my side as I pull a knife free from my holster. I turn to look at him and he nods at me, sensing my need.

I *need* to do this. Vengeance swirls in my veins, filling me with adrenalin.

I step forward and grin savagely at Jason. He pales even through the blood on his face.

"You will never touch her again," I say quietly.

And then I start cutting.

CHAPTER FORTY-SIX
HARPER

Someone is screaming. It cuts through the veil hanging over me, and I whimper.

It hurts too much.

It's me. I'm screaming.

Growls sound around me, and a hand strokes gently over my cheek.

"Little omega," someone begs.

The words pierce my heart. I moan, shaking my head. Ace is dead.

"Sweetheart," someone murmurs. "We're so sorry. We failed you."

The voice breaks.

It sounds like Rogue, but it can't be. I'm dreaming.

I didn't know dreams could hurt this much.

But I'll walk through fire to be with them again, even if it's only in my dreams.

"Rogue," I whisper. My throat burns, the rasp of my voice not sounding right.

"We're here, baby," he says. "We're not leaving you ever again."

A sob breaks through, and I feel dampness on my cheek.

Warm lips press to my forehead. "We'll get you out of here. Ace, how long?"

"Two minutes." The voice sounds strained.

This is a weird dream.

It's not real, though.

Real is an unfamiliar alpha putting his hands on me. Squeezing and pinching and *hurting*.

"Am I dead?" I whisper. The hand stroking my face pauses, and an agonized growl vibrates through my bones. My mind is growing fuzzy again, and I whimper. Don't want to leave them.

"No, love." Rogue again. "We'll be able to go home soon. Just a little longer."

My mind drags me under.

The ground vibrates underneath me. I'm wrapped securely in strong arms, and when I breathe in I'm surrounded by woodsmoke and leather.

"Devlin," I try to say, but my voice isn't working properly.

A hand smooths over my hair, achingly gentle. "Princess."

He sounds mad. "Don't be angry," I sigh, nuzzling into his chest.

"Never," he swears, voice hoarse. "Never with you."

Voices murmur around me in broken pieces. My mind feels like a jigsaw. I know where the pieces fit, but my mind can't put them where they need to go.

My pack is dead.

I don't want to be here, wherever I am.

Fingers prod at my arm, and I feel the touch of a needle.

I scream, thrashing my arm around.

No more fucking needles.

The fingers disappear, replaced by the buttery scent of freshly-baked bread with a touch of sea salt.

A hand traces my cheek.

"Come back to us, love." The voice begs.

It sounds like Gabe.

"Can't," I choke out. "Don't want to leave you."

"We're all *here*, little omega," Ace whispers. "We're just waiting for you."

That sounds perfect. Maybe I am dead.

I force my eyes to open, relieved when there's no bright light pushing them shut. Even the effort hurts, but I persevere.

A face swims into view. Bright green eyes, full of love. A black curl drops over Rogue's face as he leans in.

"Come on, sweetheart," he murmurs. "Time to wake up."

"You're dead," I whisper flatly. His face looks tortured.

"No, love," he says softly. "None of us are dead."

A small kernel of hope fills me. Maybe it wouldn't hurt to check. I've been wrong before, after all.

I force my eyes back open, staring into Rogue's glittering eyes. They look misty.

"There you are," he murmurs. His scent trickles into my nose.

He's *here*. He's not dead. Rogue's not dead.

A desperate urge fills me, pushing me to *see*. I try to pull myself up, struggling, and several sets of hands all jump in.

"Whoa, little omega. Take it easy."

I whip my head towards the sound and there's Ace, with a small, sad smile on his face.

Ace. Ace is here.

Gabe pushes him gently out of the way so he can lean in and kiss my forehead.

"We were so worried, love," he chokes.

Three. One more.

I turn and try to look around the room, an anxious whine peeling from my throat.

Rogue takes a step back and Devlin is there, lines of worry edging his forehead.

"Devlin," I whisper, as tears start to fall. Four. All present and accounted for. I hold my arms up and he's at my side in a flash, pulling me into him gently.

"I thought you were dead," I sob, and there's a chorus of disagreement. "He told me you were all dead."

"Oh, princess," Devlin murmurs, rocking me gently. "It takes a lot more than that little weasel to hurt us."

They run their hands over me gently as I cry, my face pressed tightly into Devlin's shoulder.

We're all here. We're all together.

Finally, I sit back, and Dev gives me space to look around.

All four alphas look like they've aged overnight, stress lines bracketing their mouths and curving grooves in their forehead that weren't there before. Shadows line their jaws.

"How long..." I direct my question at Rogue.

"Four days." There's so much love and agony in his expression that I want to cry again. I look to Gabe and Ace, holding on to each other like they're keeping each other standing.

"I want to touch you all," I say softly. "When I thought..."

I break off, unable to finish the words. They all move closer to the bed, climbing on gently. Rogue pulls me into his side whilst Dev lays his head gently on my legs. Ace and Gabe mirror him, and I sigh in relief when I have them all close.

"Stay with me," I mumble. I'm already drifting away.

When I wake up again, I finally feel a little more human.

Ezra arrives, his crinkled face wreathed in relief. He shoos the pack out so he can check me over, and he gently offers to do an internal examination.

Fear ripples through me, but I nod. I need to know.

I call Gabe back in, and he holds me closely as Ezra takes some swabs. I can feel the tension in his posture as he watches Ezra work.

"Hey," I say gently, pulling his face around and ignoring the twinge of pain in my shoulder. I've had much worse.

Everything from when Jason injected me with heat hormones is a blur, and although the guys have filled me in on what they know, there's still a question mark over Jackson. He told the guys nothing happened, but we don't know for certain.

I could be pregnant.

Ezra finishes and straightens up, meeting my eyes steadily. I brace myself.

"There's no internal access, Harper," he says, and my whole body shakes in relief as Gabe folds his arms around me.

"So, they didn't…" I whisper, and he shakes his head.

"No, sweetheart," he smiles at me, sadly. "They didn't."

I turn to Gabe, tears of relief sliding down my cheeks. He pulls me close, but there's a touch of something in his expression that twists my stomach. He's told me how he killed Jason, and I won't judge him for it. But I worry about what it's done to his soul.

"I would have done the same thing, you know," I murmur, and his face snaps up to meet my gaze, a protest forming on his lips. I press my finger to them and he relents, letting me speak.

"If I had the opportunity, I would have ripped Jason apart. A knife, a gun, even a fucking paper clip. You did what you needed to do, and I don't want you to waste a single more of your thoughts on him, Gabriel Winter."

He stares into my eyes, not responding as the pack tumble back through the doors. He'll need more time to come to terms with it, but I won't let this eat him up.

I'm surrounded by love, affection, warmth on every side and I breathe it in, my eyes closed.

"So… what happens now?" I ask. It's the question I've been avoiding. Jason may be gone, but the compound is still hanging over us.

Rogue smiles crookedly. "Well… my father signed off your pack membership. So you're officially no longer under the guardianship of the compound."

My mouth drops open. "Holy shit. Are you serious?"

He entwines our fingers together, his green eyes searching mine.

"How do you feel about being Harper Winter?" he asks me quietly. Ace and Gabe grin behind him. Devlin squeezes my hand on my other side, and I stare at them all, overwhelmed.

Harper Winter. Not 792. Never again.

"I'd like that," I breathe. Tears prickle at the corners of my eyes.

It means I can *stay*. No more worrying about the compound knocking on the door.

We'll still need to be careful in public, but this… this is everything.

I'm a full-blown member of the Winter pack.

I'm theirs.

And I'm free of the compound. I hesitate slightly, and Rogue picks up on it immediately. He cups my cheek with his hand, and I nuzzle into it.

"What is it?" he asks gently.

"Ava," I ask quietly. "My friend. She's still at the OC."

"We'll find out," he promises me instantly, and my unease settles slightly. Maybe we'll be able to help her.

"Princess!" Devlin calls, a teasing growl tearing up his throat.

I stifle a laugh. I'm tucked away in his bedroom behind his closet. I wondered how long it would take him to find my note.

I'm ready for my spanking now, sir.

Who needs sweet words when punishment feels this good? As it turns out, 'hide the knot' is the best fucking game ever.

Footsteps thump outside the door, and I flush with excitement as Devlin bursts in, sniffing the air. My scent is strong today, and he's found me easily. Something that I'm not displeased about.

Although…

Something clenches at my core. *Want.*

A wave of heat rolls into my belly, and I clutch it. A whine slips out of me and Devlin is there in a second. Our game is forgotten as he scoops me up, scanning my face in concern.

"Princess?" he asks worriedly. Another tug. I moan, throwing my head back, and Dev's eyes widen as he inhales.

"Oh," he murmurs, his scent rising to match mine. "Princess, I think you might be—"

"Heat," I gasp. *Devlin.*

"We've got you, baby."

Devlin tears out of the bedroom, calling for the guys as he heads towards my nest.

My nest.

My beautiful, warm, cosy nest.

I wept when the pack showed it to me. They'd been back and forth for days, carrying large boxes and ushering me into different rooms as they carried tools and materials through to the attic, casually asking me what colors were my favorite in the middle of random conversations. It was the worst-kept secret ever, and I loved every moment of it.

My nest is everything I could ever have wanted.

A low-ceilinged room lined with a huge lilac mattress instead of a proper floor, so soft that my feet sink into it when I walk. There are huge soft pillows and blankets *everywhere*, large beanbags and even a hammock strung against two walls. Low wooden shelving holds every kind of scented lotion I might want in easy reach, candles, some *very* fun toys and a small cabinet with cold drinks and snacks. I even have a chest with different pieces of clothing, all worn by my alphas and swapped out regularly, so the scents stay strong.

The best part is the lights. The ceiling and one wall are completely covered with tiny warm fairy lights, twinkling at me. It's like something from a fairy tale. I genuinely feel like a princess whenever I'm in this room, which is pretty damn often. We sleep here most nights, piled together in a huddle. None of our beds are big enough for the games we like to play.

"Is it okay?" Gabe had asked me anxiously when they took my blindfold off, his hands twisting in his shirt.

I'd carefully padded into the room, trailing my hand over

the different pieces, overwhelmed by how much care and attention they had all put in.

"Perfect," I'd whispered, my shoulders shaking. "*You're* perfect."

Now, Devlin carefully toes his boots off at the door, sweeping in and laying me down on the soft surface. Immediately I curl up, my hands fisting in the soft blanket as a moan rolls out of me. I'm so *hot*. I grab at the blankets, pulling and tugging them into a pile.

Something is missing, and I whine and stare at Devlin pleadingly. He stares back at me with panic in his dark eyes, one leg in and one leg out of his trousers, and I slide my eyes to his discarded shirt until he gets the hint and passes it to me.

A slight wave of worry fills me as I think back to the artificial heat, but I'm soothed by the sight of my alphas. I'm not on my own.

Ace and Rogue come skidding through the door, eyes wide. They catch my scent at the same time, and rumbling purrs echo through the room as they start undressing.

Gabe appears a few seconds later, beaming as he carefully carries a covered plate through the door.

"Red velvet cake. For later," he winks at me as he places it onto a shelf, and I grin at him, despite the twisting in my belly. He didn't forget.

My slick is starting. Wetness drips between my thighs and I rub them together, already seeking release. Devlin leans in and kisses me deeply, the familiar smokiness soothing me before a cramp clenches my stomach, making me whimper and squirm. The heat is settling in now, drawing a hazy mist over my vision.

He slides a hand under my shirt, massaging my belly in warm, firm strokes.

"We've got this, princess," he purrs, as he tugs at my jeans. "You're so fucking beautiful," he swears as I open my legs to him pleadingly. His hand drops to my clit, the roughness of his skin causing delicious friction that makes me keen as he rubs his palm in firm circles. It's not enough though.

Empty. Need.

We do have this. We've prepared for this.

Rogue appears, helping Devlin remove the rest of my clothes. As soon as I'm naked, Rogue tugs me into his arms, the skin contact easing the heat I can feel licking at my skin. I shift my hips over his hardness, eyes closing at the pleasure.

"Now," I beg. "Please, Rogue."

He wastes no time, pushing my thighs apart and sliding into me with one firm thrust, making me cry out in pure pleasure. His hand slides up and he pulls my face to him, nipping at my lips as he moves in fast, sure strokes.

"Who do you belong to, love?" he asks roughly.

"You," I gasp. "All of you. *Bite, please.*"

I've been waiting for this moment for weeks, and I refuse to wait a second longer. The moment I'll finally be theirs, and they'll be completely, wholly mine.

"Yes," he hisses. He lifts my ankle to hook over his shoulder, his thrusts moving even deeper as I scream his name, my first orgasm rippling through me like lightning.

Rogue roars as he pumps into me, his knot nudging my entrance. I curve my leg around him and tug hard, both of us groaning as his knot pops into my opening, filling me up. His seed floods me, the warmth and wet pulling another series of flutters from my core.

I turn my head, presenting my throat to him. He leans in and *bites*, his teeth sinking into my neck. I cry out as his bond snaps into place, a link directly from his heart to mine. It's packed full of love, and the feeling makes tears roll down my cheeks.

I'll never be alone again.

"Never," Rogue swears, and I realize I said the words aloud. He strokes his hand across my cheekbone before turning and offering me his neck and I *finally* bite down, leaving my mark on him.

Our newly-created mating bond thrums inside my chest, linking us both together forever.

Rogue keeps rocking me gently as I come down from my orgasm, my eyes drifting to half-mast for a few moments before the clenching starts again. I groan and start to move against him, my body pushing me for more.

Rogue rolls to his back, carefully keeping our bodies connected, and I throw my head back as he catches a plump nipple with his mouth and sucks. A calloused hand slips onto my other breast. Devlin rolls and squeezes me between his talented fingers. His chest fits against my bare back, dusky brown hairs tickling me as he slides his other hand down to my clit and rubs the rough pad of his finger over it. It's like a magic button, my eyes closing in bliss.

A gush of wetness runs past Rogue's knot, his glazed eyes meeting mine as his knot slowly releases me. Leaning in, he presses a kiss to my damp forehead.

"Flawless, love," he whispers. Rogue moves out of the way as Devlin places his hand on my back, gently encouraging me down and leaning in to kiss my scars, trailing his tongue over a particularly sensitive area and making me shiver.

Trailing his hand down my back and over my ass, he suddenly smacks his palm against my exposed pussy, making me cry out and drop to my elbows. I'm so sensitive that stars flicker across my eyes.

"Look at this pretty pink pussy, all wet and dripping for us," he groans.

His words send heat licking up my spine, and I wriggle, pressing myself down with a pleading whine. I want him *now.*

Lifting my ass up, I present myself to him, loving the way his breath draws in on a hiss. I *love* presenting for them. It's worlds away from the twisted directions of the compound. and I sob in relief as Devlin pushes slowly into me.

He curls a hand around my throat and gently pulls me back, fitting us together like two parts of a puzzle as he rolls his hips against mine, meeting my eyes in the mirror in front of us.

His teeth sink into the other side of my neck, and a second bond pulls my body taut, full of protectiveness. I find the spot between Devlin's thumb and finger that we agreed on. He told me he wanted his bite somewhere he could always look at.

The bond pulses through him and he pumps harder as I moan. It's like I can feel the pleasure twice over.

"So good, princess," he groans. "Feel you everywhere."

I turn to look for Ace and Gabe and my core tightens against Devlin's length, making him growl in pleasure as I clamp down on him like a glove. Ace is watching me, possession, lust and love curving into the lines on his face. His hand is on the back of Gabe's head, his fingers running through his hair, and a pulse of want runs straight to my pussy as I watch Gabe's head moving back and forth.

"Our little omega is watching us, Gabriel," Ace groans, and Gabe moans around his cock. He sucks harder, faster, and I grab Devlin's hand as Ace and I both cry out our release at the same time.

He reaches for me as Devlin slides out of me, the slick between my thighs offering a smooth entrance for my other two alphas.

Ace grabs Gabe's hand and tugs him along.

"Are you ready for this, little omega?" he whispers. I stare at him through heat-glazed eyes, whimpering mindlessly.

"Please," I whine. My core is already feeling empty, the heat still running through me.

Ace urges me up on my knees, and I mewl at the feel of his

fingers running through my slick. He coats his fingers, sucking them and offering Gabe a taste.

"Cinnamon, oranges and honey," he purrs, the vibrations going straight to my clit.

"Fucking amazing, love," Gabe groans. The sight of him sucking my juices from Ace's hand makes my knees wobble, and Ace slides an arm around my waist to hold me up. Gathering more of the fluids, he runs his other hand through to my ass, smoothing his fingers over my hole. He slides in a finger and I buck in his arms, crying out as he slides a second in.

"Little omega," he kisses my shoulder gently. "Are you ready for us?"

"Yes," I moan. I'm *so* fucking ready.

Ace lifts me gently and I feel his cock prodding at my rear. He slowly pushes in and the pressure of his entrance makes my eyes roll back as he sinks into me.

I slide slowly down to the base, adjusting to the fullness and holding my hand out to Gabe. I need them both.

He grins at me, lust darkening his eyes as Ace lays back and pulls me with him. Ace's hands slide under my knees, and he opens me wide as Gabe licks his lips. They love to take me like this. Holding me open for them.

Whining, I turn my head to see Devlin and Rogue watching us, their hands on their lengths as they pump their hands up and down. My arousal jumps up again, loving the feel of their eyes on me.

Gabe presses his mouth to my clit and sucks hard. I soar, screaming their names as Ace groans, sinking in another inch. Before I come down, Gabe thrusts gently into my pussy and my vision goes white at the feel of them both stretching me. They thrust into me gently, then harder, finding a rhythm as I rock between them, the three of us connected in a tangle of arms and fluids and pure fucking love.

Taking an arm each, they bite down on my wrists at the

same time, and stars dance across my vision as I adjust to the four bonds inside me.

It's indescribable.

They offer me their necks in turn, and I place my bite on them as they shudder against me.

Their knots slide inside me at the same time, stealing the breath from my lungs as I gasp for air, filled to the brim with them.

All mine.

They both hiss as they lock into place, my head falling back on Ace's shoulder as he kisses my cheek, pushing damp hair away from my forehead.

"We love you, little omega," he whispers.

I blink back tears as they surround me with murmurs of agreement.

My pack.

My mates.

"I love you," I whisper. "All of you."

And whatever our future, we'll face it together.

THE END

AVA

Machines beep around me, breaking up the endless silence.

A door opens. Footsteps.

A face stares into mine. It's so familiar.

Broken sounds slip from my lips as I mouth the word inside my head.

Dad.

He turns away from me, his silence worse than any cutting words.

"You're certain?" he asks. His voice is empty.

"As certain as we can be, Sir. There is always a risk—"

"I don't care about your risks."

Awkward silence.

"We have several possible options lined up. All of them have impeccable bloodlines."

"And they will produce a male." It's not a question.

"They have so far. A female would be highly unusual – but as I said, not impossible."

Silence.

The machines beep.

Whatever they've given me feels like sludge inside my veins.
I can't move. Can't speak.
I can only listen.
"Very well. Proceed."

Omega Found playlist (in order)

Find it on Spotify

Nobody Knows – Pink
You Haven't Seen the Last of Me – Cher
Only Hope – Mandy Moore
Scars – James Bay
Say You Love Me – Jessie Ware
Taking Chances – Celine Dion
Bruises – Lewis Capaldi
Take Me to Church – Hozier
Scars To Your Beautiful – Alessia Cara
Give Me Love – Ed Sheeran
Skinny Love – Birdy
Angel – Sarah McLachlan
Galway Girl – Steve Earle
Yours – Ella Henderson
All I Ask – Adele
Courage – Celine Dion
All I Need – Within Temptation
Bless the Broken Road – Rascal Flatts

A note from Evelyn

Harper, Rogue, Devlin, Ace, and Gabe.

What can I say?

I wrote an outline for this book, but you dragged me down so many different directions that it went in the bin after the first chapter. Assholes.

Whilst Harper and the pack have their HEA, there are still some loose ends to tie up, and you'll be seeing more of them in the future.

If you loved the Winter pack as much as I do, then please consider leaving a review. Reviews are like lifeblood for indie authors, and I am so grateful to my awesome readers and ARC team for your cheerleading and support for a brand-new baby author still finding her feet.

Ava is up next, and if Harper's story broke your heart, then Ava's will tear it up and burn it to ash.

Omega Lost is available for pre-order now!

Evie x

Stalk me!

Find the latest on the Omega War series, strong GIF game and many, many teasers in my Facebook group, The Evelyn Flood Collective.

Printed in Great Britain
by Amazon

37352442R00182